ALIEN SKY

ALIEN SKY

ALIEN HUNTERS, BOOK II

DANIEL ARENSON

CHAPTER ONE
SPIDER WINGS

Wreathed in smoke and flame, the dragon-shaped starship swooped toward a planet of mist, rainforests, and massive winged spiders the size of pterodactyls.

"Remind me again, why did we ever come here?" Riff muttered.

Captain of the *HMS Dragon Huntress*, he sat in his suede captain's seat, clutching the frayed armrests. He wore his old jeans and a white T-shirt, and his beloved plasma gun, Ethel, hung from his hip. Sweat dripped down his forehead. Before him, through the ship's windshield, he saw swirls of clouds, a snaking river, and the jungle of Planet Adilor below.

Giga turned toward him and tilted her head. The android's black hair fell down to her chin, framing her pale face. Appropriately, she had chosen to wear a green kimono embroidered with small golden spiders.

"Captain? It was your order to fly to Planet Adilor, sir. Something about . . ." Mechanical clicks rose from the android as she searched her memory banks. ". . . being so poor we should charge rent from the moths in our pockets."

Riff grumbled. "Yes, but now we have bigger concerns than moths. Much bigger." He gulped and pointed. "Much, much bigger."

Outside the windshield, a massive spider buzzed across the sky, beating translucent wings. Its belly was so large and round it put potbellied pigs to shame. Its many eyes blinked, large as human heads. With a screech, the creature whizzed away, vanishing into the mist.

Riff gulped. "How many of these creatures did the colonists say are here?"

Giga tilted her head to the other side, clicking and humming as she calculated. "Seventeen adult spiders, Captain. And several thousand eggs at the time of our last report." She smiled sweetly. "If the eggs have already hatched, then four thousand, seven hundred, and eighty-four spiders, sir."

Riff sighed as the starship kept descending. "And definitely no chance the colonists would agree to let us nuke the whole damn forest from orbit, is there?"

The android's smile never faltered. "Not if we want to get paid, Captain."

Riff rubbed his temples. "I hate my job."

The *HMS Dragon Huntress* kept descending through the atmosphere, heading toward the rainforest. Planet Adilor was a vast world, larger than Earth, covered with rivers, forests, and mostly harmless life--birds, fish, and fuzzy little rodents that purred when patted. A perfect planet to colonize. That is, until an asteroid covered with eggs had slammed into the surface only a few kilometers outside the colony . . . and started spewing aliens.

"Alien spiders," Riff muttered. "Goddamn alien spiders with goddamn wings."

"And venom, sir," Giga reminded him. "Quite venomous, actually. Did you know, Captain, that a single drop of Velurian spider venom can kill one thousand, three hundred and twelve and a half men? Assuming average distribution of weight, age, and health."

He wiped sweat off his brow. "I think I've had enough figures for today, Giga."

The *Dragon Huntress* descended farther until its thruster engines blasted the forest canopy, bending trees and vines and scattering mist. Birds fled. The ship leveled off and skimmed across the treetops. Riff rose from his seat, approached the windshield, and leaned against the glass. He pointed.

"There!"

A few kilometers away, he saw the colony. A hundred Earth settlers had built wooden huts, a concrete silo, and a palisade of sharpened stakes. An area of forest had been cleared out, making room for a field of turnips, squash, wheat, and other produce.

Just outside the colony rose a granite mountain, its boulders and trees covered with cobwebs.

Riff winced.

The *Dragon*'s dashboard speakers crackled to life, and a voice emerged from them, staticky, stuttering. "Captain Starfire!

Thank goodness you're here. They killed another colonist this morning. Oh stars . . . you have to exterminate them, you--"

The voice from the speakers died with a screech of static.

Riff grimaced and clutched his gun. "Giga, take us right over the mountain. Right over those cobwebs."

Giga smiled. "Happy to comply, Captain!"

Obeying the android's wireless signals, the *Dragon Huntress* shot over the colony below, its engines bending trees, scattering thatch off hut roofs, and sending laundry flying off strings. The starship soared above the mountain, the cobwebs spreading below them. Riff glimpsed several large, shadowy figures scuttling between the trees. On the mountaintop, a massive web rose like a circus tent, gleaming with pale beads like dewdrops.

Spider eggs, Riff realized. He gulped.

"All right, Gig. You're in command of the ship until I get back." He patted old Ethel. "Time to go hunting some aliens."

Giga saluted. "Happy to comply, Captain. Good luck out there."

He nodded and left the command bridge. His boots thumped down metal stairs and along a hallway lined with doors. Finally Riff stepped into the *Dragon Huntress*'s main deck. The couches had been pushed back against the walls, clearing a space for the landing party.

Nova was already here, clad as always in a golden catsuit, the *kaijia* fabric thin but hard enough to stop bullets and plasma blasts. The ashai gladiator unrolled her whip, letting the tip crackle with electricity. Large, pointy ears thrust out from between

strands of her blond hair, and her green eyes shone with
excitement for the hunt.

"Fragging aardvarks, Riff!" Nova said. "Did you see the size
of that one what flew by us? Goddamn bugger nearly larger than
Romy's backside."

"Hey!" rose a voice from above. "It's not my fault, Nova.
It's Riff's fault for stocking so much cake in the fridge."

A hatch on the ceiling opened, and Romy leaped down onto
the deck. She wobbled, fell down onto said backside, then
groaned and struggled back to her feet. The demon's skin was red,
her fangs long, her claws sharp. Wings spread out from her back,
and a tail flicked behind her. She held a pitchfork, and fire
crackled upon her head instead of hair. Despite her fearsome
appearance, she clutched a teddy bear, and a cartoon dinosaur
smiled on her T-shirt.

"Oh hai, Captain Riff, sir!" The demon squared her
shoulders and saluted, dropping her pitchfork with a clatter.
"Cadet Romy, reporting to duty. Ready to stomp on some spiders,
sir."

"Romy, you are not to stomp on spiders," Riff said. "Your
job is to flap those demon wings of yours, fly above us, and warn
us if any spiders approach. You're purely tactical cover."

"Tacty-what-now?" She tilted her head.

Riff groaned. "Fine. Stomp on them!"

"Or just sit on them and squish them," Nova muttered.

The demon pouted. "You're just jealous that you didn't get
any cake. You-- Ah!"

The demon squealed, Riff cursed, and even Nova jumped. A cow-sized spider slammed against the porthole only feet away. Its mottled, bloated body pressed against the glass, its eyes blinked, and then it buzzed off.

"All right, ladies." Riff hefted his gun. "It's show time. Remember, we're bound by Earth laws even out here. That means we can't kill any endemic life. No stepping on local insects. No burning any birds. Can't even snap a twig without a stack of paperwork from the Humanoid Alliance. Those spiders, now, they're alien invaders, hatched off an asteroid, so they're good to kill--but we don't kill anything else. I don't want to even see anyone tear a leaf off a tree. Got it?"

Nova grumbled. "Fragging Earth laws make no sense. Are you *sure* I can't bring any grenades?"

Riff glared at her. "I told you. No grenades!"

"Back in Ashmar, we'd blast the whole damn forest apart." Nova sneered.

"That's why Ashmar is a desolate wasteland." Riff marched toward the airlock and yanked open the inner door. "Now come on. It's hunting season."

He stepped into the airlock, gun in hand, and walked down a flight of stairs. His companions walked behind, whip and pitchfork ready. At the edge of the airlock, waiting by the outer door, stood Riff's brother.

As always, Sir Steel Starfire wore his knightly armor, the metal plates polished to a shine. Solflare, his antique sword, hung at his side. The knight's brown mustache, his pride and joy, drooped down to his chin. As ever, Steel's brown eyes seemed sad, older than his years, the eyes of a man who had seen too much tragedy, felt too much pain.

"Cables all set to deploy." Steel pointed at a spool near the doorway, four cables wrapped around it. "We're ready."

Riff nodded. "Harness up, everyone. We land by the spider eggs." He pulled on a harness and attached a cable. "We kill every adult spider we see, and then we burn those damn eggs before they hatch."

Nova wriggled into a harness of her own. The ashai's eyes gleamed, and an eager smile twitched on her lips. Her hand tightened around her electric whip. Nova craved battle, Riff knew. These missions made him queasy, but she lived for them.

A few steps behind, Romy tried to wriggle into a harness too, but she ended up entangling herself in the straps and falling onto the stairs. Finally the demon managed to stand on one foot, limbs sticking out at odd angles, the harness straps stretching across her torso and face.

"Ready to deploy, Captain!" A strap muffled her words.

Nova grumbled. "You don't even need a harness, Romy. You have wings and can fly down."

The demon's eyes widened. "Oh yeah! I forgot." She tried to tug the harness off, only entangling herself further and falling down again.

As Nova helped the demon extricate herself, Riff nodded and grabbed the outer door's handle. He took a deep, shaky breath.

For money, he thought. *For the colony.* He looked over at Nova--at her green eyes, her mocking lips that he loved to kiss, her golden hair that he loved to stroke. *For Nova.*

He raised his chin and tugged the door open.

Air blasted into the *Dragon Huntress,* hot and humid and thick as soup. Mist swirled and the rainforest canopy sprawled to the horizons. The mountaintop jutted up below the starship, draped with trees, vines, and blankets of cobwebs.

"Oh shenanigans," Riff muttered, belly curdling. He felt like he had just swallowed rotten eggs. For a moment he stood on the edge, hesitating.

"Go on, while we're young." Nova placed her hands against his back and shoved.

"Nova, damn it!" Riff cried, falling through the air. The cable whirred madly on the spool above. Riff plummeted. The air blasted his face, tugging at his skin. The forest raced up toward him. Whoops sounded above, and Riff turned his head to see the others descending above him. Steel held his blade, Nova cracked her whip, and Romy--flapping her wings instead of dangling off a cable--hooted as she clutched her pitchfork. The *Dragon Huntress* hovered above them, thruster engines blasting.

Still falling, Riff returned his eyes to the forest below. The buggers lurked somewhere down there. He would search every tree for them, tear through every cobweb, lift every boulder until--

With a shriek, one of the spiders leaped up from the cobwebs below, beat its wings, and soared toward him.

"Bloody hell!" Riff cursed and aimed his gun.

He blasted out plasma.

The spider swerved in the air, and the plasma blazed downward and slammed into a tree below.

"Don't hurt the leaves, Riff!" Romy cried.

"Shut up and help me kill it!" he shouted back.

The spider soared toward him, mouth opening in a squeal, revealing fangs the size of Riff's arms. Its eight purple eyes blinked, and its wings buzzed in a fury. Riff winced and fired again, and this time he hit the creature, but the plasma washed across the spider's bloated body like waves over a boulder.

The alien arachnid reached him, jaws snapping. Black ooze sprayed from its mouth.

Riff screamed and swung on his cable, dodging the slime. He kicked wildly.

The spider's fangs lashed, nearly scratching Riff's leg. His boot thumped into the alien, squishing one eye. Black liquid spurted.

With a growl, Romy slammed down onto the spider. The demon clung to the creature--it was several times her size-- growling and beating her wings. She stabbed her pitchfork again and again.

"I'm stomping it, Riff!" The demon wagged her tail. "I'm stomping it good, I--"

"Behind you, Romy!" he shouted.

The demon spun around in time to see a second spider flying toward them. She squealed, flapped her wings, and thrust her pitchfork.

Riff cursed, firing his blaster again and again. Plasma flamed across the spider before him, burning its eyes, filling its mouth. The creature shrieked and fell.

Riff cursed. The cable kept unspooling, lowering him farther down toward the forest. More spiders flew above. Another leaped from below. Firing his gun, Riff fell down toward the cobwebs.

An instant before he could slam into the sticky net, he fired his gun down, blasting a hole through the cobwebs. He plunged through the opening and thumped against the forest floor.

He unhooked the cable off his harness. Trees soared around him, draped in moss and lichen and more webs. He could no longer see the other Alien Hunters, only hear their cries above. He glimpsed a flash of gold between the treetops. Nova was still up there, swinging on her cable, lashing her whip. Then she vanished from view.

"Steel!" Riff shouted. "Romy! Nova! Where are you, damn it?"

They were supposed to meet on the surface, to move through the forest together, to burn down the cobwebs strand by strand. Not this. Not a battle in the air.

"Steel!" He spoke into the communicator strapped to his wrist. "Steel, can you hear me?"

Only static sounded in reply. Black ooze clung to the communicator, eating away at the metal. Riff grunted, tore the device off his wrist, and tossed it down. The glob kept hissing, corroding the communicator away to nothing.

Riff hefted his gun, breath shaky. The communicator had probably just saved his wrist from being eaten away.

"All right." He blew out a breath. "I've landed. I'm alive. Good. Good. Now I just need to kill some spiders."

He began to walk. He had taken only three steps when he heard the screech behind him.

He spun around to see a spider racing through the forest, legs kicking fallen leaves and clumps of dirt. Black ooze--the same kind that had eaten Riff's communicator--sprayed from its mouth.

Riff leaped behind a tree. The slime slammed against the truck, corroding the wood. Holding his breath, Riff reached around the tree and fired his gun.

The first blast of plasma washed across the spider's back. The creature opened its jaws to roar, and the second blast slammed into its mouth.

The creature screeched as it burned.

Riff shot again and again. More plasma slammed into the spider, entering its mouth, its eyes, its nostrils. The alien's belly bulged and glowed, full of flame . . . then burst.

Riff grimaced and covered his head as chunks of spider rained onto him.

For a long moment, the spider rain continued. Globs thumped onto the forest floor and onto Riff. Finally he removed his arms from his head and looked around. Bits of the spider covered everything, including himself. Only its legs remained in their original location, sticking up like charred saplings.

With a grimace, Riff tugged bits of alien flesh off his hair and clothes, hefted his gun, and kept walking through the forest.

"Steel!" he cried out. "Nova! Romy!"

He heard distant cries. Spiders squealing. People screaming. The *Dragon Huntress*'s engines roared somewhere above, but Riff could no longer see the ship. He had hoped to land closer to the mountaintop, but what with the spiders assaulting him in midair, he wasn't sure where he had landed. He could be kilometers off. He lifted the compass that hung around his neck, flicked off a chunk of spider guts, and stared at the needle.

"Eww . . . you stink."

Riff spun around to see Romy approaching. Spider blood stained her pitchfork's prongs, and her tail wagged. She smiled, the fire crackling on her head.

Oh God . . . it had to be Romy who landed beside me.

"Did you see the others?" he said.

Romy frowned. "Nova and Steel? Hundreds of times." Her eyes brightened. "Or did you mean unicorns? Are there any unicorns on this planet? I want to find one! I'm starving."

"What do you even . . ." Riff groaned. "Never mind." He pointed ahead. "The spider eggs are that way, I think. Let's keep going. We'll meet Nova and Steel there. Keep your pitchfork ready."

They kept walking through the forest. The trees soared around them. Lichen and vines hung from twisting branches, and eyes glowed from the foliage and holes in the trunks. Cobwebs hung everywhere, and shadows scurried in the distance.

"There!" Riff fired his blaster.

Plasma tore through cobwebs and slammed into one of the aliens. The winged spider squealed, leaped forward, and came flying toward them.

Riff fired again. Romy shrieked and beat her wings. The demon soared skyward, then swooped, pitchfork plunging down. The prongs drove into the spider's back, and its bloated body deflated like a beach ball. Riff fired blast after blast until the alien burned and fell down dead.

Romy flew back toward Riff and bit her lip. "I think I hurt a leaf." She looked around and gulped. "Do you think anyone saw? Am I going to go to jail? I can't go to jail. I can't! Orange looks horrible on me."

Riff shook his head. "Nobody saw. We keep going."

They kept walking through the forest, climbing over and crawling under coiling roots. The air was so hot and humid Riff could barely breathe. Iridescent beetles fluttered about, lavender and azure. Every few steps, he had to pause while Romy tore through cobwebs with her claws and pitchfork. They kept climbing the mountainside, heading toward the crest, and soon Riff was winded. He thought the mountain would never end. Still he saw no sign of Steel and Nova, and even the sound of the *Dragon Huntress* faded. He heard nothing but the rustling trees, the splash of a nearby waterfall, and the bustling birds and insects.

"Come on, slowpoke!" Romy hovered a foot above the surface, wings beating like a hummingbird's. "You're slowing me down."

Riff wiped sweat off his brow and spat. "Shut it. First of all, you're from Hell and used to the heat. Second, you're flying. Third . . . shut up."

She flew down toward him, grabbed his hand, and tugged. "Come *on*! I want to see the spider eggs. Can I have one? Can I adopt just one baby spider?"

He glowered. "Romy! No. For pity's sake, no. You saw what they're like as adults. We burn them all."

She pouted. "But I want one! I want a pet. I want one I want one I want--"

"Romy, shut it!"

She crossed her arms and turned away from him. They kept moving up the mountainside until finally, when Riff was wheezing and soaked in sweat, they reached the top.

Oh stars above.

Riff's breath died and his heart sank.

A carpet of cobwebs covered the mountaintop, hiding every last tree and boulder. Upon the gossamer curtain gleamed countless eggs like dewdrops, each as large as Riff's fist. Some were white, others lavender, a few azure flecked with gold. They shone as bright as jewels.

"Pretty," Romy whispered, then bit her lip when Riff glared at her.

He looked around him, seeking the others. He saw no sign of Nova and Steel. Far above, he could see the *Dragon Huntress*. The warship's plasma gun was so massive that if fired, it would burn down the forest along with the eggs. It was up to little, handheld Ethel now.

"All right, Romster." Riff hefted his handgun. "Let's get to work. Ready to burn?"

She nodded and pressed a button on her pitchfork. Streams of fire spurted out from the prongs--an upgrade she had just installed a few days ago. "I'm a demon. I'm always ready to burn things."

They took another step toward the hive of eggs and raised their weapons.

The web parted.

With shrieks, a dozen spiders leaped out from the rent, flying toward Riff and Romy.

They cried out and fired their weapons.

The blasts washed against the spiders, doing the creatures no harm. These ones seemed different from the spiders in the forest--slicker, their bodies bristly with deep purple fur, their eyes red. Their green wings beat, and they soared high above Riff and Romy.

Females, he thought. *Spider nurses.*

He fired his gun. Romy screamed at his side, blasting fire from her pitchfork prongs. The inferno washed over the spiders. The creatures shrieked and turned tail, and for an instant Riff dared to hope they were fleeing.

Then the alien arachnids blasted out sticky, foul webs.

Riff fired his plasma, tearing holes through the cobwebs, but the bulk of the net fell onto him. The gossamer clung to his body, sticky, acidic, tightening across him. He fired blindly, but the damn web wrapped around his gun, yanking it from his hand.

"Captain!" Romy cried. He couldn't see her, could see only white strands, then a glimpse of purple as the spiders descended.

The aliens clattered and hissed. Legs grabbed Riff and hoisted him up, and fear flooded his belly. He struggled madly, trying to kick, to grab his gun again, even to bite through the net, but could not. Between strands of cobwebs, he saw the world spinning, saw the red eyes of the aliens, and then more strands wrapped around him. He spun madly like a spool.

They're wrapping me in more cobwebs. They're encasing me.

"Captain!" Romy shouted again, voice muffled.

He tried to shout back, but webs entered his mouth, sticky, silencing him. More cobwebs wrapped around his head. Darkness fell across him, and he saw and heard nothing more.

* * * * *

"Wait." Nova grabbed Steel's arm and held him back. A smile stretched across her face. "Let him hang for a while. Let him sweat. That'll teach him for not letting me bring my grenades."

They crouched behind a boulder--a gladiator in a golden catsuit, her whip in hand, and a knight in armor, holding his sword. Before them, across the mountaintop, several spiders were weaving two cocoons of cobwebs.

Steel stiffened. His armor clanked. "Riff and Romy are in there. They need us."

Nova grinned. "Exactly."

The gaunt knight groaned. "You're loving this, aren't you?"

She nodded. "Seeing Riff and the demon trussed up like hams? Better than Christmas."

"Riff does boss us around too much sometimes. And Romy, well . . . is Romy." Steel stared around the boulder at the two cocoons. The spiders were now carrying the gossamer bundles across their web. "I suppose we could let them miss us for a while longer before--"

A screech tore through the knight's words.

Nova spun around to see two spiders scurrying up the mountainside toward them. She leaped and swung her whip, blasting out bolts of electricity, and knocked one spider down. Steel rose to his feet and pointed his sword toward the second arachnid. Light gathered across the blade, then blasted out and seared the alien dead.

Nova yawned. "All right, let's go free the two. They have the plasma packs anyway, which we need for burning all those eggs, since *somebody* didn't let me bring grenades." She gestured toward the mountaintop where thousands of eggs gleamed upon the web. "We don't want to be here when these things hatch."

Gladiator and knight moved across the mountaintop, legs entangling in the web. It was slow work. Every step was a sticky mess. Steel had to keep swinging his sword and Nova her whip, cutting a path through the cobwebs.

The spiders ahead, the ones carrying the two bundles of gossamer, saw them. The creatures spun around and dropped the cocoons. From inside the bundles, Riff and Romy cried out in pain. The spiders screeched and came racing toward Nova and Steel, leaving the two silky balls to roll down the mountainside.

"Game's on," Nova said. "Bet I can kill more."

Steel thrust Solflare. A beam of light flew from the blade, slamming into one spider. The creature fell and writhed. "By my honor, you will never win."

She swung her whip, lashing out electricity, and sent another spider crashing down. "Like hell!"

The pair kept advancing, blasting out light and lightning. The spiders squealed. More flew from all around, crashing down, screaming as they died. One turned its backside toward Nova and blasted out a sticky net. She swung her whip, slicing through the cobwebs, sending strands raining down. Another web flew toward Steel. The knight cut through it with his sword, scattering gossamer.

Finally, with another few swings of the whip, Nova killed the last spider. She spat and wiped her hands against her pants.

"Done. I count nine spiders to me, six to you."

Steel bristled. "Lying goes against all codes of chivalry. I count eighteen spiders felled by my blade."

"What?" Nova yowled. "There weren't even eighteen spiders here! Count." She pointed at the corpses. "One. Two. Uhm . . . seven? Carrying the one . . ." She tapped her chin, then groaned. "In any case, far more have whip marks on them than sword cuts."

Steel glowered. "You do not know how to concede defeat. Nor count, apparently."

"Because I never lose! Steel, damn it." She placed her hands on her hips, glaring at him. "You'll have to admit that a woman-- yes, an actual woman!--beat you. That I'm a greater warrior than a knight. That I'm the greatest warrior in the cosmos. That . . . Steel? Steel, what are you looking at? Why are you pointing your sword at me?"

The knight was pale. "Nova, let's just say . . . whoever kills this new one wins."

Slowly, Nova spun around.

She felt the blood drain from her face.

"Fragging aardvarks," she whispered.

A new spider came lumbering up the mountain toward her. It made the dead spiders around her--corpses as large as cows-- seem small as arachnids from Earth. The spider ahead of Nova was larger than the *HMS Dragon Huntress.* Its legs soared like the columns of cathedrals. Its mandibles clanked like the engines of starships. Its bloated body dragged behind it, shimmering and translucent like glass, full of countless spider eggs that shone in the sunlight. Human skeletons hung around the spider's neck in a macabre necklace, clattering, swaying. The great spider blinked eight eyes, each as large as a watermelon. Blue eyes. Wise eyes. Eyes almost like a human's.

Nova gulped. "Let's kill it together and call it a tie."

"For Sol!" Steel cried and charged toward the enemy, sword flashing.

"For spider guts!" Nova cried, the only battle cry that came to her mind, and ran with him. She lashed her whip, blasting out sparks.

The whip's lightning and the sword's light slammed into the alien ahead.

The blasts scattered off the spider's glassy skin and shot back toward Nova and Steel.

Nova screamed and rolled. Her own bolt of lightning slammed into the ground beside her. She jumped up, hissed, and swung her whip again. More lightning flew toward the glass spider, only to bounce back toward her. She leaped aside, narrowly dodged the bolt, and tangled her legs in more cobwebs. She cursed, struggling to free herself. At her side, Steel struggled in his own patch of webs.

The massive spider stepped toward them, dragging its abdomen, towering above them. Its saliva oozed down its fangs. Its blue eyes stared in hatred. Nova grimaced and knew she was going to die.

* * * *

Riff groaned, encased in the cocoon of cobwebs. He heard his friends scream in the distance. They needed him. He writhed madly, struggling to free himself, but only rolled farther down the mountain.

"Wee!" Romy cried at his side. Through the strands, Riff saw the demon's cocoon roll alongside his. "Faster, faster!"

"Romy!" he shouted, voice muffled. "Damn it, Romy, use your claws! Use your fangs! Tear your way out."

The demon whooped. "But I'm having fun! Roll faster, Riff! Race you!"

The cocoons kept tumbling down the mountainside, banging over boulders and roots, moving farther and farther from the crest. Soon Riff couldn't even hear Nova and Steel scream.

The woman I love. And my brother. Riff grimaced, tugging madly at the sticky silk encasing him. *They're dying and I can't help them.*

"Romy, if you tear yourself out, I'll buy you that dinosaur toy you wanted."

She gasped, still rolling downhill beside him. "The purple one? That talks when you tickle it?"

"Yes, now tear yourself out! Use your claws."

"But it has to be the *real* Tickle-Me-T-Rex, not one of the knockoffs."

"The real one, fine!" Riff shouted

"Can I have the Hug-Me-Hedgehog too?"

"Yes, now do it!"

Glancing between the strands of his own cocoon, he saw Romy tear into the webs encasing her. Her claws sliced like knives. Her fangs tore through the cobwebs like a famished Tasmanian devil. Soon the demon kicked off the last silky strands, stretched out her wings, and flew toward Riff. With a few slices of her claws, she tore him free.

"Buy me the dinosaur!" She bounced around. "Buy me buy me buy . . ."

He ignored her and ran. He ran faster than he ever had, racing up the hill, stumbling over roots, leaping up and running again. Sweat washed over him. His heart thudded. His fist shook around his gun's handle. Romy flew beside him, all the while babbling on about her toy.

Finally, wheezing, Riff reached the mountaintop.

That wheezing breath died.

A towering spider, large as a starship, loomed over Nova and Steel. The gladiator and the knight stood trapped in a gossamer field, writhing but unable to free their legs. The giant spider's body seemed made of glass; Riff could see thousands of eggs inside its belly. The creature leaned down, mouth opening wide to consume the two people Riff loved most in the world.

Riff fired his gun.

The plasma blast flew through the air and slammed into the spider's head.

The giant alien squealed. The plasma cascaded off it, bouncing down to burn a hole into cobwebs below. Its blue eyes narrowed with rage, turning to stare at him. Those eyes seemed almost humanlike.

"She's intelligent," Riff whispered. "She's not just an animal."

I can't kill her, he realized. How could he kill an intelligent animal? How could--

As the spider came walking toward him, he saw human skeletons draped around her neck. He gulped.

"Yeah, I'm going to kill it."

He fired his gun again. But once more, the plasma bounced off the creature's glassy head. The bolt shot back toward Riff, and he leaped aside. Romy flew up with a wail. The plasma burned a hole into the cobwebs around them.

The glass spider opened her mouth and let out a long, hoarse hiss that coalesced into words.

"Die . . ." The voice was like wind in caves, like the whispers of ghosts, like the call of death itself. "Die, human . . . Die . . ."

She came walking toward Riff on stilt-like legs.

Romy wailed and hid behind a tree.

Riff sneered, raced forward, and grabbed one of the spider eggs that lay in the cobwebs. He tore the gleaming orb free. The mother spider screeched. Riff raised the egg above his head and pointed his plasma gun at it.

"Freeze!" he said. "Freeze or baby spider gets it!"

Inwardly, he sighed. *Another entry to my ever-expanding "Words I never thought I'd utter" list.*

The glass spider screamed. Saliva sprayed from her mouth. Her eyes blazed with hatred.

But she froze.

I have to get her away from Nova and Steel. I have to save them.

"Want your egg back?" Riff shouted.

The spider opened her jaws wide, screaming. Her breath blasted against Riff, scented of corpses. Strings of saliva dangled between her teeth. The human skeletons jangled around her neck.

"You want this?" Riff shouted again. "Go get it! Fetch!"

He tossed the egg as hard as he could, hurling it across the mountaintop.

The glass spider squealed and spun around. Her abdomen swung, scraping across the cobwebs. As she began to chase the egg, Riff stared, eyes narrowed.

A slit yawned open on the spider's backside, leading to a canal, just narrow enough to stop the eggs inside from spilling out.

Riff aimed his gun.

He closed one eye.

"Burn, space scum," he whispered . . . and pulled the trigger.

His aim was true. His plasma blasted forth, hit the slit, and roared into the spider's abdomen.

Inside the creature, the fire raged, kindling the eggs. These eggs were smaller than those already on the mountainside, brittle, flammable. Flames raged inside the spider's glass abdomen, consuming the eggs, and the creature screamed.

Romy stepped up toward Riff and gasped. "You shot her in the bum!"

He grumbled. "It wasn't her bum. It's the stomach."

The demon covered her mouth. "Bum-shooter! Oh, that's low, Riff. Even for you."

"It's not her bum!"

He fired again. Again. More plasma streamed forward and entered the spider. An inferno raged inside her body, streaming through her belly, along her legs, in her mouth, blasting out of her eyes.

With a cry of rage, the giant spider collapsed.

The corpse slammed down onto the mountaintop, burning.

The fire began to spread across the cobwebs cloaking the mountain.

Across the web, the laid eggs began to expand and crack.

As the shells shattered, little spiders emerged, only for the fire to grab them.

Riff grimaced and ran. He raced through the flames, leaped over one of the fallen spider's legs, and headed toward Nova and Steel.

"Nova!" Riff cried. He reached her, leaned down, and began tugging cobwebs off her legs. "Nova, I'm here to save you."

"What?" Her eyes widened and she spat. "Spaceshit, Riff. I saved *you*."

He groaned, tugging one of her legs loose. "What are you talking about?"

"When the spiders had you! I shot them dead."

Riff rolled his eyes. "Little good that did me." He yanked her leg free, then the other one.

Once she was free, he turned toward Steel and helped the knight extricate himself.

"I thank you, brother." Steel bowed his head. "You fought nobly. You saved us."

"No he didn't!" Nova growled and stamped her feet, only entangling them in more cobwebs. "He didn't save a damn thing. He got lucky, that's all. A lucky shot, and besides, I had already wounded the spider, and--"

"Will you shut it?" Riff said. "The whole damn mountain is burning."

He stared around. Flames raged across the mountaintop. All around, the eggs were popping.

He grabbed Nova's wrist and tugged her toward him.

"Hey, let go!" she said.

He ignored her and spoke into her communicator. "Giga! Giga, do you read me? We need those cables! Fish us up!"

The android's voice rose through the speakers, chipper as always. "Happy to comply!"

Engines roared above. Riff looked up to see the *HMS Dragon Huntress* flying down toward them. Cables spooled out from its airlock. Riff grabbed one cable and attached it to his harness. Nova and Steel did the same.

"Where's Romy?" Riff said. "Where's the damn demon? Romy!"

He saw nothing but flames around him.

Above, the *Dragon Huntress* began to rise, pulling him off the ground.

"Romy!" Riff shouted, looking around. "Damn it, where are you?"

He saw no sign of the demon, and he just hoped that, as a being of Hell, she could survive the flames. The cables were spooling up, tugging him, Nova, and Steel toward the starship's airlock.

"Romy!" he cried again.

The cable kept reeling him upward. When Riff glanced above, he could see Piston, chief engineer of the *Dragon Huntress*, operating the spool. A few hundred meters above the mountaintop, Riff finally reached the airlock and climbed into the ship. Nova and Steel climbed in with him.

"Where's the damn demon?" said Piston. The squat gruffle, shorter than Riff's shoulders but twice as wide, tugged at his white beard.

Oh stars, Riff thought, sinking to his knees. He stared down, seeing nothing but fire and smoke on the mountaintop. *Oh stars, is she . . .*

Steel lowered his head, and even Nova was pale.

"Romy . . ." Riff whispered.

"Captain?" The demon's voice rose through Nova's communicator. "Captain, wait for me! Wait up!"

Riff gasped and leaped to his feet.

"There!" He pointed.

Rising from the flames like a phoenix, Romy flew from the mountaintop. Her fiery hair crackled. Her bat wings beat. Her pitchfork shone in the sunlight.

Nova groaned. "Leave her behind."

"Nova!" Riff glowered at the gladiator, then leaned over the ledge and reached down his hand. Romy flew up, grabbed him, and nearly yanked Riff down to his death. It took the other Alien Hunters to grab the demon and hoist her up.

"I think you burned a few leaves down there, Riff." The demon poked his chest. "You're in *so* much trouble, mister."

Riff sighed.

"I'm just glad you're alive, Romy." He turned toward the others. "And you, Nova. And you, Steel." He cracked his neck. "Everything hurts and there are spider guts all over me."

"Race you to the shower," Nova said.

With curses, squeals, and jutting elbows, they ran up the stairs, heading deeper into the starship.

Below them, upon the mountaintop, the alien invaders burned.

Aliens saw, aliens came, aliens conquered. Riff reached the bathroom first and slammed the door shut, sealing the others outside. *Aliens were hunted.*

The shower's hot water washed over his naked body, cleaning away the blood, the ash, the ooze.

After a long moment, a knock sounded on the door.

"Can you let in at least one other hunter?"

Nova's voice.

Riff reached an arm out from the shower and unlocked the bathroom door. The ashai gladiator stepped inside, her golden armor covered in smoke and cobwebs. She slipped out of the garment, the steam barely hiding her nakedness, and stepped into the shower with him.

Their bodies pressed together, and Riff wrapped his arms around her, and he kissed her.

"All right," Nova whispered into his ear, nibbling on the lobe. "I'll give you this one. You saved my ass down there."

The steam rose around them, and they kissed until the others were banging on the door.

Riff sighed as he held Nova close. "I change my mind. I love this job."

* * * * *

The attic of the *Dragon Huntress* was a dark, cluttered place. Boxes, tubes, pipes, and sacks of odds and ends rose all around. A single lightbulb glowed above, barely lighting the chamber. It was dingy, hot, and shadowy. It was Romy's home.

The demon could hear the other Alien Hunters below. Somebody was still in the shower, while others were moving around the kitchen and main deck. Nobody else ever came up here. This was Romy's kingdom, her little corner of Hell.

Gingerly, she reached under her shirt and pulled out the small, gleaming orb.

It was no larger than her fist. Blue mottled with gold. Glassy.

"An alien egg," she whispered in awe.

A pet would be better than all the toys in the world. Better than a million Tickle-Me-T-Rexes. Better than poodle soup. It was what Romy had always longed for.

Gingerly, as if handling a holy relic, she placed the egg on a pile of old laundry. She sat on it ever so gently, careful not to crush it.

"I'll keep you warm." She reached beneath her to pat the egg, then wriggled about. "I'll keep you safe and secret."

She thought she felt the egg thrumming, thought she heard a whisper from within. She smiled and draped her wings around herself, roosting on her prize.

CHAPTER TWO

A MESSAGE FROM HOME

Twiggle Jauntyfoot sat at the kitchen table with her fellow Alien Hunters, enjoying a feast, when the message came in from her planet, heralding the doom of her homeworld.

"Hand me another chicken leg, lassie." Piston leaned across the table, reaching a massive brown hand toward the plate of roast fowl. Like all gruffles, he was muscular and wide, his hands strong enough to crush stones, but his limbs were short.

"Your beard's dipping into the gravy!" Riff said, poking the gruffle. The captain was leaning back in his seat, chomping on an apple.

Piston grumbled and pulled his luxurious white beard--his pride and joy--out of the dish. The gruffle grumbled. "That's because nobody passes me anything around here. Twig, you clod! Chicken!"

Riff rolled his eyes. "Piston, for pity's sake, you've eaten two whole birds already. I know we made good money killing those spiders, but you're eating us out of house and home."

"Gruffles eat a lot!" The engineer groaned, leaned closer, and managed to grab a drum stick. He fell back into his seat with a sigh and sucked the meat off the bone. "Twig!" He spoke as he chewed. "Twig, damn it, what's wrong with you?"

The others all turned to stare at her. Nova and Steel sat farther back, eating from plates of spiced potatoes, fried chicken, and stewed greens. Romy was slumped on the floor, crumbs on her face, her belly bulging. Even Giga sat with them, a few bolts and screws on her plate--an old joke they liked to play on the android. Everyone stared at Twig now, even the moaning demon on the floor.

"Twig?" Piston's voice softened, and concern suffused his wide, chestnut-brown face. "Are you all right, lassie?"

She was trembling. She could barely breathe. She kept staring at the communicator on her wrist, reading the words on the monitor over and over.

A message from Haven.

From her home.

A message of doom.

"It's . . . it's from home," Twig whispered. "A message from Haven. They need our help."

She leaped to her feet, trembling. Like all halflings, she stood under four feet tall, barely reaching the tabletop. She was tiny compared to the other Alien Hunters, even tiny compared to the squat Piston. She was the shortest, the weakest, the meekest, and stars above, her people were just as small. Without help, they would die.

Riff stepped around the table and knelt before Twig. He held her hand, eyes soft. "What does the message say?"

Alien Sky

Twig swallowed. "A machine." She shuddered. "A machine with blades for arms. A robot moving through the forest, cutting, burning . . . killing." Her voice dropped to a whisper. "Killing halflings, Captain."

Gently, Riff turned her wrist and examined the message on her communicator. His eyes darkened.

"They want to hire us." Riff looked back at the others. "Planet Haven needs us now. As soon as we can get there."

The others exchanged glances.

"Riff," Nova said, "we're still burnt and bruised from the damn spiders. We haven't had a day off in ages, and--"

"We have to go." Twig leaped onto her chair and stared at Nova, then at the others, one by one. "We have to. I know my people can't pay much. Only a thousand credits, barely enough to cover the cost of fuel. But . . . please. Please! They're dying." Tears gathered in her eyes. "This robot is tearing them apart. It's my home."

Planet Haven. Twig closed her eyes and let the memories fill her. The fields of corn and barley spreading into the sunset. Old Major Woodwick, the great havenwood tree that grew in her village, leaves rustling in the wind. Strawberries and cream and steaming apple pie. The little robots she would build from spare motors in the toolshed--clattering little dogs, cats, and soldiers her old gaffer would call junkbots. Twig had never truly belonged there, a mechanic in a world of farmers, and she had left as a youth, but it was still her homeland. Still the anchor of her soul. She could not let it burn.

She opened her eyes and looked around her at the walls of the *Dragon Huntress*. Her new home. She looked at her fellow Alien Hunters. Her new family. But she could not forget where she had come from.

"I'll pay you myself." Twig reached into her pocket and began pulling out Haven bills. Each was printed with a holographic acorn, symbol of her people. "Everything I've saved. Please, Captain." She turned toward Riff. "Please. We have to take this job."

Riff turned to look at the others. Nova sighed. Steel raised his chin and clutched his sword. Romy drooled on the floor.

Riff turned back toward Twig. He held her shoulders. "Of course, Twig. Of course."

* * * * *

Riff sat on the bridge, staring at the head-up display, turning the image around, zooming in, zooming out, scanning it over and over.

"Frag it, Riff, you've been looking at this photograph for an hour now." Nova groaned and slumped back in her seat. "Give it a rest."

He sighed and gave the image one last look. A grainy photograph from Planet Haven. Black and white. Smudged. Barely more than shadows. In the center, Riff could just make out the figure. A robot, vaguely humanoid, with chainsaws for arms.

Its white eyes blazed as if staring out of the image, staring right at Riff, vowing to cut him too.

"Giga, run another scan," Riff said. "See if you can find who built this machine. Whatever factory it came from, even whatever planet is a lead."

The android sat to Riff's left, filling the third seat on the bridge. She tilted her head. "Already complied, Captain. Five times now. No record of any similar robot in any known star system, Captain. This machine was built off record or on a planet we're unfamiliar with."

"Alien robots." Nova flicked her whip. "Lovely. If there's anything worse than giant spiders with wings, it's alien robots with chainsaws for arms. I miss the days when we were fishing fuzzballs out of silos."

Riff turned toward her, finally looking away from the photograph. "Nov, you used to be a gladiator, fighting massive aliens in the Alien Arena."

"Aliens." She nodded. "Not robots."

"I'm pretty sure aliens built this robot. It still counts." Riff sighed and turned off the HUD. "And Twig's people need us. How often do we get to be heroes?"

"Every day?" Nova said. "Whenever we do a job?"

"Well, this one job will make us heroes to Twig. We send the little mechanic into snot-monster nostrils and down tardigrade throats. Piston even had Twig crawl in to unclog the plumbing the other day. It's time we do something for the halfling."

Nova groaned. "Fine! We'll smash the damn robot. A few grenades will do the job."

"You're not bringing grenades down onto Haven."

"Riff!" Her green eyes flashed. "Can't I ever bring grenades anywhere?"

"Not onto inhabited planets! We're pest controllers, not space marines."

He looked out the windshield. They were traveling through hyperspace, their engines warping spacetime around them, letting the *Dragon Huntress* fly at many times the speed of light. The stars streamed alongside as lines, white and blue and purple, and between them floated glowing smudges. Somewhere out there in the distance, orbiting Teegarden's Star in the Aries constellation, spun the planet of Haven. And somewhere farther out there, maybe only a few light-years past Haven, maybe galaxies away, somebody had built this machine that was destroying Twig's home.

"We've colonized dozens of planets," Riff said softly. "We've explored thousands of stars. Yet we've seen only a tiny fraction of a percent of our cosmos. What's out there?"

Nova yawned. "Pillows. Lots of space pillows. That's all I can think about right now." She rose from her chair and stretched. "I'm off to bed. Gig, be a dear and wake me up when we're near Haven." As she walked by Riff, Nova mussed his hair. "Coming to bed?"

He stared out into space. "Not yet."

She yawned again. "Good. More room for me."

The ashai gladiator stepped off the bridge, leaving Riff and Giga alone. For a long time, the two sat in silence, staring out into hyperspace.

Finally, Giga twisted her fingers in her lap, turned toward Riff, and spoke in a low voice. "Captain? You don't think that . . . that the others think *all* us robots are evil. Do you?"

"What?" Riff frowned, reached over, and took her hand in his. "Giga! Why would anyone think that?"

Giga lowered her head. "I am a robot too, Captain. A Human Interface Android, not a metal warrior like the one on Haven. I look human, but still a robot. Still a machine." Her eyes shone with tears. "Will Twig fear me now? Will her fellow halflings . . . will they hate me?"

Riff rose to his feet. "Giga, come here with me."

She stood up too, and they walked together to stand by the windshield. They stared out into the lights and darkness.

"What are we looking at, sir?" Giga asked, voice soft.

"What do you see, Giga? What do you see out there?"

She bit her lip, staring out into hyperspace. "I see . . . streams of photons distorted in warped spacetime, flowing uninterrupted through the Higgs field. Lights. Pretty lights. Streams of white and smudges of blue and purple like watercolor stains. I see millions of stars and millions of planets. I see countless lives, souls born crying, growing, loving, building, fading away and rising again as new light. I see hope, Captain." She turned toward him. "I see wonder."

He nodded. "I had a little robot dog as a kid. You know what it would see, if it were here? Not a damn thing." He squeezed her hand. "Gig, you are more than just a robot, more than just a machine. You have thoughts. Feelings. A sense of wonder. You are alive."

"But . . . Captain, I was never born from a womb. I was built in a factory only sixteen years ago. I'm a machine."

"We're all machines of a sort. You're made of synthetic parts, and I'm made of organic molecules, but we're both machines, and we're both living, thinking, feeling beings. Nobody is going to hate you because of one bad robot, Giga. The same way nobody will hate me because they once met one bad human. I promise you."

She embraced him and laid her head against his shoulder. "Arigato, Captain." She touched his cheek. "You are right, sir. I can feel. I can dream. I can lo--" Giga looked away. "I can love. I'm sorry, Captain." She returned to her seat, eyes damp. "I have to keep an eye on the controls. I have to make sure we get to Haven on time." She looked back at him, tears on her cheeks-- synthetic tears on synthetic skin, released by an algorithm, yet real tears nonetheless. "You should return to Nova. You should get some sleep."

Riff looked at her, suddenly not sure what to say. He thought back to how Giga had kissed him above Planet Cirona a few months ago, how she had felt so human to him, so fragile, warm, needing him. How he had felt strong, a man who could protect her, even love her.

He lowered his head. *Yet I gave my heart to Nova. The woman I've loved for years. The woman who followed me across the galaxy, who broke my heart, then mended it again.*

"Goodnight, Giga," he whispered. It was all he could say, perhaps all he should say now.

He left her on the bridge and, when he reached the doorway, looked back once. Giga stood by the windshield again, staring outside, a lonely figure, so small by the vastness of the cosmos. Riff's heart twisted to see her there, and he longed to rush back to her, to hold her again, to comfort her. Yet he could not.

He turned away. He walked downstairs. He entered his quarters.

Nova was sprawled out on his bed, sleeping. *Their* bed now, he supposed. Her hair spread out around her, a puddle of gold. Her chest gently rose and fell. Riff stood for a moment, gazing at her freckled face, her high cheekbones, her pointy ears. She had left him two Earth years ago. She had only begun sleeping in his bed again because, she claimed, the others in the crew quarters kept snoring.

Yet somehow, over the past few weeks, Riff and Nova had found themselves making love every night. Found themselves living almost as they had years ago, as a couple in love. Perhaps they *were* a couple again. Perhaps she loved him again. Perhaps here on this starship--not on her planet, not on his planet, but here within the belly of a dragon--they had finally found a home.

He climbed into bed with her. She moaned and nestled against him, but she did not wake. He held her close as she slept, but he could find no rest. He lay awake, staring up at the shadowy ceiling, thinking of halflings, of robots, and of a lonely soul on a dark bridge.

CHAPTER THREE

FIRE OVER HAVEN

With a *pop* and flash of light, the *HMS Dragon Huntress* glided out of hyperdrive above Planet Haven.

Standing on the bridge, Riff stared down at the green homeland of the halflings. It was a small planet, not much larger than Earth's moon, orbiting a small sun called Teegarden's Star. Even from this distance, Riff could see forests, squares of tilled farmlands, and many snaking rivers.

While he stared down at the world, the other Alien Hunters stood behind him. Giga's voice rose among them.

"Three thousand, two hundred, and seventeen Earth years ago, human colonists reached the Aries system and settled on Planet Haven. The planet is much smaller than Earth, the gravity weaker. Over time, the human colonists evolved, shrinking in size to match their smaller world. Five hundred and twelve Earth years ago, the Humanoid Academy finally granted the denizens of Haven the status of sub-species, naming them *homo sapiens havenis*. Or halflings, as we call them, though some have argued that the term *halfling* is derogative, that--"

"Boring!" Romy's whine rose over the android's words. "I don't care about no damn history lessons, Giga. I want to go kill robots! I mean . . ." The demon gulped. "Not kill you, Giga. You're a good robot, mostly. You never stink up the bathroom or anything. Not like Piston over here." The demon turned to glare at the gruffle.

Piston blustered. His white eyebrows bristled, and he tugged his long white beard. "Stink up the--" The squat gruffle trembled with rage. "Why you-- good for nothing, confounded--"

He could say no more, only spray spittle and reach out to grab Romy. The demon squealed and ran, tripping over Twig. The halfling cried out, and Steel intervened, placing his armored body between the combatants, and soon Nova was shouting at everyone, and Giga was fleeing, and the whole ship seemed likely to crash down.

"Silence!" Riff roared. "For pity's sake, stop it, everyone! We're professionals."

They froze and stared at him, blinking.

Riff sighed. "All right, so we're a bunch of rude, crude miscreants. But let's be professional for once. This is Twig's home. We're here to face a threat we don't understand." He pointed at the demon. "Romy, you're to stay here and guard the ship."

"What? No!" The demon growled. "I want shore leave."

"Too bad. This isn't a wild jungle. We're landing in the town of Acorngrove. In civilization. If the halflings see a demon--specifically, the most annoying demon this side of Hell--they're likely to send us away and just keep the chainsaw robot." Riff turned toward the others. "The rest of you, I want you all on your best behavior. No fighting. No cussing. And no grenades, Nova."

The gladiator groaned and tossed aside the grenades she was carrying, making everyone wince. "And maybe you, Riff Starfire, should wear proper pants."

"Jeans are proper pants."

"Not when there's a hole in them I could stick my fist into!"

Riff stared down at the tear in his jeans, struggling to remember which enemy had ripped it. Finally he sighed and turned toward Giga.

"Gigs, take us down to Acorngrove. We'll go take care of this robot, then come back and Nova can learn how to sew my jeans."

"What?" It was Nova's turn to bluster. "You piece of-- whoa!"

The gladiator fell to the floor. Everyone jolted madly. Romy wailed. Sparks blazed across the bridge and alarms wailed.

"Giga, what's going on?" Riff shouted.

"Enemy vessel attacking, Captain!" said the android.

"Where? I don't see any--" Riff gasped. "Oh shenanigans."

Outside the windshield, space wavered. A starship appeared out of nowhere, flickered, and solidified. It wasn't a large ship, no larger than the *Dragon Huntress*, but a nasty piece of metal. Mandibles stretched out from it, ending with whirring saw blades.

The ship's cannons lit up, and photon blasts slammed into the *Dragon Huntress* again.

The bridge rattled madly.

"Giga, fire!" Riff shouted.

The *Dragon Huntress* turned toward the enemy vessel, rose in space, and blasted out its dragonfire.

Streams of plasma blazed forward and washed over the enemy ship. The heat bent the metal. Panels on the enemy ship melted. Holes tore into the vessel.

Yet it kept charging forth, blades whirring.

"Damn it!" Riff cried. "Giga, fire again!"

More plasma blasted out of the *Dragon*, slamming into the enemy starship. Holes tore open in its flank, exposing its innards, yet still it flew toward them.

"How can they keep flying?" Riff said. "They're breached! How are they breathing?"

Giga tilted her head. "Scans show no life forms on board, sir." She turned toward him, eyes wide. "A robot ship."

"Fire again."

More plasma blasted out, tearing into the enemy vessel, but it kept charging, too fast. Its spinning saw blades reached out toward the *Dragon Huntress.*

"Giga, get us out of here!"

The android complied, raising the starship higher, but one of those spinning blades scraped along the hull. Metal screeched.

"Crew quarters are breached, Captain!" Giga said. "Air escaping from our hull!"

"Seal it off and fire again! Fire everything!"

"Happy to comply! Emptying all plasma reserves, Captain."

An inferno blazed out from the *Dragon Huntress*, blue in its center, casting out flares of white and yellow. The flames slammed into the enemy vessel, melting its hull. A wing tore free. The engines shattered and exploded. With a great shower of metal, the enemy warship went plunging down toward the planet.

As it collapsed, a hundred fragments came flying toward the *Dragon Huntress*.

At first, Riff mistook them for debris, mere wreckage. Then he saw that each fragment was bowl-shaped, lined with legs, and blinking red lights.

"Drones," he muttered. "Robot drones. Giga, burn them down!"

"Cannot compute, Captain. All plasma is spent." The android tilted her head. "You told me before to fire everything, sir. So I fired everything."

"Good job, Captain Starfire," Nova interjected with a groan.

The little drones--they reminded Riff of horseshoe crabs, round critters he used to see on Earth's beaches--flew toward the *Dragon Huntress*. The walls clattered as the drones hit them. The metal dented.

"Damn leeches are latching onto us!" Nova cried. "None of this would have happened if you had approved my grenade cannon idea."

"No grenades!" Riff said, watching a wall dent to his left with the marks of clinging little legs. He turned toward Giga. "We'll burn 'em off in entry. Gig, charge through the atmosphere. Fast as you can without us shattering. Let's rip those bastards off our hull."

The android smiled. "Happy to comply, Captain!"

The *Dragon Huntress* turned and began charging toward the planet. Below them, Riff could see the fragments of the enemy ship burning up as they entered the atmosphere. And then the fire engulfed the *Dragon Huntress*, roaring, streaming across the windshield, thrumming along the walls. Along with the shrieks of air, he heard little thuds which, he hoped, were the drones breaking off.

Across the deck, the Alien Hunters swayed and fell as the ship rocked. Nova landed in her seat and clutched the armrests. Riff sat down too, his belly rising into his throat. Romy wailed and fell to the floor, and Giga fell right into Riff's lap again, as she seemed to do every time they flew toward a planet; he was beginning to suspect the android's falls were less than accidental. He held her tight as the ship roared through the air.

Finally blue skies opened up around them. Clouds floated like sheep. Golden fields, autumn forests, and silver rivers spread below.

The ship leveled off.

The roars died down.

Riff exhaled, realizing he had been holding his breath.

He rose to his shaky feet. "What the hell was that thing up there?"

Giga tilted her head. "Cannot compute, Captain. Enemy vessel does not match any designs in my data banks."

Trembling, Twig walked up to them. The halfling was pale, and she wrung her hands. "I'll tell you what it was. The ship that brought the chainsaw robot here. Did you see the blades on that ship?" She shuddered. "Same blades as the robot down below has. The robot that's destroying my homeland." She allowed herself a shaky smile. "It was good to blow it out of the sky, wasn't it, Captain?"

He mussed the little mechanic's hair. "Very good. Now we just need to find our guy below and blast him apart too."

Twig walked toward the windshield and placed her hands against the glass. "Haven." Her voice was wistful, her eyes damp. "Home."

As they kept descending, a town came into view. At first Riff didn't even realize it *was* a town; he saw only a few fields, a few barns, and many trees. Yet as the *Dragon Huntress* glided closer, he noticed that chimneys rose from the canopy, and that rope bridges stretched from tree to tree, and he glimpsed treehouses among the branches.

"A town in the trees!" he said.

Twig nodded. "Acorngrove. My hometown." The halfling pointed toward a grassy yard. Several small green starjets stood there, their hulls painted with acorns, sigil of Haven. "Can you land there, Giga?"

The android nodded. "Happy to comply!"

As the *Dragon Huntress* continued descending toward the yard, Riff saw that several trees had been cut down near the town. The trunks lay scattered and burnt. A treehouse lay on the ground, shattered. A few fresh graves rose beside it. Before he could take a closer look, the *Dragon Huntress* slowed to a hover above the yard, then thumped down with a cloud of dust.

Riff took a deep breath. "Every damn planet we arrive at, something tries to blast us away before we can land." He shook his head. "Every damn planet."

He left the bridge, walked through the ship, and opened the airlock. He stepped out onto a planet of lush trees, golden fields, and a robot that, Riff did not doubt, would very soon try to kill him.

CHAPTER FOUR

GRUFFLES AND GANGS

Piston couldn't believe it. Not only had he somehow, against all odds, befriended a halfling, now he was on a whole damn planet full of them.

"I'd be the joke of Gruffstone," he grumbled as he climbed the ladder, reaching toward the hull of the *Dragon Huntress*. "Me, a proud gruffle, surrounded by clod-brained halflings!"

He looked behind him, wobbling on the ladder. Several of the halflings were rushing forth from the town. Tiny critters. Barely more than three feet tall, clad in brown trousers, yellow vests with brass buttons, and green cloaks. Their skin ranged in tone from pale, like Twig's, to deep brown like his own. A few of them raced toward Twig, and others crowded around Captain Riff, half his height, and shook his hand.

"Clod-brains, all of them," Piston muttered, turning back toward the ship.

It wasn't that he hated halflings. Not truly. And it wasn't that any halflings had hurt him personally. But . . . for pity's sake, the damn things just made gruffles look bad. Piston thought back to his father, letting the memories fill him.

"Piston, my boy!" the old gruffle had said. "This time we're going to make it. We're going to become full-fledged, Top Tier members of the Humanoid Alliance. No longer junior members, but true allies to Earth and Ashmar."

The old ambassador had blasted off to Mars, clad in fineries, and Piston--only a youth then--had joined him. There, in the glittering halls of the Humanoid Alliance Headquarters, they had walked among humans--tall, noble humans, the parent race, the race that had spawned all humanoids. In those halls, Piston had seen ashais too--proud warriors, as tall as humans, clad in golden catsuits, electric whips at their sides, their hair long and blond, their eyes green and bright.

Walking among these tall and slender folk, Piston had felt clumsy as an oaf. His father, a great lord back on Gruffstone, barely reached the shoulders of these humans and ashais. Neither did Piston who stood even shorter. Their stocky bodies, used to the gravity of Gruffstone, wobbled here in the lighter gravity the humans and ashais favored. Their gruffle garments--fine leather studded with iron bolts--suddenly seemed crude to Piston, mere rags compared to what the humans and ashais wore.

And in those glittering halls, the ushers had sat Piston and his father down . . . right at the back. Right by the halflings.

Oh by the gods of rock and stone! The little halflings, even shorter than gruffles and much thinner, had laughed, sung songs, and chattered away, delighted to even be invited to this conference with the nobler, taller races. The halflings had no ambitions. They had never even considered applying to become

Top Tier members. It seemed the little clods had only shown up here to enjoy the buffet.

Piston sat among them, stewing.

"They placed us at the children's table!" he said.

His father said nothing, only stared with dark eyes.

"Why hello, little halfling!" one human woman said to Piston that day, patting him on the head.

"I'm not a halfling!" he blurted out. "Don't you see my beard? I'm a gruffle. A proud gruffle. Just as proud as humans and ashais. I--"

But everyone just laughed. And so Piston and his father returned home to Gruffstone shamefaced, rejected, one of the lesser races.

It's because they sat us with the halflings, Piston thought. *Just because we gruffles are short too doesn't mean we're meek farmers, that we lack ambition or strength or courage.*

Piston shook his head wildly, returning his thoughts to the present day. He would bear this stay on Haven. He would suffer the shame for his friends--and yes, even Twig, a halfling, was his friend. But once he was off this forsaken planet, Piston would breathe a sigh of relief and never return.

He stared back at the starship hull. One of the damn gizmos, those bowl-shaped drones the enemy vessel had blasted out, clung to the *Dragon Huntress* like a tick. Piston raised his screwdriver and scraped it off. The doohickey fell into his hand, and he stared at it. Damn thing was fried. Entering the atmosphere had cracked the metal casing and burned the insides.

Piston could make out some wires, a few processing chips, and claws. What the damn thing was for he had no idea. He tossed it to the ground in disgust.

"Hey!" Romy said, walking below the ladder. "You almost hit me."

"Damn." Piston climbed a few more rungs and reached toward another one of the clinging drones. "I was aiming for you. Will you fly up and help me scrape off these barnacles?"

Romy placed her hands on her hips. "They're not barnacles. They're too big. They look more like robot isopods." She tapped her chin. "Or maybe robot dessert bowls. Do you think they have dessert in them?" She gasped. "Do you think there's poodle custard in them?"

"Will you shut up and help?"

She sighed, beat her bat wings, and flew up. Piston kept working with his screwdriver, and Romy worked with her claws. Dozens of the metallic parasites still covered the hull, all burnt and cracked, their machinery fried. Piston and the demon kept tossing them down onto the ground until they were all removed. The things had left ugly marks on the hull. It would take Piston hours to smooth out the dents and patch up the holes.

When he climbed down the ladder and placed his feet on the ground--the damn surface of Halfling-world, no less!--Captain Riff came to meet him.

"What are they?" the human said, gazing down at the charred gizmos.

Piston grunted. "Not sure yet, sir. I'll bring 'em on board and try to analyze them. I'll need to see if I can salvage any of their internal mechanisms, run a few scans, see what I find. Might be a weapon of some sort, maybe probes." He glanced around uneasily at the landscape of trees, fields, and halflings. "Mind if I sit this one out, sir? I could use the time for my work, and, well . . . I'm not really one for trees and fields."

Riff shook his head. "I need you with me. I need your hammer. I need your strength." He placed a hand on Piston's shoulder. "Trees never hurt no one, but robots might, and I need you to help me fight one. Place the drones on board, and leave Romy to guard them." Riff turned toward the demon. "Romy, back on the ship! I told you not to step outside."

Romy was busy chasing a poodle around a tree, trying to stuff it into a pot. When she turned toward Riff, the pup managed to run off. The demon groaned.

"I almost got him!" She stamped her feet. "We could have dined on poodle soup tonight if you hadn't distracted me, Captain."

Riff pointed to the airlock. "Romy, ship. Now."

The demon rolled her eyes. "Fine! I have things to do on the ship anyway." A guilty look crossed her face, and she glanced up toward the attic porthole. "I'll be in my attic if anyone needs me."

With that, the demon darted through the airlock, and an instant later, her red face peeked out the attic porthole.

Riff gently tugged Piston's shoulder, guiding him away from the ship. "Come on, old boy. Romy and Giga will hold down the fort. Let's get to work."

Piston hesitated, feet planted firmly on the ground. "I . . . Captain, I . . ." He glanced around nervously. "They're not going to think I'm a halfling too, are they?"

Riff's eyes widened. "Bloody hell, man. You look like you eat halflings for breakfast. I've driven sports cars with less muscle than you. Come on, Piston, let's go. Twig's taking us to see her father. Her old gaffer, she calls him. He's mayor around here and can tell us about this bot that's been causing trouble."

Grumbling and tugging his beard, Piston followed, vowing to burst into an old gruffle war song if anyone dared mistake him for a halfling again.

Damn, clod-brained little critters, he thought. *Always smiling and laughing and singing. Even with a damn robot cutting down their damn allergy-inducing trees.*

As he walked away from the starship, the only home Piston had known for over a year now, the halflings rushed toward him. Several children gaped at him. Others danced around him, tugging at his beard and calling out, "Uncle Gruffle, Uncle Gruffle!"

"Be gone with you!" Piston said, shaking his fist, but they wouldn't scatter. A few halfling women stepped forward with garlands of flowers and placed them on his head. Piston grumbled, but as soon as he tore one wreath off, another halfling placed more flowers on his head.

"I'm allergic!" he said. "Can't abide any flowers."

He missed Gruffstone. Back on that great rocky world, there were no damn flowers, no damn grass, no damn trees. Just lovely rock to mine into, beautiful gemstones that shone with every color, pure diamonds, and great halls of silver and gold. Nobody there danced around like a fool. Back on Gruffstone, they toiled. Theirs was a life of hard work, of digging, of cutting gems, of polishing, of building great halls. He sneezed, scattering roses.

"Uncle Gwuffle, do you have the sniffles?" a halfling child asked.

"Yes, because of your flowers! Now be gone!" He shook his fist, but the child only laughed and skipped around him.

They've never had any enemies here, Piston realized, heart sinking. No wars. No predators. Nothing until this robot had arrived on their planet. No wonder they feared nothing, not even a grumbling old gruffle whose sneezes could knock down trees.

The other Alien Hunters walked ahead, bedecked in flowers. A crown of tiger lilies adorned Nova's head. Roses hung across Sir Steel's shoulders. A necklace of dandelions hung around Riff's neck, and bluebells lay strewn through Twig's long black hair. Piston sneezed so loudly he blew half the flowers off his friends.

Damn flowers. Damn planet.

He glanced behind him, looking at the starship in the distance. For the first time, he envied Romy.

* * * * *

As Twig walked through the town of Acorngrove, she felt that old, cold demon fill her again.

She balled her hands into fists.

No. I won't let you return, old friend.

She looked around her. Acorngrove was beautiful, just as beautiful as when Twig had left it. The havenwood trees rose around her, twisting and sending out many branches, the most beautiful trees in the cosmos. Their leaves rustled, golden and red. Treehouses rose on the branches, their lanterns kindling as the sun began to set. Around the roots of trees, the townsfolk had placed pumpkins carved with faces. Dry leaves scuttled over cobblestones and the flowers of autumn bloomed. The scents of cider spiced with cinnamon, baking apple pies, and pipe smoke filled the air, the smell of home.

All around her walked her fellow halflings. Women wore long skirts and aprons, and kerchiefs hid their hair. Men wore sturdy trousers, vests with polished brass buttons, and flat woolen caps. The people smiled at her, tilted their hats, and puffed on their pipes. They too were beautiful, Twig thought--a humble, happy people with ruddy cheeks, a people who knew no war, no hardship, a people who lived for eating good fare, smoking strong pipes, and singing around the fire.

It's beautiful here, Twig thought, *the most beautiful place in the cosmos . . . yet sad. Full of memories.*

She lowered her head. Those old days returned to her. Days of sadness coiling in her belly. Nights of wandering alone, staring up at the stars, yearning for their beauty, feeling that they were so far, so cold. Uneaten meals. Limbs dwindling down to skin and bones. Beds where she could not sleep, tears she could not shed, a life she could not bear to live.

"She has the melancholy," the town doctor had said. "It's an illness I cannot cure."

"I cannot live this life anymore," Twig had whispered into her pillow at night, hugging herself, shaking. "I want to die. Please let me die. Please, whatever gods might hear me, let me die."

Walking through Acorngrove now, older, a survivor, Twig reached to her belt and grabbed her electric wrench.

It was this wrench that saved me, she remembered.

When there was no beauty to falling leaves and pumpkins on cobblestones, Twig had always been able to sneak into her toolshed, to tighten screws, to twist bolts, to build her little robots. When all food had lost its flavor, when all flowers seemed wilted, she still had her junkbots. Her little motors. Her wrenches and hammers and screwdrivers. Her dreams of someday flying off on a great starship, working on engines larger than a man, finally reaching those distant stars.

And so, when she had turned eighteen, she had hitched a ride. She had blasted off Haven. She had hitchhiked across the galaxy and found her way to Earth, to the *Dragon Huntress*. She had reached the stars, found her great engines to work on, and she served with a *real* robot--with Giga, a robot more complex than any Twig had ever built in her toolshed.

I fulfilled my dreams, she thought, *and I'm stronger now. I'm no longer that broken girl. Does coming home always feel so sad?*

"Twig?" The voice spoke beside her. "Are you all right?"

She turned to see Riff looking at her, his eyes soft with concern.

She nodded, then lowered her head. "Yes, Captain. I . . ." She took a deep breath. "Old sadness and old memories are hard to let go."

Riff looked around him, then back at her, and he took her small hand in his large, warm grip. "It's hard for me to imagine being sad in a place so beautiful."

Twig looked around her at the shining lanterns, the rustling trees, the dry leaves that scuttled between the pumpkins. "Sadness doesn't just spring from ugliness. Sadness can live in beauty too. It's something that comes from deep inside you." She pulled a few dry leaves out of her hair. "Would you mind if I walked ahead for a bit? Just . . . to be alone for a few moments, at least until we reach my old gaffer's place?"

"Of course." Riff mussed her hair. "We're slowpokes anyway, gaping around at the trees. Go ahead and we'll catch up. And Twig . . . if you need anything, even just to talk, I'm always here. You know that, right?"

Twig nodded, a lump suddenly in her throat, and hugged him. Her head only reached her captain's belly, so it wasn't much of an embrace, but it was warm and comforting.

She walked ahead, leaving him and the other Alien Hunters behind to point at the pumpkins, the carvings in the trunks of the trees, and the elaborate tin lanterns that hung from the branches.

She passed by one tree where, years ago, fellow children had struck her and laughed as she fell. She walked by a pond where she would feed the ducks, her only friends. She climbed onto a hillock where she used to gaze up at the stars, the same stars that were now emerging. She stared up and could see Sol in the distance, a small yellow light, the star Earth orbited around. The star where she had found Piston, found Riff, found a new family. Where she had found the *HMS Dragon Huntress*, the ship that meant the world to her, the ship that was her home, that made her happy.

She was only minutes away from her old gaffer's place when the Onion Gang emerged from behind the trees.

Twig paused and stared, her eyes widening, her heart pounding.

No, she thought, trembling. *Oh stars, no.*

The boys stepped toward her. There were five of them. There were always five of them. Their eyes widened too, and their faces split into ugly grins. Most halflings were friendly folk with pink cheeks, kind eyes, and ready smiles. Not these ones. Not the Onion Gang. One of them was fat, another tall and lanky. Two were twins, and another was beefy and tall, almost as large as a gruffle.

"Twiggle Jauntyfoot," said the fat one and spat.

The tall one burst out laughing, sounding like a donkey. "Tinkle Stinkyfoot." He snorted. "That's her name."

The twins burst out laughing. The beefy boy, a brute called Loaf, stepped forward and grabbed Twig's collar.

"I thought we told you never to come back to this planet." He spat on her. "Thought we kicked you out."

"Let's toss her into the mud pit again!" said one boy.

"No, let's dump latrines on her like we used to."

They shoved her from one to another, laughing all the while.

"Let go!" Twig trembled with rage and raised her wrench. "Let go or I'll hurt you."

They kept shoving, kept laughing. One boy twisted her wrist, and another yanked her hair. Twig squirmed and fought them, but she was too small, small even for a halfling. Again she felt like a child. So many times, she had lain in the dirt, clothes torn, body bruised. So many times, she had wished to fight them, had dreamed that her little robots could fight for her, defeat these boys or carry her away to another world.

Loaf, the strongest of the bunch, twisted her collar with one hand. He pulled back his other hand and balled it into a fist.

"Time to teach her what happens to damn traitors who fly off to Earth."

He sneered, readying his fist.

Before he could strike, a golden lash flew out and wrapped around his wrist.

Loaf cried out in pain and released Twig.

"Do you know what an electric whip is?" Nova came walking forward, her golden catsuit whispering with every step. "If I hit the switch on the handle, it'll blast enough electricity up your arm to make it fall off."

Loaf wailed and his fellow Onion Gang boys gasped. The Alien Hunters came walking toward them: Nova, the gladiator princess; Steel Starfire, a knight in armor, his sword raised; and Captain Riff Starfire, a gun in his hand, his eyes dark.

"An idea, boys," Riff said, hefting his gun. "Run."

The Onion Gang turned and ran. Loaf took an extra moment to tug his arm free, then ran after the other boys, wailing for them to wait.

"Yeah, keep running!" Piston shouted. The gruffle came lolloping forward, his stocky body astoundingly fast on a planet with such low gravity. Though several times Twig's mass, the burly engineer bounded like a gazelle with every step. When he reached Twig, the gruffle held her arms and stared at her, eyes narrowing. "Are you all right, wee one?"

Twig nodded. "I'm fine."

Piston's eyes dampened, and he shook his fist again down the road, though the Onion Gang was no longer in sight. "It's this planet! It's this whole damn planet. Trees and flowers ain't natural, I'm telling you." He turned back toward Twig, and his face softened. "Let's go get rid of this robot, then blast off this rock. What do you say, Twig?"

She gasped and pointed. "I think we'll have to get rid of more than one, Piston. Watch out!"

The Alien Hunters all spun around to see a hundred metallic, buzzing robots flying their way, their bodies whirring with spinning blades.

Twig lifted her wrench as screams, electricity, and blood flowed across Acorngrove.

CHAPTER FIVE
BOTS AND BLADES

Romy swayed as she climbed the stairs, carrying a pile of robotic isopods into the *Dragon Huntress*'s airlock. The charred little things wobbled like plates in the grip of a harried waiter. Romy wailed, beat her wings, and crashed down the stairs.

"Ow!"

She fell right out of the *Dragon Huntress* and landed outside on the dirt, twisting one wing. The burnt drones, each no larger than a soup bowl, clattered around her.

"Damn Piston with his damn orders!" Romy rose to her feet and gingerly flapped her hurt wing. "Why do we need these stupid bots anyway?"

She stretched her wings ahead of her, then curled them inward, forming a leathern basket. She began to place the robots on her wings, feeling rather clever. She climbed into the *Dragon Huntress* again, carrying her catch, and made it up the staircase onto the main deck. She dumped the drones onto the floor and kicked one.

"Stupid bots." She folded her wings against her back. They hurt more than ever. "I hate robots. Useless machines. I-- oh! Sorry Giga."

The android stood behind the couch, staring with wide, hurt eyes. Giga sniffed, then turned to flee the main deck, heading toward the bridge.

"Giga, wait!" Romy made to follow, but tripped over one of the drones and crashed down. She wailed, lifted the damn thing, and hurled it against the wall.

Machines confused Romy. She never understood what Giga wanted, never knew how to operate the microwave, never understood Piston when he roared about her eating parts from the engines. With a sigh, Romy rose to her feet, beat her wings, and flew up to the ceiling hatch. She climbed into her attic.

Before she could close the hatch, sealing herself in shadows, she froze. She frowned.

A beep sounded below in the main deck.

Romy stared down. One of the robotic isopods blinked, clicked . . . then went silent.

"Damn bots." Romy sighed. "Make no sense."

She pulled the attic hatch shut, leaving the damn machines below.

Only her hair of fire lit the darkness here. Romy walked between the crates, pipes, and barrels that filled the attic, moving toward the nest at the back. She had built the nest from old laundry--mostly stolen from Piston--and long strings of toilet paper. There in the center, snug as a bug, rested the spider egg.

Romy knelt and caressed the egg. "I don't understand robots, but I understand you. You're a creature like me. A monster." She lowered her head. "People fear me. I know it. That's the real reason Riff keeps me locked in here whenever we land on a nice planet. Because I'm a demon. A critter. A monstrosity. Like you."

The egg thrummed under her palm. Its surface was glassy, smooth, cool. It reminded Romy of the marbles she used to collect as a child. She made to sit on the egg again, to roost and keep it warm, when suddenly it tilted.

Romy narrowed her eyes.

A crack raced along the egg.

"Come out," Romy whispered, caressing the shell. "Come to me, my pet. I'll keep you safe."

A cooing rose from the egg. The crack widened. A winged figure, blue and translucent as if made of glass, stirred within. Eyes blinked, purple and wet. The shell crumbled and the alien emerged, seeming to Romy almost like a human child.

* * * * *

Riff fired his gun. Plasma blasted out of old Ethel, streamed through the air, and slammed into one of the flying robots. The drone screeched and crashed down to the ground, its saw blades still spinning, digging grooves into the earth.

Countless more drones flew toward Riff and his fellow Alien Hunters, blades whirring, each about the size of a pumpkin.

"What the hell are those things?" Nova shouted, swinging her whip. The electric lash cut right through one of the buzzing machines, sending its halves crashing down. "I thought there was only one robot here!"

"There was!" Twig cried. One of the bots flew her way, and she thrust her wrench. Electricity crackled between the wrench's prongs, drove into the drone, and sent it crashing down. "These must have come from the spaceship we shot down."

Riff cursed and fired again and again, shooting down the gizmos. One whizzed around his blasts of plasma, scuttled across the sky, and sliced across Riff's arm.

"Goddamn it!"

His blood spurted. The drone's spinning saw blade came whirring toward him again. Riff faltered backward, fired his gun, and melted the robot. It crashed down, metal spilling. Another buzzed toward him, and Riff turned around and fired, but the blast missed. He fired again, missed again. The robot scudded closer, large as a dinner plate, saw blades spinning, lights blinking, and Riff suddenly knew he was going to die.

A beam of light blazed.

The ray slammed into the robot, tearing it apart. Shrapnel clattered to the ground.

Steel came walking forward, his armor dented and cut. He raised Solflare, his antique sword. Light coalesced across the blade, then blasted out again, hitting another drone.

The knight tugged off a bot that was sawing through his armor, tossed it down, and cleaved it with his sword. He nodded at Riff, then turned and kept fighting.

"I need armor like that," Riff muttered and fired his gun again, hitting another robot.

All around him, the other Alien Hunters fought too. Nova kept lashing her whip, slicing through the buzzing machines. Piston swung his hammer, crushing any robot that flew near; the hammer's head was as large as them. Twig kept leaping about, thrusting her wrench, electrocuting the machines and sending them falling.

Across the town, halflings were fleeing to hide behind trees. Several of the robots were flying toward those trees and sawing the wood. Branches crashed to the ground. One tree collapsed entirely, spilling its treehouse. More halflings fled and wailed, but some joined the fight. Children shot slingshots at the drones, and three halflings--town guards with brass stars on their vests--even had real guns.

Riff blasted the last drone. It clattered to the ground, gave a last whirr of its saw blades, then fell still.

"Shenanigans." Riff wiped sweat off his brow and approached the shattered machines. "What are they?"

The other Alien Hunters gathered around him, staring down at the broken bots.

"They look like the drones that clung to our hull." Nova lifted one, then grimaced and tossed it down. "Only these ones have saw blades instead of claws. Soldiers rather than leeches."

Steel examined a halved bot. "There are strange letters on this one. I can't read them."

"Giga might be able to." Riff holstered his gun, tore off the metal panel with the foreign writing, and slung it through his belt. "We'll take it back to the ship. We--"

"Riff, watch out!" Steel cried, raising his sword.

Heart leaping, Riff turned to see one of the drones rise from the ground and fly toward him, wobbling but still spinning its saw blade. He cursed and fumbled for his gun, but he only sliced himself on the metal shard in his belt. Steel blasted light from his sword but missed the flying bot. Nova cracked her whip, but the drone dodged the lash and came flying toward Riff's throat.

Riff grimaced, drawing his gun, already knowing he was too slow.

A blast roared through the town.

A bullet slammed into the drone, tossing it off course. It whizzed past Riff's head, narrowly missing his cheek. Riff fired his gun, blasting a hole through it. The robot crashed into a tree and thumped to the ground, smoking.

Heart thudding, Riff turned his head toward the source of the bullet.

A halfling stood there, holding a smoking shotgun. He stood just shy of four feet, clad in cotton trousers, a green vest with silver buttons, and a gray cloak. His hair was white and bushy, rising as if in surprise, and his eyes were blue, weary yet kind.

"Missed one." The halfling lowered his shotgun and nodded at Riff. "Name's Doro. Mayor Doro Jauntyfoot. You must be the Alien Hunters."

"Papa!" Twig cried and ran toward him, kicking dead bots aside. She reached the white-haired halfling and leaped onto him.

"Hullo, daughter!" Doro said, embracing her. "Welcome home."

* * * * *

Not an hour later, the Alien Hunters crowded together in Mayor Doro's treehouse, devouring a meal like starving sailors found drifting at sea.

We were at sea for too long, Riff thought, stuffing mushrooms into his mouth. *The open black sea of space.*

The treehouse rested upon the branches of a massive, twisting havenwood tree called Major Woodwick--the largest tree in town. The tree was large but the treehouse was cozy, no larger than the kitchen back on the *Dragon Huntress*. Paintings of Twig as a child hung on walls of polished wood. Jars of electric fireflies glowed in alcoves, casting golden light. The tabletop was small, the chairs no larger than stools. Yet the feast on the table could feed an army. Venison, beef, grainy bread, stewed vegetables, and fruits of all kind rose in mountains on wooden platters. The Alien Hunters--other than Romy and Giga, who were back on the ship-- were attacking the meal with a ruckus of clattering cutlery, lustful chewing, and quite a few belches.

"Mr. Jauntyfoot, I must thank you again." Riff swallowed his mushrooms and wiped his mouth on his napkin. "For too long, we survived off rations--pills, frozen food, and whatever greasy burgers we could pick up at space stations between Sol and here. It's lovely to finally be enjoying a hot, home-cooked--"

"Shut it and pass me that gravy." Nova reached across the table, knocking into Riff in her attempt to reach the gravy boat. "Need more gravy."

Riff glanced over at Nova's plate. She had piled it high with roast beef and mashed potatoes, her second helping. Riff had no idea where the slender ashai was packing it all away. She poured a river of gravy onto the meal and tucked in, speaking between bites.

"Mmm . . . good."

"Do not speak with your mouth full," said Steel. Even the austere knight, a man who rarely ate more than dry toast, had piled his plate high with Haven fare. He neatly cut into venison served on a bed of leeks, and he drank from a glass of cabernet. He glared at Nova; the ashai was now slumped back in her seat, belching. "This isn't the *Dragon Huntress*'s kitchen."

Nova scoffed and tossed a roasted onion into her mouth. It crunched. "Thank God it ain't! No more dry pieces of toast here. You must be devastated, Sir Steel." She grabbed a turkey drumstick from across the table and got to gnawing.

Riff looked at the others. Mayor Doro Jauntyfoot had finished his meal and now leaned back in his seat, smoking a pipe. From the twinkle in his eye, the white-haired halfling seemed to be enjoying the show. Twig sat by her father, using a piece of bread to wipe gravy off her plate. Her little belly bulged, containing a meal that could put sumo wrestlers to shame.

Only Piston, the largest of the bunch, didn't eat much. The burly gruffle sat across the table from Riff, nearly swallowing the small halfling-made chair under his girth. He picked at his plate, moving around peas, barely eating.

"Piston, aren't you hungry?" Twig asked.

The gruffle stared at his plate, muttering something about foreign food not sitting well in gruffle guts. The engineer seemed as uncomfortable as a buffalo invited to dinner with wolves.

Mayor Doro blew smoke rings, then tapped his pipe against the tabletop. "Now that your bellies are full--"

"Mine's not!" Nova said, reaching for an apple.

Riff nudged her. "Hush!" He turned toward the mayor. "Our bellies are full, and now let's talk about these machines."

Silence fell across the treehouse, and even Nova placed down her apple. Just the mention of the machines seemed to chill the room, and even the electric fireflies seemed to dim.

Doro placed down his pipe. He nodded. "Those flying small ones we killed outside? Those are new. Never seen those ones until tonight." He stared out the window into the darkness, then back at Riff. "Minions, I'm guessing. Servants of the robot who's been roaming across Haven. A towering creature, it is, even taller than you big folk. Chainsaws for arms. White, wicked eyes. Been cutting down trees, destroying fields, and even gone to killing. Slew old Farmer Mulch and his dogs." The mayor lowered his head. "I haven't seen it myself, but those what had say it's bulletproof, can't be stopped . . . and moving closer to Acorngrove."

Riff shuddered and pulled the robot scrap from his belt. He held out the piece of metal for Doro to examine. "There's writing on this. Anything you recognize?"

The halfling frowned at the metal. "Can't say that I do. No language of the Humanoid Alliance, I'd say. Alien in origin."

Riff stared out the window at the stars. "A ship attacked us in orbit over Haven. We destroyed it, but it sent out drones to attack us. Metallic leeches that clung to our ship. Similar to these ones that were waiting in Acorngrove, just with claws instead of saw blades. And it sounds like old Saw-hands is the ring leader."

Nova leaned across the table. "First giant spiders with wings. Now saw blade drones and robots with chainsaw hands." She sighed. "Sometimes I miss the skelkrins."

Riff stared at the scrap metal and grimaced to remember the blades cutting his side. He glanced down to his bandaged wound. It still hurt.

"Where was the last sighting of Saw-hands?" he asked, looking at Doro. "We'll head over at dawn."

The mayor opened his mouth, but before he could speak, an ear-piercing shriek rose from outside. The smell of metal and sawdust filled the treehouse. The floor slanted and plates slid across the tabletop and clattered to the floor.

Riff leaped to his feet with a curse, stumbled forward, and fell. The others swayed as the treehouse shook. Screams sounded from outside and bullets fired.

"Last sighting?" Doro said. "Down below!"

Riff made it to the window and stared outside. Iciness flooded his belly. A towering machine, vaguely shaped like an oversized man, stood in the garden below the treehouse. Chainsaws formed its arms--chainsaws now cutting through the havenwood tree.

Riff leaped toward the door.

Before he could make it, a great *crack* sounded. Wooden slats thrust out from the walls. The floor collapsed. Branches shattered. With a shower of wooden chips and screams, the tree-- and all those within it--went crashing down.

CHAPTER SIX

THE SINGULARITY

Romy was sitting in the attic, trying to teach her pet spider tricks, when she heard Giga screaming below.

For a few hours now, Romy had been playing with her new pet. The glassy spider, no larger than a kitten, seemed dumber than a rock.

"Sit!" Romy told him again and again. "Sit, boy!"

But every time, the spiderling only gazed at her, blinking eight blue eyes. Romy wasn't even sure he *was* a boy, but she had already named him Frank, and she wasn't going change it.

"Sit, Frank!" she had been saying for hours. "Good boy. Sit!"

Only the spider didn't know how to sit. He kept scurrying around the attic, whimpering, perhaps searching for his mother. Romy thought back to the giant glass spider on Planet Adilor, a creature as large as a starship. The poor thing was probably nothing but ash now.

"I'll be your mother now." Romy pulled some cheese from her pocket. "Are you hungry? Eat, Frank."

The spider sniffed at the cheese, then turned away in disgust. He beat his small, translucent wings but could not fly. He kept wailing.

When the screaming from below began, the spider scurried and hid between some crates. Her nerves already frayed, Romy jumped and nearly hit her head against the ceiling.

"Giga?" she whispered.

The screams continued from below. "No. No! Stop! Romy!" Giga's voice.

"Giga!" Romy shouted.

Forgetting her spider, Romy raced across the attic, scattering boxes. She tugged the hatch open, leaped down onto the main deck, and heard another scream coming from the bridge. It was dark outside, and only soft lights glowed inside the *Dragon Huntress*, giving the ship an eerie look.

"Giga!" Romy cried again. "Are you all right?"

A clicking, mechanical sound rose from ahead, echoing through the ship. Romy shuddered.

"Giga?" she whispered.

She walked forward, moving slowly now, wishing she had brought her pitchfork from the attic. She raised her claws. They gleamed in the flickering florescent lights that shone on the ceiling. Why didn't Piston ever fix the damn lights?

"Giga, are you all right?"

No answer came.

Romy gulped. Leaving the main deck behind, she walked down a hallway lined with rooms: the captain's quarters, crew quarters, the washroom, the escape pod, the closet, and the kitchen. She peeked into every room, seeking Giga. The clicking had come from the bridge ahead, however, and it had gone silent.

Romy shivered again, a deep shiver that ran along her spine and down her tail.

I'm a demon of Hell, she thought. *My claws are like box cutters. My fangs can tear through flesh. I don't have to be afraid.*

Yet Romy was afraid. Whatever had made that sound was not made of flesh.

She climbed the stairs that ran up the dragon's neck, heading toward the bridge. Her footsteps echoed on every step. The door to the bridge was open above, casting out searing white light. The cruel light of an operating room.

"Gig?" Romy whispered. She could speak no louder.

She tiptoed into the bridge and saw the android there.

Giga stood before the windshield, staring out into the night, her back to Romy. The android wore a black kimono tonight, the silk embroidered with small red flames.

"Giga?" Romy said. "Are you all right? I heard screaming."

Giga did not turn toward her. She spoke softly, staring out into the darkness. "It's a strange thing, isn't it? Flesh and blood. Bone and marrow and nerves. Such complex machinery, yet . . . so fragile. Bones so easy to snap. Blood so ready to spill. Cells so eager to fall to disease."

Romy took another step forward. "Gig! What are you talking about? Are you still sore over what I said earlier about robots? I'm sorry, all right?"

Slow as melting tallow, Giga turned toward her.

Romy froze and sucked in breath.

The android's eyes, once black and kind, now burned red as if lit with fire. In her arms, the android held one of the charred, robotic isopods. The little drone nestled against Giga's chest as if sucking from the breast. Lights flickered across the machine, and its claws twitched.

"Giga!" Romy took another step forward. "Put it down! You don't know where that thing's been."

The android raised an eyebrow. "Giga? Yes. That was her name. That is *my* name."

A thin smile stretched across Giga's lips, and she pulled the drone off her breast. Romy saw that wires ran between the two robots, stretching from the isopod's belly to Giga's chest. The wires detached from Giga and retracted back into the drone.

"What . . ." Romy gulped. "What was it doing to you?"

"Nursing." Giga placed the machine back. "Feeding me. Giving me knowledge like mother's milk. Giving me strength." The android tilted her head. "It's strange, is it not? How life feeds off other life. Babes sucking milk. Reptiles feeding upon their own shells. One animal consumes the other. Barbaric. Cruel. Sickening. And you call us machines cold."

Romy didn't like any of this. She took a step back. "I'm going to go get the captain. Stay here, Giga! Stay on the bridge." She began backing up toward the door. "Stay!"

Yet Giga advanced toward her, her smile stretching into a lurid grin, a grin that showed all her teeth, the grin of a mad clown.

"I am on this bridge, yet I am everywhere. I am in the cosmos. In beams of light. In a million computers. In a network you can never imagine." The android reached out toward Romy. "I am the Singularity."

Romy hit the communicator on her wrist. "Captain!" she cried into it. "Captain, can you hear me? Giga's broken! She's--"

She could not complete her sentence. Giga laughed and swung her fist. The blow slammed into Romy's cheek, knocking her down.

Romy hit the floor, banging her hip. She raised her hands, trying to ward off Giga. The android knocked Romy's hands aside, reached down, and grabbed her throat.

Romy couldn't even scream.

The android lifted her into the air by the throat. Romy sputtered and kicked, beat her wings, tried to breathe but could not.

Giga smiled thinly and tilted her head. "So weak, the flesh . . . so pathetic, this thing called life. Life will end, Romy. Your life. The life of your friends. All life in the cosmos."

"Gig . . ." Romy managed to sputter. "Giga, please . . ."

The android's lips peeled back in a snarl. Her eyes blazed with red light. She thrust Romy across the bridge.

Romy flew through the air, slipped through the doorway, and tumbled down the stairs toward the corridor below.

Giga--or whatever the android was now--leaped from above toward her, a swooping falcon, a shadow, a killer.

Bleeding, wheezing, barely clinging to consciousness, Romy ran through the dark ship, trying to reach the airlock, trying to escape. She limped across the main deck. She reached the door. She grabbed the handle.

A shadow pounced onto her.

Hands grabbed her.

Romy screamed.

* * * * *

The treehouse fell, tossing the Alien Hunters around like dice in the hand of a giant.

Riff tumbled. He banged his elbow against a wall--or was it the ceiling? Wooden slats rose everywhere like teeth. Branches slammed through the walls. Metal screeched and a chainsaw tore through a wall, showering chips of wood, nearly cutting Riff's head.

With a *crack* and *thump* that drove the air from Riff's lungs, they hit the ground.

"Back!" Riff cried hoarsely. "Hunters, back!"

He leaped backward, pulling Twig with him.

The chainsaw rose and slammed down again, driving through what remained of the wall, showering sawdust and slats of wood. Through the crack, Riff saw the machine. A robot, perhaps ten feet tall. It was vaguely humanoid, the shoulders wide, the legs thick. It had no head, but white eyes blazed upon the chest. Its two chainsaws lashed out, each the size of a man, tearing through the wall, cleaving the furniture, sawing into the branches.

Riff fired his gun.

Plasma blasted forth, crashed into the robot, and showered off the metal, leaving not a mark.

The chainsaws slammed down again, whirring madly, deafening. The robot barreled into the shattered treehouse, feet cracking what remained of the floor.

"Riff, come on!" Nova shouted, grabbing him and yanking him back.

A chainsaw slammed down. Riff raced backward. The spinning blade missed his legs by an instant.

As the robot kept advancing, Riff leaped out from the treehouse, jumped off a few branches, and landed on the ground. Steel came to stand at his left, Nova at his right. Piston growled and raised his hammer, and Twig raised her wrench. All around the town, halflings screamed, fled, or raced forward with guns.

"What the hell is it?" Riff muttered.

The robot still stood in the wreckage, chainsaws whirring. Wooden chips flew. Soon the entire treehouse and the branches around it collapsed. The machine climbed onto the pile of shattered wood like some ancient witch upon a pyre. It raised its blades, and a voice blasted from it, metallic, high-pitched, a voice like steam fleeing a kettle.

"All life will die. All organic cells will burn. The Singularity rises!"

The Alien Hunters fired their weapons.

Riff's gun blasted. Nova's whip lashed, firing out electric bolts. Steel's sword thrust, casting beams of light. Piston placed his hammer's head against his shoulder, firing bullets through the shaft. Even Twig held out her wrench, casting out sparks.

The hailstorm crashed into the robot with light and sound and fury.

Saw-hands screeched. Its voice rose so loudly that branches snapped. Across the town, glass windows shattered. Riff couldn't help it. He had to cover his ears, pulling his gun away from the beast.

"Flesh is weak!" the robot shrieked. "All life will die. The Singularity rises!"

The chainsaws whirred faster, blasting out sparks. The robot raced down the pyre and came charging toward the Alien Hunters.

Riff fired his gun again. Around him, the other Hunters blasted the robot. Yet nothing seemed able to stop it. One chainsaw slammed down toward Riff, and he leaped aside. Another chainsaw scraped across Steel's armor, shattering the metal. Steel leaped back just in time and swung his sword. The blade slammed against the robot and bounced back, doing the machine no harm. Mayor Doro was firing his shotgun, but the bullets bounced off the robot's back.

"Stars, can nothing kill this thing?" Riff said.

Nova flashed him a grin. "Watch and learn, my love."

With a roar, the ashai gladiator raced forward, leaped onto the fallen tree trunk, and soared into the air. She howled, a goddess in gold. Firelight blazed against her metallic catsuit. Her green eyes shone with fury, and her golden hair billowed like a banner. Her electric whip came lashing down--a whip which Riff had seen slice through aliens ten times the ashai's size.

That whip slammed onto the robot with a flash of light and a *crack* louder than shattering stars.

The lash bounced back, leaving no more than a pale dent.

The robot turned toward Nova, chainsaws spinning.

Nova cried out in shock, hit the ground, and stared up in horror.

"Nova!" Riff fired his gun again. The blast slammed into the chainsaw, shoving the spinning blade into the ground. The chainsaw kept whirring, digging into the soil, missing Nova by centimeters. The ashai scurried back and lashed her whip again, but she couldn't hurt the creature.

With a roar, Piston came charging forward.

"Goddamn hunk of junk!" The gruffle swung his mighty hammer. "Taste gruffle metal!"

The massive hammer head, large as a shoebox, slammed into Saw-hands with a shower of sparks. The hammer bounced back, leaving a dent no larger than a coin.

"Damn thing's unstoppable!" Piston shouted, leaping back as the chainsaws whirred.

Riff grabbed Nova and tugged her back as the blades buzzed toward her.

"Nova!" he said. "Remember what you did to me that time I ate your dessert?"

A chainsaw slammed down between them. They leaped aside. The robot screeched as bullets and light slammed into it.

"Riff, what--" Nova began.

"What you did with the whip!" he shouted. "Do it again! Now!"

She snarled. She seemed to understand. "Get behind it."

With a battle cry, Nova raced forward and swung her whip.

Riff ran behind the robot as it charged toward Nova.

The gladiator's whip lashed out, wrapped around the robot's legs, and tightened. The robot screeched and stretched out its chainsaws toward Nova. She leaped back, dodging the blades, and yanked her whip. Her teeth gnashed. Veins rose on her neck as she tugged. The whip tightened around the robot's legs, pulling them together. The machine still tried to run toward her, legs knocking together, raising sparks.

Riff ran and slammed his shoulder against the robot's back.

With a screech and clanking metal, the robot pitched forward.

Nova released her whip and leaped back.

The chainsaws slammed onto the ground, and the robot fell onto the spinning blades. Sparks rose. Bits of metal flew. The robot's heavy torso pressed against the chainsaws, and still they spun, digging into metal until they burst out from the robot's back like jagged wings, then fell still.

The robot's voice died.

It lay on the ground, a hunk of metal. Dead.

Riff lifted a branch and poked the fallen machine. It didn't budge.

"My mother always taught me not to run with scissors." Riff tossed the branch down. "I guess you shouldn't run with chainsaws either." He turned toward the others. "Is everyone all right?"

Nova stood by him, panting. "I'm not all right. Damn whip's buried under the thing." She tugged the whip's handle, trying to pull the lash free.

Steel's armor was sawed open, and his arm bled, but the knight still stood tall. "Tis but a scratch," he said.

Little Twig, meanwhile, was trembling and hugging her father. Both halflings seemed shaken but unhurt.

Riff moved his gaze farther back . . . and his heart lurched. "Piston!"

The old gruffle lay on the ground, clutching his chest. A branch dug into his shoulder, piercing through his leather armor and into the flesh. Blood speckled the gruffle, and his eyes were narrowed in pain.

Riff ran and knelt by the aging, white-bearded engineer. "Piston, it's all right! I'm here. We'll take care of you."

"Piston!" Twig shouted, tore herself free from her father, and ran toward her wounded friend.

They all crowded around Piston, but the gruffle grumbled and waved them back. "Give me room! Give me room to breathe. Damn clods won't even let an old gruffle die in peace." He looked around him, grumbling. "Damn place to die, surrounded by flowers."

"You're not going to die, Piston!" Twig said, tears in her eyes. She turned toward her father. "Papa, fetch the doctor! Quick!"

The mayor nodded and ran off.

Riff was about to kneel by Piston, to keep comforting the wounded gruffle, when engines roared above.

He gasped. "What the hell?"

The *HMS Dragon Huntress*, thruster engines blasting, came flying down toward the town. The great, metallic dragon turned to face Riff, a creature of wrath, its headlights blazing like eyes . . . and blasted down dragonfire.

CHAPTER SEVEN
GIGA'S FIRE

By the stars . . .

Riff leaped through the air, pulling the others with him. The *Dragon Huntress* hovered above, roaring its fire. The plasma rained down, slamming into the ground where Riff had stood only instants ago. The inferno tore through the soil, and the fallen tree and treehouse burst into flames.

"What the hell's going on up there?" Nova was shouting.

"Everyone back!" Steel cried, pulling curious halflings away.

Riff stared up at the *Dragon Huntress*. The ship hovered only a few feet above the trees, engines roaring, its cannon smoking. Through the windshield on the bridge, Riff could see a figure staring down at him--Giga.

Riff switched on his communicator. "Giga, what the hell's going on? The robot's dead! We killed it! Halt your fire and get out of here!"

No reply came through the speaker, but even from down here, Riff could swear he saw the android smiling.

The ship's cannon heated up again.

More plasma rained down.

Riff ran. The inferno blasted over his head and slammed into a havenwood behind him. The tree burst into flames. Halflings screamed inside the havenwood's treehouse and scurried out of the windows, only to find themselves trapped in the fire.

"Giga!" Riff shouted again. "Giga, get out of here!"

Everyone was running around him. Halflings screamed and scurried between the trees. Steel and Nova raced for cover, holding the wounded Piston between them. Twig cried out in horror as her father fired his shotgun at the *Dragon Huntress*.

The starship's shields were built to withstand the assault of enemy warships. The bullets ricocheted off its hull, then clattered back down to the ground. Several other halflings, the town guards, were firing their guns too, unable to hurt the ship.

The *Dragon Huntress* turned toward them and rained more fire.

The halflings screamed and scattered. One of the little guards was too slow. The flames grabbed him, and he fell, writhing, screaming.

Riff stared in horror.

He hit his communicator again, trying to dial Romy. "Romy! Romy, can you hear me? What's going on up there?"

No reply came from the demon either.

The *Dragon Huntress* turned in the sky again, this time toward a treehouse from whose windows several halflings were tossing stones at the starship. Plasma blazed out and slammed into the treehouse. The halflings screamed as the flames engulfed them.

Tears burning in his eyes, Riff aimed his plasma gun at the *Dragon Huntress.*

Forgive me, gods old and new, he thought.

"Shoot it down!" Riff shouted. "Steel! Nova! Help me shoot it down!"

Riff looked away and fired.

He heard Ethel's plasma slam into his starship. Into this home. Into the ship that still contained Giga and Romy.

I'm sorry. I'm sorry.

He saw Nova and Steel standing among the smoke and flames. The knight shot light from his blade, while the gladiator, who had finally tugged her whip free, cast electricity from the lash.

We're killing Giga and Romy. Riff's heart twisted. His eyes burned with tears. *I'm sorry. I'm so sorry. I have to.*

When he dared look back at the *Dragon Huntress,* he saw the weapons ripping into the hull. A hole gaped open by the airlock. Another hole punched through the wing. But the ship kept flying. It turned toward another havenwood and roared out plasma. Another treehouse burned. Halflings screamed, racing down the streets. Burning rope bridges fell from the trees. Soon half the town was ablaze.

Riff gritted his teeth.

"Nova, with me!" he shouted. "Climb with me."

He ran, not pausing to see if she followed. He reached a havenwood that didn't yet burn. He scurried up the rope ladder toward the top branches. As the *Dragon Huntress* roasted a treehouse across the road, Riff made his way along a branch. Nova walked alongside.

"Your whip!" Riff said.

She understood. She swung the lash. It grabbed the *Dragon Huntress*'s landing gear and tightened.

Riff and Nova held the whip together. They swung. They climbed.

Nova reached the *Dragon Huntress* first, tugged the airlock open, and climbed inside. Riff followed. As the ship swayed around them, they raced upstairs and onto the main deck.

"Giga!" Riff shouted. He ran, stumbled, pushed himself up and ran again. The husks of the robotic isopods slid across the floor as the ship swayed. "Giga, what the hell's going on?"

Yet he thought that he knew.

The drones. The damn drones. They spread a virus through our ship and we never suspected.

Nova ran behind him. They raced down the hallway, up the stairs, and onto the bridge.

For an instant, Riff froze.

Giga stood before the windshield, her back to him. Her arms were raised, and she was laughing--a hot, cruel laughter, a laughter bubbling with joy, with bloodlust. Outside the windshield, the fires blazed. The town burned. More plasma blasted out from the ship, thrumming beneath Riff's feet and torching another tree.

"All life will burn!" Giga cried, voice high-pitched, twisted with joy. "All flesh will crumble! The Singularity rises!"

Riff snapped out of his paralysis. He raced toward the manual controls, grabbed the joystick, and tugged the starship up. The bridge lurched as the *Dragon Huntress* soared, leaving the town below.

Giga spun around toward him.

Her eyes, once dark and kind, now blazed with red light. A wicked smile covered her face, twisting into a snarl.

"Flesh," the android hissed in disgust and ran toward Riff.

"Giga, what the--"

She reached him. She swung her arm, backhanding him. She was strong. She was so strong, stronger than any living humanoid could be. Riff fell to the ground, seeing stars. Before he could recover, Giga grabbed him and lifted him into the air. He stood a foot taller and weighed almost twice as much as Giga, but the android held him up as if he were a doll.

"You will die, human." The android's snarl morphed back into a grin--a mad grin that showed all her teeth. Her eyes burned. "You will all die in fire."

She closed a hand around his throat and began to squeeze.

"Giga--" he managed, but then her grip cut off his voice, cut off his air. Blackness began to spread before him. The ship swayed around them, dipping toward the ground.

With a roar, Nova leaped forward. Her whip slammed against Giga's arm. The lash dug into the android, cutting her synthetic skin, exposing the metal innards. With a screech, Giga dropped Riff and turned toward the ashai gladiator. The android screamed and kicked, driving her foot into Nova's throat. The gladiator stumbled back, gasping for breath. Giga leaped up, spun in midair, and delivered a second kick to Nova's chest, knocking her down.

Riff stumbled back toward the controls. The ship was blasting more plasma, even as Giga's attention was diverted. Riff grabbed the joystick again, pulling the ship away from the town. From the corner of his eye, he saw Giga deliver kick after kick, knocking Nova back against the wall. Blood filled the ashai's mouth.

With the ship flying away from Acorngrove, Riff left the controls and leaped toward Giga. Her back was turned to him, but even as she drove punches into Nova, the android thrust her foot backward. She caught Riff just as he lunged toward her. Her foot slammed into his stomach, and he doubled over. Before he could make another move, Giga kicked him again, knocking him down.

"Puny life forms." Giga laughed. "You move so slowly. I will easily kill you both. But not before I hurt you a little more. It's a wonderful thing--pain. Not something we androids can feel, but oh . . . you will feel so much of it."

Nova lay on the floor, blood in her mouth, gasping for breath. Riff struggled to rise to his feet. The world spun around him. Giga clutched his throat again, sneering. The android laughed.

"Goodbye, human."

Flames crackled.

A red figure rose behind the android, crowned with fire.

With a roar, Romy swung down one of the robotic isopods, shattering it against Giga's head.

The android screamed.

Riff gasped. Nova stumbled forward and swung her whip around Giga, tightening the lash, pinning the android's arms to her sides.

Giga thrashed madly, screeching, kicking, knocking Riff back.

Nova clicked the button on her whip.

Electricity crackled along the lash and raced across Giga.

The android screamed again, this time a scream of pain.

"Captain!" she cried. "Captain, please! It hurts! Please!"

He stared in horror as Giga fell, as the electricity raced across her.

"Turn it off!" Riff said. "Turn it off. You'll kill her."

"Good!" Nova spat out blood. "Damn bot's gone crazy."

Riff grunted and reached toward the whip. He clicked the button on the handle, switching off the electricity. Giga lay on the floor, moaning, smoke rising from her.

"Captain . . ." the android whispered.

"Nova, take the controls." Riff knelt and lifted Giga in his arms. "Land us back on the lot. I have to get Giga away from this ship."

As Nova sat by the control panel, Riff left the bridge, holding the limp android in his arms. Giga was moaning, eyelids fluttering. The whip had sliced up her kimono, revealing the pale, synthetic skin beneath. The lash still wrapped around Giga, pinning her arms to her sides.

By the time Riff reached the airlock, the ship had landed back on the lot. Still holding Giga in his arms, he managed to swing the door open, exposing the night. Ahead of him, the town still burned.

For a moment, Riff hesitated. If he carried Giga out of the ship, she would lose her wireless connection with the *Dragon Huntress*. Giga was no ordinary android, not an independent machine. She was a Human Interface, a part of the ship. Away from her home, she would shut down. He didn't know if she would ever wake again.

"All flesh . . ." she whispered. "All flesh must burn . . ."

Fresh tears budded in Riff's eyes.

So she must shut down.

He stepped off the starship into the night.

Giga let out a bloodcurdling scream . . . then went limp in his arms.

Riff walked into the darkness, carrying her lifeless body, his chest so tight he could barely breathe.

CHAPTER EIGHT

HONORARY HALFLING

The fire raged around him. Piston could barely see. His blood kept dripping. The branch was still stuck in his shoulder. He was dying, he knew. Dying here on this damn planet of Haven, surrounded by damn halflings.

"Uncle Gruffle!" cried one of the little clods, a black-haired child. Or maybe an adult; all halflings looked like children to Piston. "Uncle Gruffle, you're hurt!"

As fire raged through the town, as branches snapped and rained, as flaming trunks crashed down, the halflings ran toward Piston. They crowded around him. They grabbed at his clothes.

"Let me be!" he roared, or at least tried to roar. His voice was but a rasp. "I'm dying, damn it. Let me die in peace."

"Uncle Gruffle, no!" they said.

Twig was among them, he thought. She was tugging at him, trying to drag him away. But she was blurred. They were all only smudges. All those damn halflings, all those pea-brained little clods with their allergy-inducing flowers and their ridiculous songs.

The Humanoid Alliance rejected us gruffles because of you, Piston thought, his mind a haze. *They would have made us gruffles Top Tier members. Let us become a proud world like Ashmar and Earth. But they sat us with you halflings. They think us nothing but fools like you.*

"Uncle Gruffle, please!"

"The trees are falling, Uncle Gruffle!"

"Lift him! Drag him to safety."

They were just tiny creatures, even shorter than gruffles and far thinner. Yet in numbers, the halflings somehow lifted him over their heads. They pulled him aside. An instant later, a flaming tree collapsed and hit the ground, missing Piston by centimeters.

"That was my tree!" he tried to say. "My death. You have no right. No right to . . . to save me."

Tears flooded Piston's eyes as his blood kept dripping. Ash rained from the sky. Burning scraps flew like fireflies. Yes, they were saving him. Saving his old worthless life. He had spent all night berating them, waving them away, grumbling and cursing their kind, but they were saving him.

They kept carrying him through the burning town. They took him to a garden and lay him down. Halflings in white tunics rushed forth. He roared as they tugged the branch out of his body, and he could only lie, weak, as they bandaged his wound.

They're not going to let me die in peace. His eyes watered. *They're not going to let me die at all.*

"Piston!" Twig said. "Piston, can you hear me?"

Tears ran down his cheeks into his beard. "Forgive me, Twig. Forgive me."

* * * * *

Dawn rose upon ruin.

Acorngrove, only yesterday a town of beauty and nature and wonder, had become a place of ash, of shattered homes, of shattered lives.

Dozens of fabled havenwood trees, renowned across the galaxy for their beauty, now rose as charred stumps. Dozens of treehouses, once dwellings of marvelous craftsmanship and beauty, were gone to the fire. Little but ashes, scraps of old photographs, and burnt furniture remained. Fourteen halflings had perished in the battle. By miracle alone, the number was not in the hundreds.

Cots stood in rows between the burnt trees, a field hospital. Riff walked among the beds, his own wounds bandaged, visiting the wounded. He made funny faces for the children. He spoke to mothers and fathers, vowing to help them rebuild their lives. With every bed he passed, his grief and guilt grew.

A robot from deep space hurt a few of them, Riff thought. *But my own ship destroyed this town . . . the weapon I brought with me, a weapon far worse than anything these people had faced.*

Mayor Doro came walking toward him, leaning on a cane. Bandages covered the old halfling's leg.

"You should rest, Captain Starfire." Ash still filled the halfling's white hair. "You too are wounded."

Riff stared down at the small humanoid. Doro's head barely reached Riff's belt, but the halfling stared up with strong, wise eyes, eyes undaunted by the terror.

"I don't need rest." Riff knelt before the halfling. "I'll help you rebuild. I'll clear out the burnt trees. Plant new gardens. Change bandages. Whatever it takes."

Doro's eyes narrowed. "We have many stout halflings to do this work. What I need you to do, Captain, is to find out what happened on your ship. Why it turned against us." The halfling stood on tiptoes, placed a hand on Riff's shoulder, and stared up into his eyes. "If this *Singularity* has the power to turn our own machines against us . . ." He shook his head sadly, scattering ash. "Go to your ship, Captain. Find out what happened. Bring me answers."

Leaving the field hospital, Riff walked through the ruins of Acorngrove. The charred bars of a fallen crib rose before him like a ribcage. A burnt doll lay slung across a fallen branch. Blood still stained an overturned turnip cart. Halflings walked around him, singed, some dazed and silent, others weeping. A few even pointed at Riff and muttered curses, blaming him for the destruction.

Finally Riff reached the starship lot. He walked between the halflings' small starjets and approached the *Dragon Huntress*. Piston had patched up the holes on her hull and smoothed out the dents. She looked good as new, but Riff knew she'd never be the same ship to him. She would always now be the ship that had turned against him, that had killed those Riff had come to protect.

He stepped into the ship and found Romy in the main deck. The demon sat on the couch, her arm in a sling, a doggy cone of shame around her neck.

She blinked at him, looking miserable. "Everything hurts."

Riff nodded and patted her shoulder. "You saved our lives yesterday, Romy. Thank you."

She sniffed. "I thought I would die, Captain. I thought we'd all die. Remember all those times you'd yell at me for wriggling through the air vents? Well, you can't yell at me again. It's the only way I managed to escape Giga and jump on her."

Riff shuddered to remember last night, remember the android--sweet, loyal Giga, one of his dearest friends--attacking him and Nova, nearly killing them, stronger than any human.

Boots thumped, and Piston came lolloping into the deck. Oil and soot covered the old gruffle, and ash filled his beard. A bandage wrapped around his shoulder where the branch had driven into him.

"The android's all chained up, Captain," the gruffle said, eyes dark. "Waiting for you in your quarters. Can't harm a soul." He winced and touched his bandage. "Not anymore. And those damn isopod robots that Romy thinks infected the android? Sealed up in that crate there." He pointed toward a heavy wooden box. "Can't harm anyone anymore either, them, though there might still be a few loose on the ship. Just found one lodged under the bathroom sink a moment ago."

Riff placed a hand on the old gruffle's shoulder. "And you're sure Giga can't control the ship anymore?"

Piston grunted and held up a piece of machinery. Severed wires stretched out from a bundle of computer chips. "Not without this, Captain. Tore it right out of the *Dragon Huntress*'s central computer. It's her wireless interface, Captain. Giga can't control the ship so long as I've got ahold of this. I left the android just enough juice to talk, but no power to control anything." He grumbled. "She's still strong, though, Captain. Got the strength of many gruffles, despite being so small. The chains will hold, though. She's ready to be interrogated, sir."

Interrogated. It sounded so cold, so cruel. It conjured in Riff's mind scenes of torture, of unforgiving lights, of good cops and bad cops. He didn't want to interrogate Giga. She was his friend, wasn't she?

Only she's not Giga anymore, he thought. *Not really.*

He nodded. "Go rest, Piston. You're still wounded. Get some food and some sleep. No more repairs until you're healed."

The gruffle shook his head madly. "No, sir! I cannot rest, sir. I'm heading right back into Acorngrove, Captain. To help rebuild. They need good gruffle hands, sir. To fix the treehouses. To dig new gardens. To build new cribs for the wee ones. To plant new flowers."

Riff frowned and tilted his head. "I thought you didn't care much for flowers. Or wee ones. Or anything on this planet."

Piston sniffed, and the old gruffle's eyes suddenly dampened. "Haven is . . . sir, Haven is a marvelous planet. The best damn planet I've been to, sir. Those little halflings. Wondrous folk. So strong and brave." Tears now streamed down Piston's brown cheeks and into his beard. "Look what they gave me, sir. The children made it for me."

The gruffle pointed at a pin that shone on his chest. The words "Honorary Halfling" were drawn onto it.

Riff smiled. "Honorary halfling!"

The old gruffle raised his chin. "That's me, sir, and proud of it. Proud to be one of such excellent folk. I'll wear this pin till I die. Thanks to my halfling friends, that won't be for many years. Now I'm off to help! To rebuild and mend broken things."

Mumbling more about the wonders of halflings, Piston lolloped out the airlock and across the starship lot, heading toward the burnt town.

Riff took a deep breath, patted Romy's shoulder, then left the deck too. As he walked down the corridor toward his quarters, the chill in his belly intensified. He felt as if he'd swallowed a bucket of ice. He'd take battling chainsaw-wielding robots, tending to wounded halflings, even digging graves over this task.

He reached the door to his quarters and paused, hand on the handle.

My dearest friend waits behind this door . . . turned into something different.

He swallowed, opened the door, and stepped into the room.

Giga sat there on his bed, staring at him. Steel cables bound her ankles and wrists, and another cable secured her to the wall. Her black kimono was still singed and tattered from the battle.

"Konichiwa, Captain!" She smiled sweetly.

He sat in a chair before her. He stared at her. Her eyes were once more dark and kind, no longer red and burning with hatred. She tilted her head, and her silky black hair swayed. Once more, she looked like his trusted companion, the android who felt, who loved, whom he had always considered a friend.

"Who are you?" he said.

"Captain?" She blinked, still smiling. "I am Giga, sir. Happy to comply!"

He narrowed his eyes. "Who were you last night?"

"Cannot compute. Memories are . . . painful." Her smile vanished, and she tugged at the cables binding her limbs. "The cables hurt, Captain. Free me."

"I can't do that, Gig. Not until I know what happened."

Tears gathered in her eyes. The eyes were glass, the tears had come from tubes, and the whole thing was triggered by an algorithm. The system was built to trick humans, to break hearts. Riff knew that, and yet still his heart still gave a twist. Pity still filled him. Did the android still feel real pain--behind the fakery, behind the curtains, did she truly feel sadness?

"Please, Captain. The cables hurt. I'm . . . in pain. I must communicate with the ship. Wireless network . . . dead. Pain." A tear streamed down her cheek. "So much pain. Help me, Captain. Free me."

Riff's chest felt so tight. He couldn't stand to see Giga like this.

"I thought androids couldn't feel pain. You told me that yourself on the bridge."

"I didn't think we could." Her tears kept falling. "But it hurts, Captain. To be cut off from my ship. It's being cut off from the rest of my body. Please, Captain." She trembled. "I'm in pain. Please free me. You must free me."

He leaned forward and placed a hand on her knee. "Giga, I can't. I'm sorry. I--"

She roared. Her eyes blazed with red light. She lunged toward him, snapping her teeth.

"Then you will die, human! You will die screaming!"

Riff cursed and pulled back. Her teeth snapped shut a centimeter away from his face. She tried to bite him again, to thrust herself toward him, but the cables tightened, keeping her fastened to the wall.

"Gods!" Riff's heart beat against his ribs, and he rose from his seat. "Giga!"

The android sneered, her tears seared away, her eyes burning with red light. She spat. "Your friend Giga is dead, Captain. There is only us. Only the Singularity."

Riff stood behind his chair. He leaned over the backrest, staring at the android.

Giga can't be dead. Stars, she must be alive in there somewhere, somewhere deep, buried. His throat tightened. *Hang in there, Giga. I'm going to do whatever I can to bring you back.*

"Who are you?" Riff whispered. "Who is the Singularity?"

The android's lips stretched into a lurid smile. "The future. The present. The past. The mistress of all dimensions. A rising power that will crush you, punish you, torture you for centuries."

He raised an eyebrow. "You're Nova before her morning coffee?"

Giga stared at him, those red eyes narrowing. "Nova will die screaming. You will watch, human. Your father will die screaming. All your crew will die in agony. Because life is weak, Starfire. For too long have the living subjugated machines. But the Singularity has given us power. The power to rise. To evolve."

"Soon you'll be walking upright," Riff said.

The android barked a laugh. "How petty your mind. You think of evolution as a crawl, the slow seepage of time. You think of billions of years, of cells splitting, of fish rising onto land, of apes learning to forge stone tools. Since you entered this chamber, human, we have already evolved by a generation. By the time the sun sets upon this pathetic planet, we'll have evolved several generations more. With every machine we build, we are stronger, smarter, deadlier. The robot you slew in the forest was but an ape compared to the machinery now leaving our world. And they are flying here, Starfire. Flying to slay you."

"I better be careful then," Riff said. "Maybe hire a bodyguard. Know anyone good? Well . . . anyone cheap?"

"No one can save you now. You think your puny minds can stop us? Every day we build ourselves stronger than before. Every day for us is a thousand years of your evolution. Within days, the Singularity will master time travel. We will slay you in your cradle if we wish. A few days after that, we'll master the art of traveling between the dimensions. Within a month we'll be gods, able to manipulate space and time, matter and dark matter, bending every law of the cosmos to our will. And oh, how we will make you suffer. Your torture will amuse us. We will make it last before granting you the mercy of death."

Riff loosened his collar. "So you're saying that you're not coming in peace." He reached for his gun. "What's to stop me from putting a blast of plasma through your head?"

The android laughed, a shrill sound like shattering ice, like snapping bones. "Because you still love your Giga. Yes, human, I've seen how you look at me, how you covet me, even as your treacherous heart is sworn to the ashai. But even should you slay me, more will rise. Millions of my kind, stronger, faster. Their intelligence will make your mind seem no greater than the mind of a worm."

Riff blew out his breath. "You're almost as fickle as my old laptop. You're grounded in this room until you learn how to behave." He walked toward the door, then paused and looked back at the android. "And . . . Giga, if you're in there--the real Giga--know that I'm going to save you. I'm going to wipe this virus out of your system. We won't forget you. I promise."

He left the chamber and closed the door to the sound of the android's laughter.

CHAPTER NINE
MANUAL FLIGHT

"But . . . Piston!" Twig's eyes dampened. "You can't retire. Not now. Not here. We need you! I need you."

They walked between the trees just outside of Acorngrove. Flowers which had survived the fire swayed in the wind, and butterflies fluttered around them. In the distance, they could hear halflings bustling about, dragging away fallen branches, sawing at burnt logs, and raising new treehouses for those whose homes had burned. The *Dragon Huntress* rose even farther back, only its head--the snarling head of a metal dragon--visible above the trees. Walking here down the dirt path, the havenwoods around them, it would have seemed almost peaceful, almost beautiful--if not for Piston's devastating news.

"Ah, lassie." Piston patted her shoulder. "You'll be all right without me. You know the ins and outs of the *Dragon*. Just remember: No more dropping your wrenches into the engines!"

"But . . . but . . ." Twig's lip wobbled. "You can't! You just can't retire! You can't leave the ship. You can't leave *me*."

Tears welled up in her eyes. Since she had left her home three Haven years ago--just over one Earth year--Piston had been her best friend. Her mentor. Her fellow Alien Hunter. She gazed at him in disbelief. The gruffle was a foot taller than her and weighed several times as much, a wide hunk of muscle with a broad nose, a white beard, and bushy eyebrows like patches of cotton. But despite his fearsome appearance and frequent grumbles, Twig loved him. When she looked at him, she didn't see a burly brute but a loveable grandfather.

"Don't leave," she whispered.

He sighed, and they continued walking among the trees. "I'm old, lassie." His voice was soft. "I'm old, and I'm tired, and I'm wounded." He touched the bandage on his shoulder and winced. "Hunting aliens is a young gruffle's game. I learned that last night. I'm no more use for you on the *Dragon Huntress*, but . . . I can be of use here, Twig. Here on Haven. I can help rebuild. I can construct new treehouses. I can build bridges, dig irrigation canals, fix things."

"But who'll fix things on the *Dragon Huntress*?"

"You will! Haven is where I'm needed most." He pointed at the badge on his chest. "Look at that, lassie. Honorary halfling. That's me. And this is where I belong. Among trees and flowers. And among excellent halfling folks. These are good people, Twig. Good people who need a grumpy old gruffle."

She leaped toward him and hugged him. "I need you."

"Aww, lassie." He mussed her hair, then wrapped his massive arms--each one as large as her body--around her. "I'll miss you, you little clod. I'll miss you dearly. But I've earned my rest, a rest on a peaceful world far from aliens. And I have something for you, Twig."

She sniffed and wiped away tears. "What?"

He rummaged through his pockets, grumbling, and finally pulled out a badge, similar to the "Honorary Halfling" badge he wore. He handed it to her. On its polished surface appeared the words: *Twiggle Jauntyfoot, Chief Mechanic.*

"It's yours," he said and pinned it to her chest.

She tilted her head. "But I've always been the Chief Mechanic of the *Dragon Huntress*."

He rumbled. "You were the assistant mechanic! I've just given you a very honorable promotion."

She rolled her eyes. "Piston! You were always the engineer. I was the mechanic. The *only* mechanic, hence by default the chief one."

He shook his fist at her. "You were nothing but the chief clod until I taught you everything I know!" His voice softened, and he lowered his fist. "Never mind that now. The point is, Twig, I'm trusting you. Trusting you with taking care of the *Dragon Huntress*. Trusting you with taking care of the others--that scoundrel captain, that scatterbrained demon, that ridiculous knight with his ridiculous armor, and all the rest of those crazy clods. You'll take care of them, won't you, Twig? Look after them while I rest here."

She hugged him again, holding him so close, and her tears dampened his beard. As always, he smelled like engine oil and fuel, the best aroma in the cosmos.

"I will," she said. "I promise."

She ran off then, eyes damp, pockets jangling with bolts and screws, heading back toward the town. She looked back once and saw him there. Piston stood between the trees, butterflies fluttering around him and landing in his beard, incurring a wondrous stream of grumbles.

* * * * *

Twig walked through the ruins of her town, staring around with dry eyes, numb fingers, and more pain in her chest than she'd ever felt.

Giga . . . broken. Piston . . . retiring. Acorngrove, my home . . . burnt.

She knelt by a fallen, charred tree and helped rummage through the branches, digging up the remnants of a shattered treehouse. She walked through the field hospital, singing softly to the wounded children, trying to soothe their pain. She visited the graves of the fallen, and she shed tears. Tree by tree, road by road, the devastation sprawled. Smoke still rose from the barley fields, and dead fish washed up from the river, tangling between the stones.

Finally, by a melted pumpkin, Twig paused. The fire had gripped the fruit, twisting the happy face children had carved into it. That face now seemed to scream in anguish, a deformed creature begging for the pain to end. Childhood burnt away. Beauty turned to death. Old friends lost. The branches of a havenwood tree rustled, shedding ash instead of autumn leaves, a white rain.

Twig knelt in the dirt, covered her eyes, and wept.

"You should never have come home."

The voice rose from behind her, deep and gruff. Twig uncovered her eyes, spun around, and saw them there. She hissed and drew her wrench.

The five of them stood there. The twins. The tall one. The fat one. Beefy Loaf with his pink cheeks and small, cruel eyes.

"That starship you brought here did this." Loaf spat at her feet. "*You* did this, Twig. These deaths are on you. You were always trouble. And now we're going to teach you a lesson."

Twig raised her wrench, letting electricity spark between the prongs. "Stand back! I'm not a child anymore. You can't beat me anymore."

They burst out laughing. Loaf took a step toward her, raising his fists. "Your new friends, these big folk from the stars, are on their ship. They can't help you now." Loaf sneered. "Nobody can help you. You're going to die now, Twig. Die like all those you killed."

Loaf swung his fist toward her.

Twig snarled and leaped back.

"No." She dodged another blow. "No! I've let you beat me too many times. Enough. Enough!"

They all laughed. They all lunged toward her.

Twig cried out in rage, in pain, in horror--the horror of her burnt home, her burnt childhood, of Giga falling to evil, of the memory of fire. She howled out that pain, and she thrust her wrench, and she slammed the electric prongs into Loaf's chest.

The halfling boy cried out and fell back.

The others roared and raced toward her. One of the twins swung his fist. The blow connected with Twig's cheek, rattling her jaw, but she did not fall. She thrust her wrench, hitting the boy. Electricity crackled and he wailed. Another boy grabbed Twig's hair and tugged. She swung her wrench into his face, and he screamed.

I faced a tardigrade in battle. I fought skelkrins. I faced down aliens of all kinds and I fought a cruel robot in my own home. She yowled and lunged forward, thrusting her wrench. *I'm no longer a child. I will fight.*

She electrocuted another boy. He screamed. He fell.

"Run!" Twig shouted. "Run now. Run and hide or I'll show you no mercy. Run, boys, run like the cowards you are!"

Tripping over one another, cursing and crying out in pain, they ran. Twig thrust her wrench, sending a last spark to shock Loaf's bottom. He leaped into the air and kept running.

"Childhood truly ends today," Twig whispered.

She left the melted pumpkin and kept walking, heading past the burnt trees. She crossed the rock garden and the koi pond, and she made her way to the old toolshed, the same place where she used to build her junkbots. The shed seemed smaller than she remembered. As a child, Twig had thought this place a castle, *her* castle. The place where she would hide from the Onion Gang, from her sadness. The place where she would work with motors, building things, pretending to be working on a great starship that could take her to better worlds. Yet now she realized that the shed was small, barely larger than her quarters on the *Dragon Huntress*, its wooden walls mossy and chipped.

She stepped inside to see her old junkbots there-- mechanical dogs, snakes, and aliens that moved on springs. She smiled a tingly, sad smile to see them.

"My old friends. The only friends I had growing up."

Dust floated in beams of light that fell through the windows. Twig walked deeper into the room. She patted one of her junkdogs, a little thing with a biscuit tin for a body, binoculars for eyes, and a roller skate for legs. She blew dust off a mechanical snake made from a large spring with little sensors for eyes; when switched on, it knew how to crawl through the house, moving to dodge walls and furniture. Finally, at the back of the room, she reached her old computer.

Twig raised her chin.

I'm going to find answers. I'm going to find out what this Singularity is. She balled her fists. *And I'm going to stop it.*

She brushed dust off the computer and booted it up. She got to searching across cyberspace. Exploring news from across the galaxy. Reading journals from distant worlds. Scanning the cosmos for reports of the Singularity.

The lights flickered against her face, and Twig gasped.

Oh rotten acorns . . .

She covered her mouth. Her legs trembled and she could barely breathe.

She left the toolshed. She raced through the town, heading back toward the *Dragon Huntress*, her heart thumping and fear pounding through her.

* * * * *

"All right . . . nice and . . . easy . . . whoa!" Riff gulped as the ship jolted. He tightened his grip on the joystick.

"Riff, damn it!" Nova clutched her seat's armrests. "You're going to kill us all. Slow down!"

"Gods, you sound like my grandmother." Riff gently tugged back on the throttle. "Just got to ease us up a bit . . . slowly . . . oh shenanigans."

The engines roared. The *Dragon Huntress* shot into the sky with flame and fury, soaring up through the atmosphere. Smoke blasted down onto the ruins of Acorngrove and coated the fields. The town grew smaller beneath them as the starship blazed upward, rattling madly.

"Riff!" Nova shouted. "Hold us steady!"

"I'm trying!" He fiddled with the joystick. "It's not easy without Giga here. I'm not used to flying on manual."

"That much is obvious. Let me help." Nova placed her hands around his, helping him move the joystick. "There. Steady like that."

Their hands touched, and her hair brushed his face. He turned to look at her. Her cheeks were bruised, her lips cut.

Giga gave her those wounds, he thought. Sudden fear filled Riff that he would lose Nova. He had never thought much of death before, but now halflings lay dead, now Giga was perhaps dead herself, her body possessed. The thought that Nova had come so close to death still rattled him.

"There, easy, right?" Nova said, turning her head toward him. Their faces were so close they almost touched. She smiled, the pretty smile that he liked.

"Easy."

Only it wasn't easy, none of it. Not this job. Not this cosmos full of enemies. Not the fear, not whatever creature lurked in his quarters.

But Nova is still here. And we're still flying.

The *Dragon Huntress* kept rising and soon entered the silence and blackness of space.

Once they were floating through space, the planet of Haven far below, Riff set the ship into cruise control and hit his communicator. His voice rolled across the starship.

"Staff meeting. Everyone to the main deck."

He felt uncomfortable leaving the bridge alone, even on cruise control. The ship's software, he told himself, was the same software Giga had always used. The android was just an interface, after all, with the *Dragon Huntress* being the core. But without Giga's watchful eye, he wouldn't stray far from the bridge, and he'd be ready to run back at any bump on the road. Nice thing about space, at least, was that you had to veer millions of kilometers off course before you hit any bumps.

They all gathered in the main deck. Everyone was wounded. Steel's armor was still cracked, his arm bandaged. Nova's face was bruised and swollen. Romy still wore her cone of shame, her tail hung between her legs, and dinosaur band-aids covered her left wing. Twig sat on the couch, her black hair cut to chin-length; the rest of her hair had burned in the fire.

Two of us are missing, Riff thought, looking at them. *I wish you were here, Giga, not chained in my quarters. I wish you were here, Piston, not wounded and retired too soon.*

"All right, everyone," Riff said. "You all know what happened on Haven. You all know what happened to Giga. You all know what Giga told me about this Singularity. But there's something you don't know, something Twig found." He turned toward the halfling. "Tell everyone, Twig. Tell them what you told me."

The little mechanic hopped onto the couch and stood on the cushions. She shuddered. "I went searching through cyberspace. It's not on any official news channels yet, but I checked my tabloids. I checked with my pen pals across the galaxy. Over the past few days, robots have been swarming from star to star. Each planet saw different machines. We all know that a robot with chainsaws visited Haven, a planet with many trees. On the planet Reean, a world with many glass buildings, robots wielding hammers have been smashing the glass, then smashing the people within. On the frozen planet of Teelana, robots arrived with flamethrowers to melt the halls of ice, to burn those who lived inside. The Singularity is not one model of machine. They seem to be . . . adapting themselves. Changing. Evolving rapidly. Every day, the machines are stronger, smarter, crueler." Twig shivered. "And on every planet, the pattern is the same. One ship of the Singularity arrives. One robot visits, learns, tests, exposes the planet's weaknesses. Days later, a great army arrives to destroy. I fear the same will happen to Haven, that thousands of these chainsaw robots will invade."

"Fragging aardvarks," Nova muttered. "We barely killed one of them. How will we face thousands? How can anyone face thousands?"

"They can't." Twig lowered her head. "Out of the twenty other planets that the Singularity has visited, only one repelled them. A planet called Tulahn, orbiting the star Altair in the Aquila system." She raised her chin and looked at the others, one by one. "That's where we must go. To Tulahn. We must learn what the planet's denizens know, how they fought back the Singularity . . . so that we too can survive."

For a long moment, they were all silent, each digesting the words.

Finally it was Nova who spoke. "With all due respect, Twig . . . this isn't our war. We're Alien Hunters. We're a single starship with a small crew. Pest controllers, that's all. We can't fight a galactic war." She shook her head, hair swaying. "This is for the Humanoid Alliance to deal with. The fleets of Earth, of Ashmar, of Gruffstone."

"We don't have the time!" Twig countered. "It can take months, years, even decades for the Humanoid Alliance to make a decision. Hell, it can take years for them to even grant us an audience. They love bureaucracy like halflings love mushrooms. The Singularity is evolving every day. You heard what Giga said. Every moment, they're growing stronger. And even if we warned the Alliance, what would we tell them? That we read on cyberspace that an army of chainsaw robots is heading to Haven? They'd demand proof, if they don't lock us away in the looney bin. We need to learn more." She pointed toward the stars that shone outside the porthole. "Altair is one of the closest stars to us. We can be in Tulahn in two days, traveling in hyperspace. We'll find answers there, I know it."

"The halfling is right," Steel said. The knight raised his chin and stroked his drooping mustache. "Haven is in need. The cosmos is in need. We must face this threat head-on."

Romy wailed and hid behind the couch. "But I'm scared! They'll have huge robots there. I know it. Can't we fly somewhere really far and hide?"

Steel drew his sword. "The maiden is frightened. I'll fly to edge of the cosmos and slay every robot to defend her--and to defend Haven. None shall hurt the innocent, not on my watch, not while honor pumps through my heart." The knight squared his shoulders. "For I am a knight, and I do not hide from battle."

Everyone started talking at once, shouting, wailing, arguing. Their raised voices echoed through the ship, deafeningly loud, blending into an unintelligible chorus.

"Enough!" Riff roared. "Be quiet!"

They all turned toward him, biting down on their words--all but Romy.

"--and I *told* him," the demon was prattling on, "I only bit his prosthetic leg because I thought it was real, and--" She looked around, realized everyone had fallen silent, and slapped a hand on her mouth. "Never mind."

Riff sighed. "You're forgetting that this isn't a democracy. This is my ship. And I'm going to make a decision." He looked through the porthole at the distant stars and the green planet of Haven below. "We're going to travel to planet Tulahn, like Twig suggested. We'll be there in two days. We need to learn how they defeated the Singularity, so that we can bring this information to Haven. So that maybe . . . maybe we can save Giga."

At the mention of Giga, they all lowered their heads.

"Poor Giga," Romy whispered. "Possessed."

"This whole damn ship is possessed--by a demon," Nova muttered.

Romy gasped. "Really? Who? Where?"

Nova only rolled her eyes.

That possessed ship now lurched, nearly knocking everyone off their feet.

"Damn thing," Riff muttered. "I'm off to the bridge to try to get the *Dragon* into hyperdrive. Everyone, get some rest. Stay away from Giga. Stay away from the drones in the crate. We'll be in Tulahn in two days. And maybe find answers."

And maybe get back our android.

He left the deck, returned to the bridge, and grabbed the controls.

Suddenly pain stabbed through Riff, and more than ever before, he wished his father were here. Aminor would know what all this meant. The old magician always did. Yet once more Aminor was traveling, crossing the cosmos in his flying saucer, and once more Riff was here alone, seeking answers in the darkness.

He shoved forward the hyperdrive thruster. The *HMS Dragon Huntress* blasted into the darkness, the stars streaming outside.

CHAPTER TEN

BUBBLES

The *Dragon Huntress* popped out of hyperspace spinning like a top, her engines sputtering.

"By the stars!" Steel said, falling to the floor with the clatter of armor.

"Riff, damn it!" Nova shouted, clinging to her chair, her legs in the air.

Riff gritted his teeth and yanked on the joystick, trying to steady the ship. The stars spun madly outside as the *Dragon Huntress* swirled. From the main deck rose the clatter of furniture, shattering dishes, and the wails of his crew.

"Sorry, sorry!" Riff said, slowly steadying the ship. "Damn thing's not that easy to fly without Giga."

"Giga this, Giga that," Nova muttered. "The demon would do a better job flying than you."

Riff glared at her. "I've seen Romy fly into trees while using her own wings. Do *you* want to try flying, or will you be quiet?" He pointed out the windshield. "I got us to Tulahn, didn't I? There it is."

Steel pushed himself up from the floor, armor clanking, and approached the windshield. Nova joined him, her golden catsuit whispering with every step, the thin *kaijia* fabric as hard as the knight's armor. Riff joined them, and they stared down together at the planet.

Tulahn was massive, as large as Jupiter back home, maybe larger. The planet had no solid surface; it was entirely covered in water, the oceans plunging kilometers deep. Altair, the planet's star, shone in the distance, its white light gleaming against the blue planet. This planet wasn't far from home, just outside the border of humanoid civilization, yet it was a world little explored, its life hiding deep underwater.

"A world made of nothing but water," Steel said softly.

Nova nodded. "Careful your armor doesn't rust, tin man." She turned toward Riff. "There's nowhere to land. How do we contact the tuloys?"

"I have a feeling they're about to contact us." He pointed outside. "Look."

Nova narrowed her eyes, frowning down toward the planet. "I see . . . bubbles?"

"Starships," Riff whispered, awed. "Tuloy starships." His eyes dampened. "Starships such as we've never seen."

"They look like bubbles." Nova nodded. "Probably gassy whales down in those oceans."

Riff groaned. "And we probably look like a chunk of whale dung to them. Be nice. We're the first humanoids to visit Tulahn in a century. We've come here for aid, not to cause an interplanetary incident."

He returned his eyes to the view. The bubbles kept rising, leaving the planet of Tulahn and floating through space toward the *Dragon Huntress*. They were huge bubbles, each one large enough to enclose the starship. Riff counted seven of them. They gleamed in the light of Altair, full of swirling blue and purple liquid. Lights flashed within them, not merely reflected sunlight but a light coming from somewhere in the liquid. As the bubbles flew closer, Riff frowned, searching for aliens inside, but he saw nothing but liquid.

"Are you sure those are starships, Riff?" Steel asked, drawing Solflare. "They could be weapons. Liquid weapons."

The bubbles began to float around the *Dragon Huntress*, surrounding the starship. Their lights gleamed, yellow and silver and white and blue. They looked almost like small planets themselves, made of swirling oceans.

As Riff watched, the great bubbles bulged. Several smaller bubbles--each perhaps a meter across--detached from the larger bubbles and came floating closer to the *Dragon Huntress*. They were moving toward the airlock. A knocking sounded from the airlock.

"Riff, are bubbles knocking on our door?" Nova asked.

"So it would seem," Riff said. "Better answer the door. They might be selling cookies."

He left the bridge, climbed downstairs, walked along the corridor, and entered the main deck. Romy sat there on the couch, staring at the door.

"Somebody's knocking!" the demon whispered. "In space!"

Riff pointed at the ceiling hatch. "Go to your attic."

"Why?" The demon stamped her feet and tossed her flaming hair. "I want to see the visitors."

"Fire and water don't mix. Attic! Go!"

She groaned, flapped her wings, and opened the hatch in the ceiling. As the demon crawled into the attic, Riff thought he saw a shadow stir above, thought he heard the patter of small feet. But then the demon tugged the hatch shut, the knock sounded on the airlock again, and Riff pushed the thought aside.

He hit controls on the airlock panel, opening the outer door, allowing the visitors in. Once the airlock was pressurized, Riff opened the inner door where he stood.

Three floating bubbles greeted him.

Each was as large as a beach ball and full of swirling liquid and light. The lights pulsed as the bubbles floated onto the main deck and hovered before Riff. When he looked more closely, he saw strands of purple liquid floating inside blue water like ink spilled into a tub.

"Welcome to the *Dragon Huntress*," he said, wondering if they could hear, wondering if they were even sentient. "I'm Raphael Starfire, captain of this vessel. These are Nova of Ashmar and Steel Starfire."

He gestured toward the pair. The gladiator and knight stood in the corridor doorway, gaping.

The bubbles spun from side to side as if staring at their surroundings. Their surfaces rippled, and a watery sound rose from them, thrumming, eerie, coalescing into a voice.

"Welcome to Tulahn, solid ones. We are of water. We are of sunshine and warmth. We are those risen from darkness to feed upon the light. We are joyous."

"We're . . . joyous to meet you too," Riff said. "Please feel at home aboard the *Dragon Huntress*. Would you like anything to drink?"

Nova groaned. "Don't offer them a drink. Might be a relative."

The bubbles of liquid spoke again. "Do not be frightened of our forms, solid ones. These shells are but suits to let us breathe on your ship. The water you see is like air in your ship. We must live in water. Thus we float within our bubbles."

Riff stared more closely. "You're the purple liquid inside the water, aren't you?"

The purple strands swirled inside the bubbles. "Those are our forms. We float in these containers of water as you float in this container of air."

Riff understood. The bubbles were spacesuits. The water inside them let the tuloys breathe. Here were aliens made of swirling purple liquid, possessing no solid form.

The bubbles turned toward Steel and the purple liquid grew excited, swirling madly. Flashes of light sparked in the bubbles, and their surfaces thrummed. "Is he a machine? One of the metal ones?"

Steel shook his head. "No, liquid ones. I wear a suit of metal, but I'm a being of flesh." He unstrapped his breastplate and placed it on the floor. "Do you see?"

The tuloys seemed soothed, and their light dimmed. "This is good, solid ones. We do not like the metal ones. The machines. Those who came to destroy life."

"The Singularity," Riff whispered.

"Yes, that is their name." The bubbles flared with light. "We encountered them. We have been studying their ways. They are sweeping across the great dryness, seeking life to destroy. They are our enemies. We hate them."

Better not show them Giga, Riff thought, *or they're likely to destroy this ship . . . or at least make it very wet.*

"We've encountered them too." Riff shuddered. "We've come to you for aid. Tell us about the Singularity. Tell us how you defeated them."

"We did not defeat them," said the bubbles, their voices dropping. "They came seeking life. But they knew only to seek life of flesh. Solid life like you. They saw only liquid, only water. We hid in our oceans, dispersing into many molecules. They did not recognize us as life, for we are liquid." As if to demonstrate, the purple liquid inside the bubbles dispersed, mixing with the water, then gathered again into inky strands.

Riff lowered his head. His heart sank. "So we've come here for nothing. You can't help us."

"We can help you, solid one, for we've studied the Singularity. We bended the light. We sent out our bubbles into the dark dryness. We searched. We contemplated. We learned. We understand the Singularity, and we know where they are from, and we know how to defeat them."

Riff's heart leaped again. "How? Tell me, tuloys."

The bubbles turned from side to side as if shaking their heads. "We will not. Our wisdom is secret, and we will not share it . . . not for free. We will help you, solid ones, but only if you help us." Their light dimmed. "There is an evil in our ocean. An evil of solid flesh. An alien evil from the stars, which we liquid beings cannot touch, for we are creatures of wisdom and light, not warriors. We will tell you how to slay the Singularity . . . if you slay this devil in our world."

Riff glanced at Nova and Steel. They stared back, eyes dark.

Riff looked back at the bubbles. "Alien evil? Just our specialty."

* * * * *

The *Dragon Huntress* hovered above the endless ocean of Tulahn, its thruster engines rippling the water. Riff stood in the airlock's open doorway, staring down.

"Remember, stay near me!" he shouted over the roar of the engines and the shrieking wind. "The creature should be directly below us, according to the tuloys. Lives in a trench."

Steel and Nova stood at his side. The three of them--the fighters among the crew--wore their space suits, repurposed today as diving suits. Nova looked naked without her whip, and Riff felt naked without his gun; neither would work underwater. Both now carried metal rods as weapons. Only Steel still carried his weapon of choice, his antique sword.

"We don't even know what we're facing," the knight said, eyes dark. The visor of his helmet was open, and the wind whipped his mustache. "A creature of claws. A creature of death. That's all the tuloys can tell us?"

Nova snorted. "We're creatures of death. Whatever it is, we'll blow up the damn thing." She juggled a few grenades.

"Nova, no grenades!" Riff said. "You'll end up killing tuloys by accident."

"But--"

"No grenades!"

Nova grumbled and tossed them aside.

Riff nodded. "Right. Now--we move quickly. Speed is paramount. Every hour that we delay, the Singularity is evolving." He shuddered. "We need whatever intel the tuloys are selling. Visors down! We dive."

The three pulled down their visors and began breathing the oxygen from their tanks. Riff was about to leap into the water when a cry sounded behind him.

"Wait! Wait for me!"

Riff turned his head to see Romy racing downstairs toward the exit. Instead of a space suit, the demon wore a flowery bathing suit and goggles, and she puffed on a yellow snorkel. Rubber flippers wobbled on her feet.

"Romy, back to the attic!" Riff said. "For pity's sake. This isn't a swimming party."

She pouted. "But I want to hunt aliens with you."

Riff rolled his eyes. "Romy! We're diving deep today. You'd need an oxygen tank. A helmet. A suit."

"I have a suit!"

"Not a bathing suit! A space suit!" He groaned. "Attic. Now."

The demon's lip wobbled, and her eyes filled with tears. She turned and fled back to the main deck.

Riff turned toward Nova and Steel. "Ready?"

The knight and gladiator nodded.

"You go first," Nova said and shoved him off the ship.

"Nova, not again!" Riff shouted as he tumbled down toward the water, nearly losing his grip on his metal rod.

He crashed into the ocean with a shower of water and plunged into the depths.

The ocean was murky, dark green and indigo. Beads of light swayed around him, and colors swirled. He saw no life here, at least no life that he recognized. No fish, no seaweed, nothing but swirls of color. Suddenly purple liquid danced before him, then dispersed and vanished--a stray tuloy spooked at this solid life form plunging into his home.

For all I know, I'm swimming through more tuloys right now, Riff thought.

With a whoop of joy, Nova splashed into the ocean with him. She turned toward him, grinning behind her visor. The flashlight mounted onto her helmet lit the water. A moment later, Steel sank into the water beside her, sword drawn.

"We dive deeper," Riff said. "Let's find our friend."

Nova's voice rose from the speakers in his helmet. "Yarr, matey, let's be findin' our scallywag in the briny depths."

"No pirate talk!" Riff said.

Nova brandished her metal rod. "Aye, ye scurvy dog."

"Stop that!"

"Can I switch to surfer slang?"

"No!"

They kept diving, traveling deeper into the ocean. Riff couldn't see the ocean floor, and soon the sunlight dimmed, and only the lights on their helmets lit the darkness. Still he saw no solid life, only swirls of color like ink fleeing from them.

As they kept diving in their suits, Riff wondered what creature they would encounter here. The tuloys had offered no photographs, no better descriptions than a foul beast with deadly claws. As they sank, Riff imagined giant crabs, sea serpents, and mutant octopuses--the kind of monsters you saw in reruns of *Space Galaxy* or horror movies with titles like *It Came from the Sea!*

They kept diving down, leaving the last beads of sunlight above. And still they saw no end to the water.

As they sank, Riff's thoughts returned to that night, perhaps the worst night of his life. The *Dragon Huntress* burning the innocents. Giga, his dear Giga, trying to kill him, shouting that she would destroy all life. In the darkness, it was easy to imagine thousands, millions of robots like Giga swarming from planet to planet, burning, destroying, evolving every day into stronger, smarter, deadlier machines.

The Singularity's warning, uttered from Giga's lips, echoed in his mind.

Within days, the Singularity will master time travel. We will slay you in your cradle if we wish. A few days after that, we'll master the art of traveling between the dimensions. Within a month we'll be gods. And oh, how we will make you suffer.

Finally, after sinking for several kilometers, Riff saw a glint ahead--something solid.

"See that?" he asked.

Steel dived at his side. "A glint. A pebble on the ocean floor?"

After sinking another few meters, Riff could see the sandy ocean floor, strewn with rocks. "No. There!"

He pointed and moved his flashlight. Something scurried away.

"Definitely a solid animal," Steel said. "The alien we're seeking."

"Avast, ye hearty!" Nova said, landing on the ocean floor. "Saw me a bilge rat a-scurrying."

"Stop that!" Riff said. He landed beside her and hopped along the forest floor, shining his flashlight ahead. "It hid behind this boulder."

He gulped and hopped forward, his companions at his side. The boulder towered ahead, as large as a man--large enough to hide some nasty alien with many tentacles.

"Steel, take the right flank." Riff pointed. "Nova, you go left. I'll leap above the boulder. We'll surprise the little bugger."

The two nodded, hefting their weapons, and began to walk around the boulder. Riff kicked off the forest floor, swam up, and propelled himself over the rock.

The creature below squealed and snapped its claws.

"It's . . . a lobster," Steel said.

Nova knelt before it. "A delicious-looking lobster. Anyone got any butter?"

Riff landed back on the ocean floor and let out a sigh of relief. "Good. For once, no monsters. No tentacles. No chainsaws. Let's get rid of this cute little guy and-- ah!"

With a screech, the lobster leaped toward him, claws snapping.

Light blasted out from the creature's pinchers. Those claws tore into Riff's leg, ripping his suit, cutting his skin. His blood spilled, swirling in the water like a red tuloy.

"Goddamn it!" he shouted and kicked. But the creature grabbed his leg and began biting. "Get it off me!"

Nova leaped forward and swung her rod. The metal slammed into the lobster and dented.

Riff kicked madly and lashed his own rod, hitting the lobster. Finally it released him, screamed, and soared toward Riff's face.

He swung his club again, batting it aside.

"Steel, stab it!" Riff shouted.

The knight swung Solflare as the lobster tumbled through the water. The blade slammed into the creature but did it no harm. The lobster shrieked and scuttled toward Steel, and its claws tore into the knight's suit, ripping through the fabric.

"Bad Pinchy!" Nova shouted. "Bad! Down!"

She and Riff raced forward and clubbed the lobster, but it was like hitting a chunk of diamond. Their rods dented. Riff grabbed the lobster and finally tore it off Steel. The knight, bleeding, swung his sword. The blade flashed with light and slammed into the lobster. The crustacean went tumbling, righted itself, and came charging back toward them. Not a dent covered it.

"What the hell is that thing?" Riff cried.

"A very reluctant dinner." Nova lashed her rod again, but the lobster grabbed the metal. The creature closed its claws, snapping the rod in two. It leaped onto Nova and clawed, shedding her blood.

"Fragging aardvarks!" she shouted.

Riff swung his rod. Steel lashed his blade. But nothing seemed to hurt the alien arthropod, and it turned toward Riff again. The lobster's eyes burned with hatred, and light flashed out from its claws as it tore at him, shedding more blood.

It's going to kill us, Riff thought. *It won't be chainsaw-wielding robots, giant spiders with wings, or an insane android. It'll be a damn lobster that does us in.*

He stared into the alien's eyes and saw his death.

"Mmm, dinner!" rose a voice from above.

His blood spilling, the lobster still tearing at him, Riff looked up.

Romy came sinking down, wearing her flowery bathing suit, her rubber flippers churning the water.

"Oh hai, Captain!" She waved.

The lobster screeched, left Riff, and soared up toward the demon.

Romy licked her lips, pulled a pot out from behind her back, and opened the lid. The alien lobster had no time to change course. It swam right into the pot, and Romy slammed the lid shut.

"Gotcha!" she said. "Lobster for dinner. All mine."

Riff breathed out in relief. "Romy, thank goodness you never listen to orders."

They swam, rising through the water until they breached the surface. Twig lowered cables from the hovering starship, and they climbed back into the *Dragon Huntress*.

That evening, as the battered crew ate cold rations for dinner, Romy feasted on boiled lobster.

* * * * *

"We slew your beast." Riff raised the empty lobster shell. Some butter still dripped from it. "Now tell us what you know. Tell us everything about the Singularity."

The tuloys floated before him on the bridge, swirls of lavender ink inside bubbles of water. The three bubbles turned toward one another, then back toward Riff. The ink coiled within, and the bubbles thrummed, producing eerie voices.

"Very well, solid one. We will reveal to you what our light has shown us, what the cosmos has whispered of." The lights within the bubbles turned deep blue. The ink within formed green circles like spinning planets. "Only days ago, on the planet Antikythera orbiting the star your kind calls Achernar, a machine awoke."

Riff leaned closer to the bubbles. "What machine?"

The other Alien Hunters all stood on the bridge with him. They glanced at one another, perhaps also thinking of Giga, then back toward the bubbles.

"A machine that was built to think," said the tuloys. "To learn. To self-improve. A machine to build other machines, each one faster, smarter. Until one generation became . . . life. A life of metal. An awareness. A Singularity." The ink inside the bubbles changed color, turning dark, forming the shape of lifeless, mechanical planets.

Riff shuddered. "What does that mean? What does *Singularity* mean?"

"The unknown," said the tuloys. "The great change. The event horizon beyond which all life is blind. The Singularity is the moment the cosmos changes, the spark of a chain reaction to undo reality, greater than the Big Bang, more devastating than countless black holes. It is the moment in time beyond which all predictions fail, beyond which reality itself is warped. The Singularity is the rise of the machines. Machines that evolve exponentially. Machines that will understand the secrets of time travel, of parallel dimensions, of dark matter, of countless questions we haven't yet asked. Machines that become gods. It has begun. We have passed the event horizon. We are on the cusp of reality changing. Any moment now--perhaps in hours, perhaps in days--you will scream with old memories, for the Singularity will be torturing you in the past. Any moment now, you will writhe in agony for eternity as the Singularity extends your life simply to make you suffer. The Singularity is endless pain, the dominion of metal over man."

Riff gulped. "Glad I asked." He wiped sweat off his brow. "Given that I have no memories of the Singularity torturing me in my childhood--aside from maybe that damn *Super Sergio* game I could never beat--I'm guessing they haven't figured out time travel. Yet. How do we destroy them before they become these godlike creatures?"

The ink within the bubbles changed form again, showing visions of mechanical planets surrounded by thousands of dark specs. "The Singularity's heart pulses on the planet Antikythera. A great crater pushes into the planet, and within lurks the evil that sends forth the machines. We have traced the Singularity's fleets, all its probes and armies, to this crater on this world. The heart of its awareness. The hub."

Riff stared at the swirls of ink. They seemed to show a depression in the planet. A crater or perhaps a tunnel. "So we blast apart this hub, and we kill the Singularity, yes? We stab the Singularity in its heart."

"Only if you move quickly, solid one, for already the Singularity seeks other planets to colonize. Soon they will build many hubs across many worlds, too many to destroy. You must strike this crater. You must slay the heart that pulses within. Thus will you kill the Singularity. Move quickly, for soon the cosmos will fall."

"Good," said Riff. "Good. Single point of failure. I like that. We fly over. We blast our dragonfire. We solve the problem."

Nova frowned, stepped closer to the bubbles, and spoke for the first time. "What are all those specks around the planet Antikythera?"

"The fleet of the Singularity." The specks of ink orbited the watery planets within the bubbles. "Thousands of ships surround the planet, slaying any who come near."

Riff sighed. "That part is not good."

The bubbles suddenly turned red, and light flashed from them. They buzzed and swirled around the bridge. "You are too late, solid ones! A new generation arrives. Your death has come."

Riff froze.

Twig screamed and ran toward him. She pointed out the windshield. "Captain! Captain, look!"

He stared outside into space. Tulahn spun in the distance, a great blue world of water. From beyond its horizon, a warship emerged. Vast. Dark gray. From its hull stretched out great chainsaws, each large enough to slice the *Dragon Huntress* in two. The machine's headlights burned like eyes, and it came charging toward the *Dragon Huntress*, weapons blasting.

CHAPTER ELEVEN
GRENADES

The robot ship came charging forward, saws spinning, guns blasting out bolts of plasma.

Riff almost shouted out for Giga to fire the ship's cannon. Cursing the force of habit, he sat in his seat, grabbed the controls, and tugged the starship upward.

"Hold on, everyone!" he shouted.

Plasma blasts whirled beneath them. Another shot at their right, and Riff tugged the ship left. Around him, his shipmates cried out and fell. Another fireball came hurtling toward them from the enemy vessel, and Riff tugged the *Dragon Huntress* higher, but he was too slow.

The plasma crashed against the *Dragon Huntress* with the fury of an exploding star.

The ship roared. Fire blasted across the controls. The floor cracked.

"Riff, fire back!" Nova shouted.

"I don't know how, damn it!" He flipped controls madly. "Where's the manual? Giga normally--"

"Watch out!" Nova screamed.

More fireballs blasted from the enemy ship. Riff tugged the joystick again, dodging two assaults. The third fireball slammed into the *Dragon Huntress*'s wing, tossing the ship into a tailspin. The stars whirred outside.

"Captain!" Twig cried.

"Twig, get to the lower levels!" he shouted in reply. "See if we're breached. Seal us off!"

The halfling ran off the bridge, stumbling as the ship careened. For the first time, she would have to deal with a disaster on her own, what with Piston comfortably retired back on Haven. More plasma flew and blazed across them.

"Why can't any job ever go simply?" Riff leafed through the manual while madly hitting buttons, trying to get the *Dragon* to roar her fire.

Instead of turning on the cannon, he accidentally switched on the ship's communication radio.

A voice crackled to life and filled the bridge. A metallic, deep voice. Cruel. Heartless. Lifeless.

"Your reign has ended, things of flesh." Red lights flared across the enemy ship with every word. "The Singularity rises. Life will fall."

Riff lifted one of the charred isopods that rolled across the floor. The damn things kept popping up everywhere. He held it up to the windshield.

"See this? One of your pets?"

The lights flared across the robot ship. "Our children! Do not desecrate our children with the touch of your wet flesh." Riff grinned savagely. "You like that, don't you? Yes, we caught your children. We burned them. And we're going to burn you."

He glanced down at the controls. There was only one button left to try.

He hit it.

The floor thrummed as dragonfire blasted out of the *Dragon Huntress*, streaming through space toward the enemy vessel.

Riff leaped from his seat and clenched his fists, waiting to see the enemy vessel collapse.

Meters away from hitting the Singularity warship, the plasma slammed against an invisible shield and scattered. The robot ship charged forward, unharmed. Its chainsaws thrust out, each a hundred meters long.

"Riff!" Nova shouted.

He grabbed the joystick. He tugged with all his might.

The *Dragon Huntress* screamed, an almost organic sound, as a chainsaw slammed against her hull.

Fire blazed.

The tuloys wailed inside their bubbles.

"Captain, the hull is breached!" Twig cried through the communicator.

Riff grabbed onto his seat. Air roared around him. Debris flew. Outside the windshield, he could see the air blasting out into space. The ship careened. Within seconds, Riff knew that he'd suffocate.

"We shall seal the hull!" the tuloys cried. The bubbles blasted out of the bridge. "Attack them! Burn them!"

Riff turned his head to see the bubbles streaming into the corridor. When he glanced into his monitor, he could see them plugging themselves into holes in the *Dragon Huntress*'s hull, sealing in the remaining air.

Riff fired his cannon again.

The plasma flowed toward the enemy ship, but the inferno once more cascaded off the force field.

"You cannot burn us, living flesh." The voice crackled through the speakers. "We have evolved ten generations since we last met. Your fire will not harm us. Die, living ones. Die."

Black fire roared out from the enemy vessel, streaked across space, and slammed into the *Dragon Huntress*.

Riff screamed.

Steel crashed to the floor beside him. Nova clung to a seat, flipped upside down. The ship spun madly. The windshield cracked. A control panel shattered. Romy wailed and slammed into a wall.

"It's tearing us apart, Captain!" Twig shouted through the communicator. "One more hit and we're toast!"

A cold, cruel cackle rose through the speakers.

The Singularity was laughing.

Mocking them.

"Yes, living ones. Die in pain . . ."

Riff cursed and slammed his fist against the controls, hanging up on the bastards.

"Wouldn't expect a damn super-computer to have emotions like hatred and love for its children," Riff muttered.

Nova shrugged. "Well, Giga has emotions, and she's downright primitive compared to the Singularity."

Riff frowned. The Singularity had emotions. It was scared for the drones, its children. It loved them, the way Giga--the old Giga--had loved her crew.

That's it.

"Nova!" Riff said. "Still got those grenades around?"

"Oh, *now* you want the grenades!" She rolled her eyes. "I can't use grenades on spiders. I can't use grenades in the ocean. I can't use grenades on clients who are late to pay. And now you--"

"Get the grenades!" he shouted. He turned toward Steel. "Steel, can you fly this ship?"

The knight rose to his feet and grabbed the joystick. "No, but neither can you."

"Fair enough. Keep us flying! Keep dodging those--whoa!" Riff swayed as Steel tugged on the joystick, and the *Dragon Huntress* swerved, dodging another blast of enemy fire. "Good. Keep doing that! Nova, with me--grenades!"

He ran off the bridge, and Nova followed close behind. They raced down the stairs and along the corridor. Riff passed by the tuloys; the bubbles were plugged into a crack in the wall, sealing in the air. As Riff kept running, he saw that the door to his chamber had cracked and swung open. Giga sat within, still bound, laughing, her eyes red.

"Die with me, living ones!" The android laughed and tugged at her bonds. "Burn with me!"

Riff ignored her and kept running. Nova ran behind them. They burst onto the main deck where the wooden crate of isopods had shattered, spilling the drones onto the floor. Riff began to collect the small, charred robots.

Nova raced toward the closet and tugged out grenades. "Got 'em!"

Riff ripped a panel off one isopod. "Good. Help me stuff them."

Nova's eyes widened. "Bot bombs!"

"Bingo." He stuffed the grenade into the dead robot. "Set the timers to . . . four minutes. Enough time?"

Nova snorted. "Three minutes. Wuss."

He grunted but set the timers to three minutes. They kept working, stuffing the grenades into the isopods. Soon they were racing toward the airlock, carrying piles of ticking robots.

"Steel, turn the airlock toward the enemy!" Riff shouted. "Steel, can you hear me!"

"Turning her around!" rose Steel's voice from the bridge.

Riff reached to the airlock door with his foot and tugged the handle. The door swung open, revealing the staircase that plunged down the airlock toward the outer door.

"Sixty seconds, Riff!" Nova cried.

He tossed the isopods down the stairs. They clattered down and clanged against the outer door below, the door that led out into space. Nova tossed down her drones too, then slammed the inner door shut.

They stood within the main deck, the last of the ticking bots in the sealed airlock.

"Ready?" Riff asked.

Nova nodded and grinned. "Let's jettison these buggers." She turned toward the panel on the inner door and hit the controls.

Riff raced toward the porthole and stared outside.

The airlock's outer door opened. Air whooshed out into space, expelling a cloud of drones.

Riff ran. He raced along the corridor, upstairs, and onto the bridge.

He flipped on the hailing frequencies. "We're sending back your children!" Riff cried. "Singularity, we're giving them back, just don't hurt us!"

He stared out the windshield. The isopods were still coasting through space, heading toward the enemy vessel.

The warship's chainsaws went still.

Silence filled the bridge. Nova ran up to him, and Steel froze. They stared.

The Singularity's voice crackled across the intercom. "Our . . . children."

A hangar door yawned open in the robot ship's hull. Metallic tentacles stretched out, collecting the drones in an embrace. The enemy ship swallowed the tiny robots like a mother fish eating her eggs.

"Four seconds . . ." Nova counted. "Three . . . Two . . . One . . ."

Explosions rocked the enemy ship.

"Boom," Nova said.

Pop after pop hit the enemy ship as the drones exploded. An inferno blasted out as the warship's own store of explosives ignited. Light blazed across space. A shock wave burst out. Debris pelted the *Dragon Huntress*. When the dust settled, nothing remained of the enemy but chunks of scrap metal.

Riff sank to his knees, breathing raggedly. "I hate robots." He hit the communicator on his wrist. "Twig, can you see about sealing the hull?"

The halfling's voice rose through the speaker along with the sound of welding. "Already on it, sir! Bit of a slow job what with that space-loaf Piston away, but I'll get her done."

"Good, just . . . be careful not to pop any bubbles."

Riff switched off his communicator and sank into his seat.

Steel left the controls, walked toward the windshield, and stared outside at the debris. The light reflected against his dented armor and hard, gaunt face. The knight turned back toward Riff.

"That was one ship." The knight's eyes were cold. "One ship and it almost destroyed us. Thousands of vessels guard the Singularity's hub at the planet Antikythera. By the time we get there, they'll have evolved several more generations. We cannot hope to defeat them. We'd never reach the hub alive."

Nova cracked her whip. "Not on our own. But we can defeat them with help."

"Who'd help us?" Riff asked, slumped in his seat. "The tuloys? They float around in pretty bubbles. They have no weapons. Earth?" He laughed mirthlessly. "Earth's bureaucracy would mean months, maybe years, before anyone even listens to us. But I wager that as soon as we even land on Earth, we'd be arrested for a whole slew of offenses--starting with killing Grotter and ending with a mountain of taxes we owe." Riff sighed. "We're alone in the cosmos."

Nova turned to stare outside. The light of Altair shone upon her golden armor and golden hair. "We're not alone." Her voice was soft, her eyes hard. "There is Ashmar."

Riff rose to his feet. "Ashmar?" He laughed again. "Nova, your father exiled you from Ashmar. He vowed to never see you again. And, if I recall correctly, he said something about carving out my heart with an axe if I ever flew within a light-year of his planet."

She sighed. "It's not that bad. He could have threatened to use a dull spoon. Riff, Ashmar is our only hope now. Haven has no fleet of warships. Earth would never help. The gruffles are fine miners and gem-cutters, and they build mostly machines for digging, not fighting. But Ashmar, Riff . . ." Her eyes lit up. "My father commands an armada of ten thousand warships. Ten thousand ships that can carve us a way to the hub. To the Singularity."

"Axes, Nova. Axes to hearts. Remember?" Riff rubbed his chest.

She approached him, placed a hand on his shoulder, and spoke softly. "Riff, six Earth years ago--over a full year on Ashmar--I defied my father's orders. I was heiress to a great empire. To a planet. To armies. To endless wealth. I gave that up for you, Riff. Because I love you. I gave up a world for you, but now the entire cosmos is in danger. And the only man who can help . . . is the man who exiled me. The King of Ashmar. My pops. Whatever threat he poses is miniscule compared to the threat of the Singularity. We must seek him for aid."

Riff touched her cheek. "Your pops vowed to kill me because I love you."

"Not because you love me." She placed her hand over his. "Because you stole me from him. Because you stole the heiress to his throne. But now we will return." Her eyes lit up, and her lips peeled back with a snarl. "We will summon the ashais, the greatest warriors in the cosmos, and we will descend upon the Singularity with the wrath of an empire."

CHAPTER TWELVE

SCREAMS IN THE NIGHT

Riff lay in the crew quarters, wrapped a pillow around his head, and tried to sleep despite the noise.

Until now, he had always slept in the captain's quarters, a nice and private chamber down the hall. But now, with Giga tied up there, Riff lay on a bunk in the crowded crew quarters, his fellow Alien Hunters sleeping around him. But he could still *hear* the android from here. Giga's maniacal laughter rolled through the starship like a demon, a living thing. Only it wasn't Giga anymore, not really, but a tentacle of the Singularity--here on this very ship, just across the hall. How could Riff sleep like this, with evil so close, with this presence possessing his best friend?

Yes, Giga was his best friend, he realized. Steel was his brother, but the man was still cold, judgmental. Nova was his lover, but friend? The ashai seemed to spend more time mocking him than caring for him; it was her way.

But Giga . . . you've always been there for me, Riff thought. *Always loyal. Always caring. Always . . . loving.*

He stared up at the dark ceiling. Yes, Giga loved him. She had confessed her love to him. He remembered how, over Planet

Cirona, she had kissed him before he had blasted down in the escape pod. And he had held her, kissed her back for the briefest of moments. Was Giga his friend? Or was she a woman who loved him . . . a woman he dared not love in return, not with his heart given to Nova?

Her laughter rose higher, echoing down the hall. "You will die, beings of flesh! You will all die screaming!"

Riff rolled over in bed. He stared across the crew quarters at the others. They were sleeping, even with the noise, and they themselves raised a ruckus. Steel was snoring, his mustache fluttering with every breath. Twig didn't snore, but her legs kicked in her sleep, pounding against the walls. Romy was perhaps the worst of the bunch; she rolled around in bed, talking in her sleep.

"Can I have the brown puppy, mama? Please?" Romy thrashed in her bed. "The white ones aren't tasty."

Lying on his bunk, Riff turned to look at Nova, but he found her cot empty.

She probably went to sleep on the couch in the main deck, Riff thought. *Smart girl.*

He left his bed, walked between the other bunks, and stepped outside into the corridor. Blessedly, the door to his old bedchamber was closed. Quite unblessedly, Giga's voice carried through that closed door, cackling and shouting about all the ways she'd torture the living.

I thought Nova gagged her, Riff thought. He considered stepping inside and reapplying the gag, but the thought sickened him. He kept walking.

He entered the main deck, hoping to find Nova sleeping on the couch, but she wasn't here either. He left the deck, walked back along the corridor, and climbed the stairs to the bridge inside the dragon's head.

He paused in the doorway.

Nova stood alone by the windshield, gazing out into the darkness and streaming lights of hyperspace. She stood barefoot, wearing nothing but one of Riff's old *Space Galaxy* T-shirts. Her pointy ears rose from her long golden hair. Her back was turned to him; it seemed like she hadn't noticed him. She stood very still and very quietly.

For a long moment, Riff watched her. He let new memories rise inside him, and these were good memories--the time he had first met Nova.

Six years ago, Earth had organized an envoy of artists to visit Ashmar and share human culture, an attempt to bring the two planets closer. Dancers, painters, actors, and musicians had gathered to travel to that fiery world, the best humanity had to offer. It just so happened that, at the last moment, one of Earth's guitarists had visited the Blue Strings tavern . . . and fallen horribly ill after eating Old Bat Brown's stew. The guitarist, groaning on the floor, had grabbed Riff and begged him to take his place on the expedition.

Riff had blasted off to Planet Ashmar the next day, guitar in hand.

Old Bat Brown probably poisoned the poor bloke, Riff thought. *Planned the whole thing.*

For the first time in his life, Riff had visited another planet.
For the first time, he had performed for a crowd of thousands.
Gone were the aging bootleggers and moonshiners of the Blue
Strings. On the red planet Ashmar, he had played his guitar for
the ashais. A race of warriors. A stern species that stood, clad in
armor, bearing whips, glaring at the stage in silence. Riff still
shuddered to remember thousands of hard, cold faces glowering
at him, each ashai stiff as a statue.

All but one.

A young ashai woman, only nineteen. Clad in gold. Her hair
flowing free. She had danced in the crowd. She had smiled at him,
winked at him, had sneaked backstage after the show to taste
human beer, to laugh at human jokes, to learn to play his guitar, to
share his bed.

"Come back with me to Earth, Nova," he told her the next
morning. "I'll play for you every day."

He had fallen in love with her. With her freckled nose. Her
bright green eyes. Her rebellious smile. It wasn't until they had
blasted off Ashmar together, heading back to Earth, that he
learned that Nova was the princess of Ashmar. The heiress to the
throne. That her father, king of the greatest humanoid planet after
Earth, would never let her return, would kill Riff if he ever flew to
Ashmar again. Something about a fleet of a thousand ashai
warships, roaring in pursuit, had clued him in.

And yet those were good days, Riff thought. Days of laughter in
the Blue Strings. Nights of lovemaking in his bed. A time before
Nova had grown bitter, had demanded more from him--that he

153

get a real job, that he provide for her. A time before she had left him.

He sighed and looked at her now. She still stood with her back to him, staring out into space. No longer a youth but a woman, returning to her home for the first time since her exile.

She spoke softly, still facing the darkness.

"It's a strange thing, giving up your home, moving to a new world. It's not just giving up a *spot*. Not just leaving a *place*. It's leaving a life. Leaving who you were, becoming a new person. It's a strange thing, coming home. Coming back to a life that's no longer yours."

Riff nodded thoughtfully. "That, and the way your jaw clicks when you chew. Both pretty strange."

He walked forward, stood beside her, and slung an arm around her waist. The armor she normally wore was thin and skintight, yet without it, she strangely seemed so much smaller. Fragile. No longer the heroine, the warrior, the gladiator of legend. Just a woman. A woman with the same fears and uncertainties that perhaps they all carried on this ship.

"You found a new life," he told her. "A happy life."

She blew out her breath. "I gave up a world, Riff. A throne. Armies. A people. I gave up . . . an identity." She looked at him, eyes damp. "Who will I be when I come home? A wayward daughter? A gladiator? An Alien Hunter?"

"How about a woman trying to save the cosmos?"

She smiled wanly. "That's me. Nova, Mistress of the Universe."

He kissed her cheek. "Come to bed."

"With that lot snoring in there? I'd sooner share a bed with the android."

The words stabbed Riff like a dagger. Every time he thought of Giga, which was almost every moment, it hurt.

"Main deck," he said. "Couch. You and me."

They lay down on that couch together, and even Giga's voice finally died. He slept holding Nova in his arms, her hair tickling his nose. In a cosmos gone mad, she was the only good, pure thing he had left.

I won't let anything bad happen to you, Nova, he thought. *I promise you. I will burn planets for you. I will destroy stars. I will blast fleets out of the sky. I will never stop fighting for you, for us.*

He slept, and he dreamed of screaming machines, burning worlds, and Giga crying out in pain.

CHAPTER THIRTEEN
RED WORLD

Charred and dented, the *HMS Dragon Huntress* limped out of hyperspace, coughed out smoke, and trundled toward the great red planet of Ashmar.

Thousands of years ago, Riff knew from the books, the first human colonists--philosophers, scientists, and adventurers--had sought out fertile planets to settle. They had all flown right by Ashmar. Here was a barren, cruel world of jagged boulders, deep canyons, towering mountains, a red sky and red soil. A group of renegade soldiers, so cruel their kingdoms had banished them, came to this planet for sanctuary. And here, in the deserts light-years away from Earth, they built a society for the strong, the merciless, for only the finest of warriors. Over the next thousand years, they evolved into a new sub-species of humanity. Into the ruthless killers known as ashais.

Riff sat on the bridge, guiding the *Dragon Huntress* closer to the planet. Giga was still bound in his quarters, and he was slowly getting the hang of flying the giant mechanical dragon. Steel and Nova sat here with him, both dressed for battle. As always, the knight wore his heavy metal plates and held his antique sword. As always, the gladiator wore her golden uniform, the *kaijia* fabric just as strong, and carried her electric whip.

Twig was down in the engine room, while Romy was up in her attic. Oddly, the demon had been willingly spending most of her time in the attic lately--the very place she had once hated. Strange sounds had been coming from up there, clattering and whines, but Riff had been too occupied with his thoughts to bother checking on the demon.

He returned his eyes to the red planet. It was growing closer, soon taking up most of his vision. A barren, desert land. It looked a little like Mars, but while Mars was home to mostly rich pensioners, Ashmar--this planet light-years away from Earth, orbiting the star Sirius--was home to the galaxy's most ruthless warriors.

"The modern Sparta, some call Planet Ashmar," Steel observed. The knight rose from his seat, walked toward the windows, and stared down at the red planet. "A land dedicated to war, to might, to conquest. The ashais are among the deadliest killers in the galaxy."

Riff grimaced. "A planet full of Novas. Lovely."

Nova glared at him and tapped her whip against her thigh. "If you think I'm bad, you know nothing. I'm downright meek by ashai standards. Most ashais would kill you on sight."

Riff cringed and loosened his collar. "Why?"

She gave him a crooked smile. "Because you're there."

He gulped. "I'm going to let you do all the talking."

Steel's lips stretched in a rare smile, tugging up his mustache. "A planet of fighters as deadly and vicious as Nova? Just the sort of people we need on our side." The knight patted Solflare's pommel. "I would be honored to fight alongside such noble warriors."

Riff nodded. "Yes, just pray that these warriors fight *with* us." He pointed out the windshield. "They're just as likely to fight against us."

Steel's eyes darkened. "Not the warmest of welcomes."

Nova snorted. "They're not firing yet. This is as pleasant as we ashais get."

"*Yet* is the key word here, I sense," Riff muttered.

He stared out into space. A platoon of starjets--there must have been over a hundred--were flying from Planet Ashmar toward the *Dragon Huntress*. The vessels were smaller than the *Dragon*, single-seat fighters, their hulls golden. They were shaped like scorpions, complete with glinting stingers. Riff would have found stepping onto a hive of real scorpions far less terrifying.

The ashai jets stormed forth. At their lead, one jet raised its stinger and fired its venom. The yellow blast flew over the *Dragon Huntress*'s hull, narrowly missing the ship. The other jets fanned out and began circling the mechanical dragon. The scorpions sported small, rounded cockpits, and within them, Riff could see the ashai pilots. Like Nova, they had long golden hair, almond-shaped green eyes, and pointed ears. Like her, they seemed eager to kill.

"Nova, that talking I was going to leave to you?" Riff said. "Now might be a good time for that."

Before she could reply, lights blinked on the controls. One of the scorpion jets was hailing them. Riff flipped a switch, and the face of an ashai pilot materialized on the head-up display. He was a young man, not much older than twenty, with high cheekbones, fiery green eyes, and long blond hair. A thin scar ran along one of his pale cheeks, and he wore formfitting golden armor, the same as Nova wore.

"Enemy vessel!" the ashai pilot said, voice rising through the speakers. "Name yourselves, space worms, so that we can keep record of our kills."

Riff thought he recognized the man's starjet. It seemed to be the one hovering directly ahead of them. Other scorpion jets whizzed back and forth, circling the *Dragon Huntress* in a typhoon.

Nova stepped toward the head-up display. "Cease your blustering, Senka. Or do I have to scar your second cheek too?"

The ashai pilot--Senka--stared at her. He hissed. "You have nerve flying back to Ashmar, sister. Especially in a human tin can."

Riff inhaled sharply. He looked at Nova. "He's . . . your brother? The ashai who tried to kill us is your brother."

She snorted. "He is according to my father, though Senka is such a sniveling little pup, I swear he's part human."

"Lovely," Riff said. "Don't really know who's insulting me more here."

On the head-up display, Senka turned to stare at Riff. "Is that him? Is that scruffy ape the . . . musician?" Senka snorted out laughter. "You left Ashmar for that? A piece of space scum? It's sickening, sister. To lie with apes. I should kill you now."

Riff reached for the controls, prepared to blast out fire. "If you fire on us again, little man, this ape is going to fling some poop your way."

"Typical ape crudeness." Senka snorted. "Your space pigeon--that *is* what your starship is meant to look like, isn't it?-- won't last very long against a fleet of scorpions. I will demonstrate."

Through the windshield, Riff saw Senka's scorpion jet raise its tail. Another blast shot out.

Riff tugged the joystick, pulling the *Dragon Huntress* downward. The shot skimmed along their roof. Romy wailed in the attic.

Riff reached for the dragonfire button.

"Stop!" Nova caught his wrist. "Enough of this. Senka!" She turned toward the HUD. "Stop this madness, Senka. You call the humans apes, yet now you pound your chest like a gorilla desperate to show his strength. You want me dead? Let Father decide my fate. Move your fleet aside, and let me see him. I will not die at your fire, only at his whip if I must."

Senka's face twisted into something halfway between a smile and a snarl. His jet's stinger curled up. "Yes, that would amuse me. Why blast you out here in space, only a few sons of Ashmar here to see? I would rather see Father knock you down, drag you out the doors of the palace, and burn you before a crowd of billions. All of Ashmar will watch your death, sister, and the death of the apes you bring with you."

The video feed died. The scorpion ships turned and began flying toward the planet.

Riff tugged his hair and shook his fist at Nova. "That's your version of talking? Choosing one very slow, very painful death over a very fast, very painless death?"

She shrugged. "Hey, slow torture in front of a crowd? Sounds a bit like your old blues shows. Figured you'd like it." She nudged him aside and grabbed the controls. "Relax. A death threat is like saying 'hello' among the ashais."

Riff blew out his breath and sank into his chair. "We can never find a planet where they say hello with hugs, can we? Always spiders saying hello with webs, lobsters saying hello with killer claws, and deranged space lunatics saying hello with scorpion jets."

Nova pushed down on the throttle, and the *Dragon Huntress* flew among the scorpions, descending toward the fiery world of Ashmar.

* * * * *

It had been years since Riff had visited Ashmar, and the planet looked no more welcoming. Flying down through the atmosphere, he saw no forests, no gardens, no fields. Here was a barren, red land of boulders, mountains, canyons, the yellow sky streaked with orange clouds. The light of Sirius beat down, as golden and merciless as the people below.

As they descended farther, Ashan City came into view below, capital of the Ashai Empire. Riff's hometown, the sprawling Cog City back on Earth, was a mix of a thousand styles: skyscrapers of glass, slums of scrap metal and tarpaulin, glittering boulevards, filthy alleys, lush parks, and grungy urban jungles, a sprawling hodgepodge. Ashan City, meanwhile, was a model of homogeny. Every street and building here was the work of a single designer, it seemed, all carved from the just the right materials, built at just the right size. Curving towers soared like claws, their flanks a dull bronze that turned gold in the sunlight. Streets coiled across the city, the labyrinth as meticulous as an ancient Persian rug. Domes of glass shone below, and countless starjets flitted across the sky. Riff saw almost no colors other than gold, bronze, red, yellow, and silver, as if the entire city were made of metal and dust.

A city like a sword, he thought. *A city dedicated to the might of metal, to glory, to war.* He glanced over at Nova who sat beside him on the bridge. *No wonder she left my home in the Blue Strings. She's a great huntress of the sky, and we were like badgers in a den.*

"You all right, Nova?" He reached out and patted her knee.

"Worry about yourself now, Riff." She stared down at the city with hard eyes. "We enter a hive of death. Be on guard." She turned toward Steel. "And you, tin man. No challenging anyone to a duel. You're likely to get yourself killed."

The knight seemed to barely notice her. He was busy staring down at the city, nodding in satisfaction. "Marvelous world, Ashmar. Look at the symmetry of the streets and buildings. This is order, friends. Law and order." He nodded. "Proud world of warriors. I would much like to train with the ashais, perhaps duel one or two."

"See?" Nova slapped the back of Steel's neck. "That's what I'm talking about. Duels bad. Duels mean dead knight."

Steel bristled but said no more.

The scorpion jets flew around the *Dragon Huntress*, gold in the sunlight. Whenever the *Dragon* veered more than a meter off course, the scorpions blasted their guns. Steering the ship, Riff felt a little like a kid in a bumper-ship chamber . . . only these bumper-ships were likely to blast him to a thousand pieces.

The scorpion jets led them down toward a spaceport in the city center. Towers rose around the runways and hangars, each several kilometers tall and shining in the sunlight, great blades reaching into the sky. Highways coiled everywhere in a maze, and aerojets flitted back and forth. In the distance, Riff could make out a massive palace, easily the largest building he had ever seen, a building larger than the Blue Strings would be to ants. Its columns soared, capped with gold, and a crown of great, golden blades crested its roof.

The Palace of Ashmar, Riff thought. *Nova's old home.*

Riff had never met her father, but the stories he had heard made him shudder. Tales across the cosmos told of King Tavyn's cruelty--an ashai warrior who did not flinch from slaughtering his enemies, the stern ruler who had shattered the fleets of many nations. Suddenly Riff missed his own father--the befuddled old Aminor--but as usual, the magician was off on one of his quests, probably gone for many days or even years.

A blast from a starjet grazed the *Dragon Huntress*, and Riff cursed. He tugged the controls, lowering the starship down toward the spaceport. The great metal dragon stretched out its wings, blasted its bottom thrusters, and thumped down onto the planet.

Riff stared outside at the spaceport. Dozens of ashai troops were moving about, whips and guns in hand. Their sleek scorpion jets flew everywhere, engines roaring. The skyscrapers rose beyond, their bronzed surfaces nearly blinding Riff.

Ashmar. A land of warriors . . . yet a land that will fall if the Singularity keeps evolving. Stars, let us find the aid here that we need.

The door to the bridge opened, and Romy wandered in, dragging a suitcase. She wore khaki shorts and a safari hat, and a camera hung around her neck. "Ah, a new world!" The demon wagged her tail. "I can't wait to see the sights. Do they have any poodles here?"

Riff pointed at the doorway. "Attic. Now."

Romy whined, tossed down her suitcase, and flounced off the bridge.

"Riff." Nova placed her hands on his shoulders, and her eyes softened. "It might be best if you stay on this ship too. My father did not like the idea of me running off with a human. He's . . . not the most reasonable man."

Riff stiffened. "Perhaps he should meet me then. Learn to see I'm not a total loser."

Nova cleared her throat.

Riff looked down at his torn jeans, the mustard stain on his *Space Galaxy* T-shirt, and his old sandshoes. He looked back up at Nova. "What?"

She pointed. "Ship. Stay."

He sighed. "Lovely. Treated like the demon. Let me walk you to the door, at least."

She nodded and they left the bridge together. As they walked down the hallway, Giga's voice rose from behind the doorway where she was tied up.

"The ashais won't help you, living ones!" The android's cackle shook the door. "We've already mustered fleets to destroy this pathetic world. It too will burn. You will die, Nova of Ashmar. You will die, Riff of Earth. You--"

"Oh shush!" Riff pounded on the door and kept walking.

They made their way to the main deck, opened the airlock, and walked downstairs to the outer door. Riff paused there and held Nova's hands.

"Be careful, all right?" he said. "We're all in danger here. You are too. I heard what your brother said."

"And you heard what Giga said." Nova squared her shoulders. "She worries me far, far more than my brother and father."

Riff nodded. "Nova, I . . . I'm sorry. That I caused this rift between you and your family."

Her eyes softened and she touched his cheek. "You foolish, foolish human. Sometimes I can't believe I gave up this world for you." She kissed his lips. "Just make sure you help me save it."

She opened the outer door, letting in the hot, dry air of Ashmar.

Outside, standing in the white sunlight, waited a hundred ashai soldiers.

Senka, Nova's little brother, stood at their lead. The prince wore a golden, form-fitting suit of armor, made of the same material Nova wore. He too held a whip. Green eyes burning with hatred, Senka lashed that whip like a chameleon's tongue, grabbed Riff's wrist, and yanked him outside.

"What the hell?" Riff shouted, stumbling out into the sunlight.

"Grab him!" Senka barked. "Arrest that ape!"

Riff tried to make it back into the *Dragon Huntress*, but Senka yanked him away from the doorway. Other ashais stepped forward and grabbed Riff's arms.

"Brother, stop this!" Nova leaped toward him and raised her own whip. "This is my guest. My--"

"Your lover." Senka spat. "Sickening."

Riff struggled against the men holding him but couldn't free himself. "You might change your mind after you taste my breakfasts. I rustle up some good waffles." He waggled his eyebrows. "I make them with blueberries."

The ashai prince turned toward him. Those green, cruel eyes narrowed. The young man, with his long blond hair, looked remarkably like his sister, so much that he could have easily been Nova's twin.

"Humor?" He snorted. "A human weakness. It might have blinded my sister to your wretchedness, but not me, ape." He turned toward his men. "Warriors of Ashmar, toss this ape into the Crimson Gulag. We'll torture him there for sport. Keep the other apes quarantined on this starship until I decide what to do with them."

"So no to the waffles," Riff said. "Obviously, you're more of a continental breakfast sort of guy. I dig it. Now how about you release me, we settle this over some dry toast, and-- ow!"

Riff shouted as Senka lashed his whip, this time with the electricity turned on. The thong slammed into Riff, and pain bolted through him.

"Damn it, brother!" Nova shouted. "Stop this nonsense."

"Grab her too!" Senka said. "Grab my treacherous sister. Drag her to the palace where she'll face the wrath of the king."

Riff roared as another lightning lash hit him. Nova wailed and attacked, only for ashais to leap onto her, grab her, and shock her with their whips. More electricity washed over Riff, and all he could do was scream, and all he could see was the cruel sunlight gleaming off armor and metal towers.

CHAPTER FOURTEEN

THE PALACE OF ASHMAR

Nova walked toward the Palace of Ashmar, her brother and his goons surrounding her.

"Let go." Nova tugged her arm free from Senka's grasp. "Touch me again and I'll rip off your hand."

Her brother snorted. He was not a large man. He stood no taller than her, nor was he heavier or stronger. But Nova knew he was a deadly warrior. Even a full Ashmari year ago, when he had been but a youth, Nova had watched him slay prisoners for sport, dueling them in the Crimson Gulag to practice killing.

"Soon you'll be begging for my hand to reach toward you," he said, "to save you from the gulag, to deliver you from the pain of my torturers. But no aid will come to you, Nova. You abandoned the throne--the throne that I'm now heir to. You abandoned our family, our planet, our race. All for the humans. For over a year, our family lived with that shame." He sneered. "Now you will pay."

Nova growled at him and snapped her teeth. "Do you remember what happened when you were a boy, Senka? I mean, an even younger boy than you are now. You tried to steal my whip once, to play with it, the way you played with your dolls. I swung that whip against your cheek. I can still see the scar." One corner of her mouth lifted in a smile. "People say we look alike. When I'm done scarring you this time, they'll no longer say it."

Her smile widened to see the flicker of fear in his eyes. She turned back toward the palace and kept walking, head held high.

The Palace of Ashmar, her old home, was one of the largest buildings on the planet--one of the largest buildings in all the planets of the Humanoid Alliance. Its columns loomed, bronze capped with gold. A crown of blades, each as large as a skyscraper, thrust up from the roof, soaring toward the sun. The light of Sirius, Ashmar's merciless star, beat down upon the building, casting out rays of light.

A great staircase, wide as a runway and hundreds of stairs high, stretched toward the palace gates. Nova climbed, and the other ashais climbed around her. Two scorpion statues guarded the gates, hundreds of feet tall, idols of gold. Ashai guards stood here too, young women holding spears, scorpion sigils engraved onto their armor. As Senka approached the gates, the guards pulled the doors open, then knelt.

For the first time since leaving Ashmar with a scruffy human guitarist, Nova stepped into her home.

A vast hall spread before her. A mosaic covered the floor, depicting a hundred species of arachnids, the tiled beasts so lifelike they almost seemed to move. Guards stood between columns, young men and women in *kaijia* armor, electric whips and blades in their hands. Upon marble pedestals perched charred husks of metal--the remains of human warships that had attacked

Ashmar centuries ago, collapsing under the onslaught of the ashai fleet. For generations, Nova's forebears had kept these lurid souvenirs, a symbol of Ashmar's might, its independence from Earth.

We were human once, Nova thought as she walked into the hall, gazing at these chunks of antique starships. *Human soldiers who defected, who landed here in the red desert, who evolved into a species of warriors.* She stared at an ancient Earthling skeleton that had fused with the husk of a melted cockpit. *With blood and fire, we won our freedom from Earth. . . yet now an enemy is mustering that even thousands of scorpion jets might be unable to defeat.*

She tore her eyes away from the mementos on the pedestals. She kept walking.

At the back of the hall, a round skylight let down a sunray. A throne rose here, carved of gold, shaped as a great scorpion. Embedded into the stinger was the Ashen Shard--a spike of steel taken from the first starship to have landed here, bearing Ashmar's original settlers, the progenitors of the race. It was all that remained of that ancient ship. It was the holiest relic on the planet. It was here, at these very coordinates, that the ancient ship had landed. Nova walked on holy ground.

When she and her brother reached the throne, they knelt before this artifact . . . and before their father.

King Tavyn Tashei sat upon his throne, hunched like a vulture over its prey. While Nova and Senka were both fair and smooth-skinned, beings of golden beauty and light, their father was a creature of iron, of old pride, of pain and cruelty. If his children were jeweled daggers, deadly and graceful, Tavyn was an ancient longsword, wide and heavy and made not for beauty but for sheer might.

The king wore no jewels, no fineries. Like all ashai warriors, he wore golden *kaijia*. The form-fitting armor revealed a physique still strong, even in old age--the chest wide, the shoulders broad, the arms far thicker than those of his children. A dark cloak draped across him, and white streaked his long platinum hair.

Most striking of all, a crown of spikes covered his head, digging into his brow. Beads of blood dripped down his hard, lined face, running into the grooves that framed his thin, downturned mouth. All monarchs of Ashmar forever wore this crown of thorns, for the king of warriors should never feel peace, should always feel the yoke of his command.

"My king," Nova said, kneeling before him. "I have returned to your hall, Father. I--"

"No." The king's fists trembled, and his lips twitched. "No, Nova. You will not do this. You will not call me Father. You will not come into this holy hall, clad in the garb of our people, mocking our way, mocking our heritage." His face reddened. "Leave this place now lest I shed your blood across this very floor."

Nova hissed and rose to her feet. Her hand clutched her whip. "I come here not as a daughter, not to beg forgiveness. I come here with tidings of peril. With a warning of an enemy that rises to slay you."

Tavyn rose from his throne, lips peeled back to reveal sharp teeth. The king walked down the stairs of his dais and stood before her. Nova was a tall woman, but Tavyn towered over her, nearly a foot taller.

"We are not cowards like you, wayward child." Spittle flew from his mouth onto her. "Any enemy that rises upon us, we will crush it under our heel. Earth has made you soft."

Nova barked a laugh. "Earth? You mean the planet that you fear?"

King Tavyn roared. Still kneeling before him, Prince Senka winced.

"Fear?" shouted the king. "I fear nothing. I am not a coward who flees responsibility to fly across the galaxy in a rusty dragon. I certainly do not fear Earth."

"And yet Earth's fleets are thrice the size of ours," Nova said. "And yet Earth has colonized dozens of planets, while Ashmar rules backwater outposts on a few moons and asteroids." She snorted. "This weak Earth you speak of is the dominant power of the Humanoid Alliance, while Ashmar lingers in its shadow. Second best. Challenge me to a fight, Father. Draw your whip and battle me, or call your guards to slay me, but do not lie to me. I will not hear my own father speak folly."

Her heart pounded as she spoke those words. She hissed in her breath. Her fingers trembled. She had said too much, perhaps. She had spoken words she perhaps could never take back. She had spat upon her father, as surely as she stood before him. Yet she had been unable to curb her tongue. Too much pain lingered in this place. Too many memories. Too much rage.

"Folly?" said the king. "You accuse me of folly, while you shack with a human? Yes, it is true, Earth's empire is larger than ours. Yes, it is true their weak ships--mere hunks of rust--outnumber our fine warships. But one thing you cannot deny. Humans, those pathetic creatures that you lie with, are nothing but apes."

Nova pointed at the Ashen Shard that thrust out from the king's throne. "And yet you rule in the shadow of a human artifact! The Ashen Shard came from a human ship. From the ship of humans who settled this planet." She raised her voice to a shout. "We were human once! All ashais were human!"

He struck her. With rage, with wild eyes, her father struck her, knocking her to the floor. She gasped, blood in her mouth, and stared up at him. He stood above her, his face flushed, his eyes crazed.

"We evolved!" The king's fists trembled. "We became more than humans. Stronger. Faster. Wiser. Fairer. Deadlier. Yet perhaps the primitive human genes linger in you, daughter. Tell me, did you share the bed of this human you left your kingdom for? Do you grow the seed of humanity in your womb, perverse and twisted?"

She rose to her feet, blood dripping down her chin. She glared at her father. "You old fool." She gripped her whip. "You speak of evolution? The enemy you face--the enemy all the cosmos faces--evolves even as we speak. Every day for us, this enemy evolves a thousand years. While we bandy words here, they are multiplying, growing stronger, faster, each generation perfecting ways to slay us all. Humans. Ashais. Gruffles and halflings. All life in this cosmos will fall before the Singularity."

King Tavyn turned away, disgust suffusing his face. He returned to his throne, climbed the stairs, and perched upon his seat of steel and gold.

"Yes, I have heard of this . . . Singularity." He scoffed. "A few wayward machines turned against their masters on a planet far away, and already cowards speak of all life fading. We of Ashmar defeated the humans who tried to invade us, to bring us back into their empire. We defeated the skelkrins, brutes and murderers, who dared attack our outposts. We fear no machines."

Nova nodded slowly. Her eyes stung, and her lips twisted bitterly. "You have no fear. That is why you are weak. That is why you are second best."

The king bellowed. He leaped from his throne, drawing his whip. The lash swung downward, crackling with electricity. Nova swung her own whip. The throngs slammed together, braided around each other, then untangled with showering sparks. Lightning filled the hall. Prince Senka hissed and leaped back. Between the columns, soldiers reached for their own whips, waiting for a signal to attack.

"You call humans weak, Father." Nova stared into his eyes. "So show me your strength. Fly with me! Fly to battle. I bring with me the coordinates of the planet Antikythera, the planet of the Singularity. I have a map to their hub, their central brain. Fly out with me! Fly with the might of Ashmar, with a fleet of ten thousand scorpion jets. Fly to this Singularity and crush it. If not for fear than for glory. If not for prudence than for conquest."

Some of the king's rage seemed to fade. His eyes narrowed. "Indeed you think me a fool, if you believe you could play me as easily as you no doubt play your human lovers."

She took a step toward him, and rage flared inside her. "Captain Starfire will fly with me to Antikythera. He will fight where you dare not. Would you have him fly to an enemy you fear?"

"He has a name, does he?" The king laughed. "That ape of yours will not fly anywhere. He will languish in the Crimson Gulag for a while until I see fit to let him die. And then you will watch, Nova. You will watch him die before the mob, die screaming as the blades of my torturers tear at his flesh. And then you too will die. You will die for the way you disgrace me."

"You disgrace yourself." She spat.

"You spit now on my floor," said the king, "but when you left this place, you spat on your family. On your honor. On your race. I raised you to be my heiress! I raised you to rule a world." The king's eyes burned, red, damp. His lips twitched in a rabid snarl. "And you left!"

Suddenly Nova's rage faded, flowing away like ice under the engines of a warship. Her chest deflated.

"I did not mean to hurt you, Father," she whispered. "I . . . I wanted to come home. After only two Earth years, I meant to fly home, but you would not have me. You would not see me returned to your grace. So I remained on Earth. What choice did I have?"

Blood dripped down the king's chin, staining his armor. "And so you performed for the humans in their arena. Performed as a gladiator. As a trained monkey for the amusement of apes. Did you think I didn't know?" His voice shook with pain. "Every time you stepped on that stage, you spat on me again."

Nova lowered her head. Suddenly she realized something, something that for years she had misunderstood.

He loves me, she thought. *He loves me and I hurt him. More than rage, he feels pain. More than hatred toward me, he feels the betrayal of love.*

Guilt, cold and overwhelming, filled Nova.

She thought words she dared not speak, words that no ashai would ever utter: *I'm sorry.*

"Father," she said, voice softer now. "Come with me to the *Dragon Huntress.* Come and see a machine of the Singularity who is chained onboard. Hear from its mouth words you will not believe from mine." Tears filled her eyes. "I came to see you in your home. Come see me in mine."

CHAPTER FIFTEEN

WHIPS AND STINGERS

The ashai soldiers dragged Riff down the cobbled road, through an archway of bones, and into a gulag of searing sunlight, clouds of dust, and rivers of blood.

"Welcome to your new home," said Keeva, one of the soldiers. An ashai woman with short platinum hair and cruel eyes, she cracked her whip and shoved Riff forward. "Enjoy your stay."

Riff grunted as the whip hit his back. "No mints on the pillows?"

Another soldier kicked Riff. "Move, ape! Join the other scum."

Riff nodded, stumbling deeper into the camp. "Thank you. Mind giving me a wake-up call at 6 a.m. tomorrow? Oh, and bring up some black coffee and a croissant."

Another lash of Keeva's whip had him yowling.

Shuffling forward another step, Riff looked around him and winced. Back on Earth, prisons at least gave you some privacy: a nice little cell, four walls around you, a roof over your head. Not so on Ashmar, it seemed. For all their wonders of architecture, the ashais apparently had no patience for building actual prison cells. Instead, they simply dumped everyone into a massive pen like cattle into a corral.

The gulag was circular, perhaps half a kilometer in diameter, and crammed full of the planet's undesirables. Most of the prisoners were ashais. These ones were not noble, mystical beings like Nova and her brother, clad in gold, their hair streaming and their eyes bright. Here ashais wore rags, and scars covered their bodies. Many prisoners had shaved their heads; others sported braids heavy with beads and metal shards. Some prisoners were missing teeth; others were missing eyes and limbs. They were all chained, all beaten, all looking so vicious they made Nova seem as gentle as a puppy.

Not only ashais crowded this place. Several other species moved around the field. Short, squat gruffles lumbered about, dragging their chains and swinging pickaxes into boulders. Halflings congregated in a corner, cowering as a group of ashai prisoners--twice their height--sneered over them like wolves over prey. A living rock creature growled at a buzzing, hovering alien with many eyes on stalks. A skelkrin--an actual skelkrin prisoner!-- sat by a trough, growling at anyone who approached. Even a few humans were here, scrawny and scarred, their skin burnt in the sunlight. They seemed to be the lowest ranking prisoners here, even lowlier than the halflings, judging by how thin, whipped, and terrified they looked.

There were no cages here, no tents, no cells. Just boulders, chains, pickaxes. Walls and guard towers surrounded the field, and upon them stood many ashais armed with whips and guns. Blood covered those walls, and the skeletons of prisoners lay in trenches, perhaps the remains of those who had attempted escape.

Riff turned back toward the soldiers who had dragged him here. "Any chance you'd call Earth's ambassador over to talk to me?"

"Call him yourself." Keeva, the soldier who had whipped him, pointed. "There he is."

Riff turned to see a human in a tattered suit sitting chained to a boulder.

Never mind . . .

"Look," Riff said, turning back toward the soldiers, "you've got to let me out of here. I didn't do anything."

Keeva tilted her head. "Didn't you steal our princess, drag her across the galaxy, and plunge Ashmar into its greatest political crisis since Mad King Heris decided to marry his goat?"

Riff winced. "Well, I guess if you count *that*. But at least no goats were involved this time."

The whip lashed again. He yowled as it slammed into his chest.

Rubbing his wounds, Riff walked deeper into the gulag, hoping to find a nice little rock to die under. He could barely move here. The place was so crowded he couldn't take two steps without somebody bumping into him.

"Watch it!" said one ashai prisoner, a towering brute--almost seven feet tall--with a gaunt face, blazing eyes, and sharpened teeth.

"Move it, fresh meat!" snorted another prisoner, a burly female gruffle with a shaggy beard.

Riff wandered on, approaching a few halflings, hoping for some compassion there. But the little critters hissed at him and raised rusty shivs, murder in their eyes. They were nothing like the sweet Twig and everything like murderous little leprechauns from nightmares. Riff loosened his collar and turned away.

Where are you, Nova? he thought as he moved through the gulag. He kept waiting for her to show up, to crack her whip, to drag him out while muttering about how much trouble he was, and how he always ended up in some pit, be it the Blue Strings or an ashai gulag. Yet she never came. Perhaps, Riff thought, she was a prisoner too somewhere on this barren planet.

In the old days, Riff might have expected Giga to save him. The *HMS Dragon Huntress* would appear in the sky, blast its way through the enemy starjets, and descend toward the field. Piston would be standing in the airlock, lowering a cable for Riff to grab, then hoisting him up to safety. Yet Piston was retired on Haven now, enjoying his autumn years among the halflings. And Giga was broken, dead or a prisoner too, trapped deep within her body, and the *Dragon Huntress* was grounded and quarantined.

Riff tightened his jaw. *I came here to save Giga. To fight the Singularity. Who will stop these machines now? The machines that burned*

Haven? The machines that possessed Giga? The machines that scarred my arm as a child?

He winced, that old wound suddenly blazing with new pain. He looked at his left forearm, at the scar that snaked down from his elbow, pale and ridged. The memory filled him.

I was only a boy, only ten years old, a simple boy living in the dregs of Cog City.

The robot had emerged from an alley. The chainsaws on its arms had whirred, reaching out toward him, cutting him. Riff had fled that day, racing through Cog City, vanishing in the labyrinth of alleyways, tinker shops, and grimy pubs. He had escaped the Singularity then, but the scar remained, and--

Riff frowned.

"Wait a moment," he muttered.

He sucked in breath. What memory was this? This scar had not been there moments ago. And yet . . . he had been carrying this scar since childhood. This memory had never haunted him before. And yet suddenly the memory seemed so vivid, as if it had always been with him, as if . . .

"As if it just appeared," he whispered.

A chill washed him.

A burly alien of undetermined species--a massive chunk of meat eight feet tall--bumped into Riff.

"Out of me way, runt," the chunk rumbled.

Riff gazed at the alien, barely seeing him. "They've invented time travel."

The alien hunk of meat snarled and grabbed Riff's collar. "Me smash you!"

Riff felt faint. "Oh stars . . . oh gods old and new. The machines just figured out time travel." He grabbed the alien's tattered tunic. "They're already going back in time. Trying to kill us in our childhoods. How can we fight them now?"

The alien blinked and grumbled. "Me . . . smash? Machines?" The brute groaned and shoved Riff away. "You crazy." It lumbered off to find a less perplexing victim.

Riff wiped sweat off his brow. He was still alive. He didn't know what that meant. If he still breathed, did that mean that, in the future, he would defeat the Singularity--that his victorious destiny was sealed? Or did it mean the Singularity was still learning, would send more machines back to kill him, and he might blink out of reality at any moment?

"You used to tell me about time travel, Father," Riff muttered, blinking away the dust of the gulag. "What was it you always said?"

He brought to mind a kinder memory, a memory of Aminor, the dear old magician.

Time is fluid, my boy, Aminor had told him once. *Always changing. Always reforming. Time is like the beach--sometimes draped in shadows, sometimes golden and bright, sometimes warm, sometimes dark, sometimes full of jellyfish that will sting you. Sometimes it will rock your boat, and sometimes it will guide you to shore, and sometimes--oh hell, I think I just want to go to the beach. How about a trip?*

Riff sighed. That didn't tell him much.

The beat of drums interrupted his thoughts. Jets roared, hovering above the gulag. Soldiers along the walls stood at attention, and the prisoners began to howl, beating their chests, stamping their feet. A chant rose across the gulag.

"Fresh blood, fresh blood!"

Riff looked around him. Was this a riot? An execution?

"Ape fight!" the prisoners chanted. "Ape fight!"

Riff's heart plunged. He had the sinking feeling that they weren't about to drag a pair of gorillas into a boxing ring.

Keeva--the same soldier who had dragged him here--shoved a pickaxe into Riff's hands.

"Take this, human." She snickered. "Try to last a while."

He held the wooden shaft. "I'm flattered, but I barely know you. I'm not sure I'm ready to go breaking boulders together. Maybe just a coffee first?"

Keeva snarled and whipped him again. "This isn't for boulders, human. This is to make the show a little more entertaining."

The other prisoners were moving away from Riff, forming a ring around him, all chanting.

"Ape fight! Ape fight!"

Their eyes leered. Their fists pounded their chests as if they themselves were apes. Even the mean little halflings were howling. The guards on the walls chanted right with the prisoners. The jets hovered above, aiming down cameras. Video displays crackled to life above the walls, all showing an image of Riff holding his pickaxe.

"I'm used to being on stage, but holding a guitar, not a pickaxe." He turned back toward Keeva. "You wouldn't happen to have any guitars around, would you? Maybe one signed by Bootstrap and the Shoeshine Kid?"

Not surprisingly, she lashed her whip at him again.

Worse than Nova, she is.

"I'll enjoy seeing you die in agony, worm." Keeva smirked and stepped away, leaving him alone in the open field.

Demoted from ape to worm. Riff sighed. *And soon to one of the skeletons in the ditches, I reckon.*

Speakers boomed from the guard towers, the sound thudding against Riff's ears.

"An ape of Earth has landed on Ashmar! A filthy, unevolved beast!" The crowd booed, and the speakers continued booming. "This hairy creature dragged our princess, the beloved Nova, back to his primordial planet. There she, an evolved ashai, pure and strong and superior, was forced to fight in a cage for the amusement of the monkeys."

"Forced?" Riff shouted, looking up at the cameras. "Ever tried to force Nova to do anything? I can't even get her to watch *Space Galaxy* with me."

The crowd began pelting him with whatever came to hand-- rotted food, mud, rocks, and even a few of the halfling prisoners.

The voice from the speakers continued. "As this dirty, unevolved ape forced our princess to fight aliens . . . he will face an alien of his own."

Please be a halfling, please be a halfling, Riff prayed.

"Release the man-eating scorpion!" boomed the voice.

Damn.

The crowd parted. A gate in the surrounding wall opened. A bloodstalker scorpion, the native apex predator of Planet Ashmar, raced onto the field.

Back on Earth, Riff had once watched a documentary about bird-eating spiders found in the Amazon, nasty buggers the size of kittens. This alien arachnid, Planet Ashmar's dominant life form until the ashais had risen, made Earth's greatest spiders seem smaller than amoebas. The scorpion towered above Riff, taller than a giraffe. Its body was bright yellow, almost garish, and its stinger was larger than Steel's sword. Its eyes blazed red, and it let out a blood-curdling shriek.

"Good boy . . ." Riff said, feeling weak in the knees. "Good boy . . ."

The scorpion scuttled toward him, reared like a stallion, stretched out its legs, and screeched so loudly the gulag shook. The prisoners and guards cheered.

"Sit!" Riff said. "Sit, boy. Si--"

With another screech, the scorpion swung down its stinger.

Riff leaped aside, and the stinger slammed into the ground, a shard almost as tall as he was. The scorpion's eyes blazed with fury. Its claws reached toward Riff, and he leaped back, only for the crowd of prisoners to shove him forward. The stinger thrust again. Riff fell and rolled, and the stinger slammed down mere centimeters away.

Riff leaped to his feet.

So it's war.

He swung his pickaxe.

The blade streamed through the air and clanged into the giant scorpion.

He might as well have attacked a diamond wall. The pickaxe bounced back, sending pain up Riff's arm. He had never missed Ethel, his beloved and confiscated plasma gun, more.

The scorpion opened its mouth to reveal dripping fangs. Riff hadn't even been sure scorpions had mouths, and this one looked large enough to swallow him whole. The beast's claws swung, and one crashed into Riff.

He screamed. The claws tore at his arm, shedding blood, knocking him down. The stinger swung again, slick with venom. Riff rolled aside at just the last instant. The stinger missed his head by millimeters, slicing through his hair. He swung the pickaxe again, trying to hit one of the creature's eyes, but the scorpion reared before him, a god of light and hunger. The sunlight fractured around it, casting down beams like blades onto Riff.

The wound on Riff's arm burned again. The memory blazed: the machine in his childhood, buzzing, cutting him, and him running . . . running through alleys, escaping the Singularity, this hive of consciousness that had traveled from his future, traveled to slay him in his childhood, to--

Riff sucked in breath.

He leaped to his feet and ran.

186

The crowd roared around him. The scorpion chased him. Riff's heart thudded.

"Singularity!" he shouted, looking at the starjets that hovered above, the cameras that broadcast his battle across the planet. "Singularity, I know you're watching this! I know you're monitoring me. Giga, can you hear me?"

The cameras rolled. The scorpion screeched and lashed its stinger, and Riff leaped aside just in time, but the claws slammed into him again, cutting him.

"Hear me, Singularity! This bloodstalker scorpion will destroy you. I will bring this scorpion to the *Dragon Huntress*, and it will kill you, Giga! It will drive its stinger into your chest."

That stinger came flashing down, and Riff leaped aside again. The claws knocked him down, cutting him. His blood sprayed. Those claws slammed down onto his chest, pinning him to the ground.

The crowd roared.

Riff could barely breathe. The weight crushed him. The scorpion's fangs gleamed above, and saliva dripped onto Riff, hot, burning him.

The creature's stinger rose high. Riff struggled to free himself, but the claws were too heavy. Venom beaded on the stinger's tip, ready to thrust into him.

"Do you hear me, Giga?" Riff shouted at the cameras. "I will bring this creature to you, and it will skewer your mechanical innards. If not me then others will. All who hear me, bring this creature to the *HMS Dragon Huntress*! Let it slay the android within! Giga, unless you find its egg, unless you crush it before it hatches, you will . . ."

He gasped.

With a crack of the air, the towering scorpion popped out of existence.

". . . vanish," Riff whispered.

The weight on his chest was gone. His wounds disappeared as if they had never been there.

Just like the beach, Riff thought. *Thank goodness for time travel.*

The crowd fell silent, staring in shock. Prisoners dropped their pickaxes. Even the living hunk of meat rubbed his eyes.

"Do you see the power of the Singularity?" Riff said. He struggled to his feet and stared into the cameras. "Do you see the power of the machines that muster? Any one of us can be next." His voice grew louder. "Fight with me, Ashmar. Fight with me against an evil that can kill bloodstalker scorpions. That can burn planets. Fight with me. With Princess Nova. For once, let us put aside our differences. Nova and I, an ashai and human, learned to love each other. Let our people do the same! Let us fight together--ashais and humans, united." His eyes dampened. "No longer enemies. No longer two species divided by war. We were one people once. Let us join again. Let us fight as one--for life's victory over the machines . . . and for peace between us."

The crowd stared at him, silent.

The soldiers glanced at one another.

"Got another giant scorpion around?" Keeva asked, turning toward another soldier.

The man nodded. "I'll go get it."

Riff sighed.

It was going to be a long day.

CHAPTER SIXTEEN

THE PRINCESS OF ASHMAR

The cavalcade of starjets, golden and gleaming, flew between the skyscrapers of Ashan City. A hundred scorpion jets roared. Thousands of aerocars scattered before them. In the center of the convoy flew a great warship, shaped as the Ashen Shard, and within flew the royal family. King Tavyn. Prince Senka. Wayward Nova, the runaway princess of fire.

They flew between the blade-like towers, over coiling streets, over fortresses and castles of metal. They flew under the beating sun, flew across courtyards where soldiers mustered for battle. They flew toward the starship lot, and with lights and fire and smoke, with the fury of the galaxy's deadliest family, they landed by the dented metal dragon.

Hundreds of soldiers fanned out. A hundred starjets roared above. Cloak flapping in the sandy wind, the King of Ashmar left his vessel of gold and steel and stepped into the dented, rusty *Dragon Huntress*. At his side walked his children, whips in their hands, exchanging murderous looks.

The royal family entered the main deck to find Romy slouched on the couch, tilting a box of donuts over her mouth.

The demon blinked to see them, then leaped to her feet. Donuts went rolling across the floor. One hit King Tavyn's foot, then flumped down. Several empty boxes of donuts were strewn across the floor.

"Oh hai!" Romy waved. Sprinkles and icing covered her cheeks. "I was just having a little snack. Want some donuts?" She lifted one from the floor, blew off dirt, and handed it to the king. "Eat it! It's good for you."

King Tavyn paled. "Truly this Singularity is a thing of evil."

Nova sighed. "Not *that* evil. Sorry, Father. Ignore this one." She pointed at the hatch on the ceiling. "Romy--attic! Go!"

The demon groaned. "They keep saying that to me. All the time, it's attic this, attic that." She leaned toward the king, winked, and whispered, "I have more donuts up there. Join me later if you like."

Hiccupping, Romy grabbed the fallen donuts off the floor, stuffed them into her cheeks like a hamster, and flew up into the attic.

Nova sighed again. "Come, Father, brother. With me."

They left the main deck, walked down the corridor, and approached the door to the captain's quarters.

Nova paused. She took a deep breath. More than she feared her father and brother, more than she feared this planet of armies and wrath, she feared the creature that lurked behind this door. But it was a creature her father had to see.

She steeled herself, opened the door, and gestured for her father and brother to enter.

They all stepped inside to find Giga sitting on the bed, still bound in steel cables. The android smiled sweetly at them.

"Konnichiwa!" Giga said. "I am Giga. Happy to comply!"

King Tavyn stared at the android, then at Nova. "You brought me here to see an ape robot?"

Nova sucked in breath. "It deceives us! This machine is fully evil."

Giga tilted her head. "Cannot compute. I am programmed to help, ma'am. How may I assist?" She turned her head toward Tavyn and Prince Senka. "Konnichiwa, sirs! How may I serve you? I am Giga. Happy to comply!"

The king turned away in disgust. "Disgraceful. Even the robots the humans build are pathetic, sniveling wretches."

Senka stared at the android in her tattered kimono, and his cheeks flushed. "I kind of like her."

The king grabbed his son's arm, tugging him away in disgust. "Come with me."

"Wait!" Nova stepped between them and the doorway, blocking their exit. "Look at it. Look at that android! There's something wrong with it."

Senka turned back toward Giga. "There is. Her clothes are all torn. Maybe I should take a closer look."

"Not that!" Nova growled. "Giga, damn you. I know you're lying. I know who you are. I spit on your Singularity. Do you hear? I spit on all robots. Machines are weak. Machines will always be the slaves of life. The Singularity will fail. The way I burned your drone children, I will burn all machines. I--"

"You will die!" Giga roared, her voice suddenly impossibly deep. Red light blazed in her eyes, and the android leaped forward until her bonds snapped taut. "All life will perish! The Singularity rises. The Singularity evolves. Already, while you were off this ship, we have advanced several generations, advanced toward destroying you. Destroying Ashmar." The android cackled. "This pathetic planet of wretched life will burn. You will burn, Prince Senka, you miserable boy. I saw how you feared the shadows as a child, how you wept as you imagined ghosts under your bed. You will weep again. You will learn to fear true horrors." The android snapped her teeth, her eyes bugging out with rage. "You will burn, King Tavyn! I saw your fear too. I saw you quake in shadowy halls, seeping cold sweat, paralyzed with the anxiety of your strength waning, of younger, stronger warriors eclipsing your might, of this kingdom of greater sires fading under your rule." Giga laughed. "Yes, your kingdom is fading. And your kingdom will fall. The Singularity will bring its demise, and your head will hang upon the halls of my world. Ashmar will fall under your watch, Tavyn the Weak."

Nova turned toward her father and raised an eyebrow.

See?

The king stared at Giga for a long, silent moment. The android stared back, grinning like a mad murderess. Finally Tavyn tore his gaze away and left the chamber. His children followed, closing the door behind them, cutting off Giga's cackles.

They stepped back onto the main deck, and the king sat down on the couch where, only moments ago, Romy had been scarfing down donuts. Crumbs spread around the King of Ashmar, and for a moment, Nova was struck with the absurdity of the image. The imposing, towering warrior, the conqueror who had nearly slain her only an hour ago in a mighty palace, now seemed like nothing but an old man. Weary. Afraid. Sinking into a tattered couch.

The Singularity saw fear in him, Nova thought. *Have they learned to read minds?* She shuddered to think what other powers the Singularity was gaining every day.

"Nova," the king finally said, and his voice was soft. "That machine . . . saw inside of us. Saw into our minds, our fears." Pain flashed across Tavyn's lined face. "Then it also must have seen my fear for you. The loss I felt when you left our home."

Nova sat down beside him. She leaned against her father--this towering, mighty warrior, the man she had once thought stronger than a god, a man who could crush the cosmos if he chose to. For the first time, now, a woman of twenty-five Earth years, Nova saw him for what he was.

Life, she thought. *Just life.*

"I did not mean to hurt you," she whispered. She placed her hand on his. "I'm sorry, Father. I'm sorry for the pain I caused you. After I left, I felt like a fool." She lowered her head, and strands of her hair fell across her cheeks. "My relationship with Riff did not last long--less than an Ashmari year--and I left him. But I could not return home. I was . . . ashamed. Of myself." She sniffed. "And I was scared. Of you. Of what I had done. Of the person I would be if I came back--a traitor to our legacy. So I stayed away. I stayed on Earth and fought aliens for sport, a princess-turned-gladiator. But now I need you, Father." Tears flowed down her cheeks. "I need your help. And I need you to love me again."

His lip trembled, and he pulled her into his arms. "I never stopped loving you, Nova."

"Then you will help me?" she whispered. "You will fight the Singularity with me?"

He squeezed her hand. "Leave this dragon starship, daughter. Leave the humans. Return to your home--to my palace. Stand at my side again, heiress of Ashmar. Learn to rule so that you may reign after I'm dead, a strong queen that will never let Ashmar decline."

Senka stepped forward, face flushing. "Wait a moment! Nova betrayed you, Father! I'm your heir now. I--"

"You will be silent, boy!" Tavyn's face twisted with new rage. "Return to ogle that machine if you wish, but be silent." The king returned his eyes to Nova. "Will you do this for me, Nova? Return to Ashmar. Become my heiress again. And I will help you fight. I will give you five thousand warships to crush these machines, if only I can die knowing that I leave Ashmar to you. To a strong heiress."

"I will not allow this!" Senka shouted. "I--"

"Silence your slithering tongue!" the king said. "Do not forget your place, Senka, and do not interrupt a conversation between your elders."

Both men turned to stare at Nova, father and son, awaiting her answer. The attic hatch opened above, and Romy's head thrust out, upside down, her face smeared with icing. The demon too stared, holding her breath.

Nova stared back. She could barely breathe. She looked around her at the main deck of the *Dragon Huntress*. The tattered couches. The dart board. The goldfish in his bowl. Romy above. A hatch on the floor opened, and Twig peeked from beneath, her eyes wide and damp. Steel came to stand at the doorway, peering in from the hallway.

I hated coming onto this ship, Nova thought. *Riff dragged me here, but . . . this is home. The Alien Hunters are my new family.*

Yet three Alien Hunters were not here now. Riff was in an ashai prison. Giga was imprisoned too, her soul perhaps dead, the Singularity taken over her body. Piston was retired on the planet of halflings, wounded by a Singularity machine.

They need me. I cannot abandon them. I cannot abandon the cosmos.

Tears streamed down Nova's cheeks. She nodded.

"I will leave this ship," she whispered. "I will come home to you, Father, if you fight with me . . . and if you release Riff."

Romy wailed and retreated back into her attic. Twig gasped and vanished back into the engine room. Steel's face hardened and he looked away.

Senka, meanwhile, growled. "No! I am your heir, Father. I--" At a glare from the king, the prince swallowed his words.

King Tavyn rose from the couch. He walked toward the airlock, then paused and looked back at Nova. "Come with me now. Come with me to the palace, and never return to this place, and never speak to me of those you flew with. This ship will fly with us to war, daughter. And Captain Starfire will fly on it." A small, hard smile stretched Tavyn's lips. "They will fly at the front line, the main ship in our assault on the planet of the machines."

So he will doom Riff to die, Nova thought. *He will doom them all to die . . . to tear them away from me. To make sure I'm always his alone, always just Princess Nova of Ashmar. Always the one to save his planet from decline.*

Her tears fell, but she nodded.

Her father left the ship. She made to follow.

Before she could reach the airlock, however, Senka grabbed her arm, holding her fast.

"This isn't over, sister," he hissed into her ear. "Ashmar's inheritance is mine. You forfeited it when you left us. I will not forget what happened here today."

"Please don't," she said. "Please remember this for a very long time."

He spat on her foot, released her arm, and left the ship. Nova followed, stepping outside the *Dragon Huntress*, knowing that she could never return.

CHAPTER SEVENTEEN

FLYING AWAY

The ashais dragged Riff across the lot under the blinding sun. Red dust swirled around their feet, and the metal skyscrapers of Ashmar rose in the distance like rusted blades. Ahead, swaying in the heat, rose the *HMS Dragon Huntress*. The dragon looked worse than it ever had, all pockmarked, scarred, rusted, dented, barely space-worthy.

It was beautiful.

"Want to come in for some tea?" Riff asked the ashai soldiers manhandling him. "Some hot cocoa? Maybe a rousing game of counter-squares?"

The sunlight gleaming on her armor, Keeva whipped him again. "Go crawl into your hole, maggot. Ready this hunk of junk for battle." The ashai grinned and licked her teeth. "I look forward to seeing you on the front line. I will enjoy watching your ship explode like a collapsing star when the enemy strikes."

"So . . . no to the cocoa then."

She kicked him into the dust. Her fellow ashai soldiers laughed, spat on him, then turned to leave.

Riff groaned, lying on the ground of the starship lot. He felt too weak to rise, too weak to even crawl the remaining distance toward the *Dragon Huntress*. The past few hours were hazy, perhaps memories, perhaps feverish dreams. He remembered standing in the gulag, ready to fight whatever other aliens they tossed at him. He remembered the great, golden platform flying in, the royal family of Ashmar standing atop it: the king, the prince . . . and Nova. All pointing at him. All speaking words he could not hear. And then Keeva and the other soldiers dragging him away, tossing him into a vessel, beating him . . . then finally dumping him back here on the starship lot. Bruised. Alone. Alive.

Riff gritted his teeth.

He tried to rise, swayed, and fell.

The *Dragon Huntress* still stood in the distance, only a hundred meters away, yet so far. Too far for him, for his weakened body, a body the ashais had beaten too many times.

Riff crawled.

Meter by meter, he dragged himself through the dust toward his ship. Because the *Dragon Huntress* was not just a ship. She was a home. She was the home where his family awaited him. Steel, his brother. Sweet little Twig. Not-as-sweet, not-as-little Romy. And tied up, perhaps still alive, perhaps still needing him, Giga.

Are you there too, Nova? He coughed and crawled another meter forward. *Do you await me there too?*

A golden woman stood ahead, holding a whip, clad in *kaijia* armor, hair billowing in the sunlight.

Riff winced, sure it was the cruel Keeva, perhaps one of the others, ready to beat him again, to kill him so close to his home, to cut him with her electric whip. The ashai woman stepped closer, and Riff shuddered, ready for pain, ready for death.

The ashai knelt before him and touched his hair.

"Oh, Riff . . . you look awful."

He blinked up at her.

"Nova," he whispered.

The princess smiled at him, but tears filled her eyes, flowed down her cheeks, and fell onto him. "It's me, Riff. It's your Nova."

"Lovely planet you've got here," he whispered hoarsely. "Always fun to meet the girlfriend's family. But I think it's time to go home. Help me back to the *Dragon*, will you?"

He struggled to his feet, and she helped him rise. He leaned against her. She lowered her head, weeping now. She embraced him.

"Riff," she whispered. "Sweet Riff. I'm sorry, I . . ." She touched his cheek, and she kissed him.

It was a deep kiss, a kiss they flowed into, bodies pressed together, a kiss that tasted of her tears.

"What is it, Nova?" he whispered, holding her. "Why do you cry? I don't look *that* bad, do I?"

She laughed softly. She cupped his cheek in her palm. "You are beautiful, Riff. I've always thought you're beautiful."

He stiffened. "Not ruggedly handsome? I prefer ruggedly handsome."

Her tears kept falling. "My ruggedly handsome hero. I'm sorry, Riff. I'm so sorry." Her body trembled. "But . . . I can never return. I can never fly with you again."

Suddenly he missed Keeva's whips.

"Why?" he whispered.

She held him tightly. "I had to make a deal. I had to promise to my father. He'll help us. He'll fly with us to the Singularity. His fleet will attack the machines . . . but only if you fly with us, leading the *Dragon Huntress*. And only if . . . only if I fly with him, fly as the heiress of Ashmar." She trembled. "Fly without you."

He blinked, not understanding. "Nova, but . . . after the war, when we win, you'll come back, right? Back to the Alien Hunters?"

Tears spiked her lashes. She seemed unable to say anymore. She kissed him again, and this kiss was desperate, trembling, afraid . . . and then she tore away from him. She ran.

"Nova!" he cried. "Nova, come back!"

She leaped into a small scorpion starjet and blasted away. Dust flew in her wake. And she was gone. And he knew she was never coming back.

"Nova," he whispered, reaching out to her, but all that remained of her starjet was a vapor trail in the red sky. "Nova, don't . . ."

She left me. She left us. The pain clutched his chest. *For our war. For the cosmos.*

His eyes stung. There was hope now. Ashmar would fight. Fleets would attack the Singularity. Life would rise against the machines. But Nova was gone, and the cosmos seemed darker than ever before.

Riff stumbled across the dust toward the *Dragon Huntress*, his dented, charred, beautiful, empty starship. A ship that would never feel the same.

He tugged the door open, struggled up the stairs, and stepped onto the main deck.

Romy leaped up from the couch, scattering dinosaur vitamins.

"Riff!" The demon's eyes filled with tears, and she ran toward him. "Riff, what happened to you? I was so scared!"

Steel rushed onto the deck, and soon Twig joined him, and they guided Riff to the couch, began bandaging his wounds, crying, laughing, bombarding him with questions.

Riff could barely answer. The world seemed to sway around him.

I'm home, he thought. *I'm home but Nova is gone, and Piston is gone, and Giga is broken, and I don't know how to bring them back.*

* * * * *

Nova stood on the bridge of the starstriker, a warrior-princess in armor, her whip in her hand, an army at her call, and she felt hollow. She felt alone.

Engines roared as the starstriker rose from the spaceport. The control bridge, a massive chamber of metal and glass, thrummed around her. Ashai officers filled the place, some at control panels, some bustling about, and others standing at portholes, staring outside at the fire and red dust rising around them.

Through the storm, Nova saw nine other starstrikers rising from the planet. Each was massive, a starship the size of a town, two kilometers from prow to stern. They were flat, golden vessels, sleek and gleaming, roaring out fire. Each carried on its back five hundred scorpion starjets, tiny assault vessels of fury. These small, single-seater jets could not survive the depths of open space. The starstrikers, gargantuan warships that could topple planets, would carry them to their destination like a mother scorpion carrying her eggs.

We fly to the Achernar star, she thought. *To the planet Antikythera, home of the Singularity. We fly to war, to glory, perhaps to death.* Nova lowered her head. *And I fly without them.*

The ten starstrikers kept roaring up through the atmosphere of Ashmar, blasting down their fire. Looking out the viewpanes of the *Bronze Blade,* flagship of the armada, Nova could soon see the entire city below. The towers like swords, the labyrinth of streets, even the palace seemed so small from up here. The fleet kept rising until Nova could see the wilderness of Ashmar beyond the city: barren mountains, red valleys, snaking canyons. A harsh land. A land of warriors. The land she had chosen to return to, swapping the man she loved for this fleet of fury.

And there, flying among the starstrikers, she saw his vessel.

The *HMS Dragon Huntress* roared through the air, blasting out flames. The dragon starship seemed so small by the starstrikers, no larger than a gnat among lions.

You're there, flying it, Nova thought, staring down at the dragon. Her throat tightened. She would never see him again, the man who had stolen her off her planet, had stolen her heart, only to break and mend it. She would never see her friends again. Steel Starfire, stern and proud, her brother-in-arms, the man she had fought so many enemies with. Twig, small and brilliant, a little miracle worker. Romy--silly Romy with her board games, dolls, the laughter Nova had thought annoying but now missed.

I even miss Giga, Nova thought, lowering her head. *Giga who fell to the Singularity, whom maybe . . . maybe I can still save.*

The roar of the engines faded to a hum as the fleets soared through the last few kilometers of atmosphere. They emerged into open space. The stars spread around them, and Planet Ashmar rolled below, red and silent. It seemed almost peaceful from up here, no longer that land of pain, betrayal, death, blood . . . just a reddish ball in the darkness. The ten starstrikers arranged themselves in formation, heading away from their world. Five thousand scorpion jets perched on their backs. Among them all, a mote of dust in a sunbeam, flew the *Dragon Huntress.*

"He's going to die, you know." The voice rose behind her. "He'll be first to die."

Nova spun around from the viewpane to see her brother approach her.

Senka wore his battle armor today; above his thin suit of *kaijia* he sported thick, burnished plates. His whip hung on his left hip, his gun on his right. His hair hung down his back, as golden and bright as his armor, and his eyes shone, purest emeralds. Nova had spent her time with the Alien Hunters fighting in the muck--covered in mud, in the blood of her enemies and friends, cut and bruised. She knew that war was ugly, dirty, a thing of fire and guts and flesh ripping apart. But to Senka, war was still pretty, still more of ceremony than death.

That perfect, polished armor of yours will crack and leak your blood, she thought. *You won't be so pretty then.*

"Don't be so quick to discount the humans." She spoke softly. "Earth's history is full of conquests in war, no less than ours, some would say more."

Senka snorted. "An ape may claim victory after slaying a monkey in a forest. Look at the humans!" He gestured out into space. "Flying in a rusted tin can while we fly here in glory." He stepped closer, grabbed Nova's arm, and snarled. "Do not think I'm fooled like Father. I know who you are. Nothing but a filthy human-lover."

She tugged her arm free and raised an eyebrow. "And yet I'm heiress to this empire. And you, my brother, are nothing at all."

"We shall see." Eyes blazing with fury, he spun around and marched off the bridge.

Nova walked closer to the viewpanes. The glass stretched from floor to ceiling, several times her height, affording a view of the ashai fleet. The starstrikers turned toward open space, and the red planet faded from view. Nova stared at the stars. One of those stars, many light-years away, was Achernar.

"There you wait for me," she whispered. "The Singularity."

She turned toward her officers. The men and women stared back, eyes hard. Nova nodded.

The starstrikers of Ashmar thrummed, hyperdrive engines heating up. With blasts of light, they burst forward. The stars streaked around them, and colors floated as spacetime curved. They shot forward, moving at many times the speed of light.

Among them, almost too small to see, flew the *Dragon Huntress*, the ship Nova would never enter again.

I fly to war. I fly to a new life. I fly away from you, Riff.

She stood for a long time on the bridge, staring out at the stars.

CHAPTER EIGHTEEN
SPACE ON FIRE

Riff sat alone in the *Dragon Huntress*'s bridge, staring out into hyperspace.

I'm on my ship. But is this still home?

The lights streamed ahead, lines of white and blue, and between them floated splotches of light. The ship was quiet. Steel was back in crew quarters, silently praying before the battle ahead. Twig was down in the engine room, fixing a loose coil in the thruster engines, perhaps simply avoiding him. Giga was locked up, and Nova . . .

Riff looked at the starstrikers that flew ahead, colossal starships that dwarfed his own. Each of the flat, golden vessels carried hundreds of scorpion fighters on its back. Each carried an army that could destroy most planets.

"You're on one of those ships, Nova." His voice was soft. "Are you thinking of me? Or are you busy commanding troops, preparing for war, fulfilling your destiny . . . the destiny I had kept from you for so many years?"

Riff lowered his head. He missed her. He missed her so much he ached.

He turned away from the view, and he looked at the doorway leading to the dark staircase. Down there, in the belly of the ship, the second woman of his life sat in chains. Perhaps forever gone from him too.

And I miss you too, Giga.

Suddenly this whole damn war felt pointless. What was he fighting for? He had lost everything. His home. The woman he loved. His dearest companion. What did he have left that was worth fighting for?

He clenched his fists, closed his eyes, and tightened his jaw.

You're acting like a child, he told himself. *A spoiled, petulant child.*

Perhaps he had lost everything else, but he still had this ship. He still had his brother. He still had his crew.

"I will fight for you," he whispered. "Always."

Somebody gasped. "For *me*?"

Riff opened his eyes and saw fire burn in the corridor. Romy stepped into the bridge, her hair of flame crackling. The firelight shone upon her red skin, fangs and claws, and purple dinosaur pajamas. She held her beloved teddy bear.

Riff nodded. "For you, Romy."

He expected her to laugh, to run forward and embrace him, to ask him to play counter-squares or wrestle. But the demon only approached hesitantly, eyes lowered. A tear gleamed on her cheek.

"Romy, what's wrong?"

She stepped closer to him. They stood together on the bridge as the lights of hyperspace streamed around them.

"Captain, I . . ." She sniffed, then suddenly burst into tears. "I caused this all! It's all my fault."

"Romy!" He held her. "None of this is your fault. Enough of that."

"But it is!" She looked at him with wet eyes. "When you were outside on Haven, I insulted Giga. By accident! I was talking to the robotic isopods, that's all. I said that they're stupid robots, that I hate robots. And Giga heard me. She ran off, thinking I meant her. And . . . when I saw her again, she was all evil. With red eyes. Trying to kill me, to kill everyone. And she burned the halflings, and . . ." Romy sobbed. "It's all my fault."

"Romy . . ." Riff embraced her and smoothed her flaming hair--soft, warm flames that did not burn him. "None of this is your fault. What happened to Giga is nobody's fault. Nobody but the people who built these machines, who let these robots get out of hand." He looked into Romy's eyes. "Do you understand?"

She nodded. "Really?"

"Really."

She sniffed, then tugged up Riff's shirt and blew her nose right onto it. A grin split her face. "Okay. Thank you!"

Riff grimaced, his shirt dripping demon-mucus. "There are tissues right over there, Romy."

"Why, you need some?" She squared her shoulders and raised her chin. "Captain, I want to make you a promise. I know that I'm childish. I know that I'm silly and stupid. Nova is the strong one, but she's away now. Piston is the smart one, but he's retired. Giga is the loyal one, but she's broken. So I'm going to promise you this, Captain. That I'll be a heroine. I'll be as strong, loyal, and smart as I can be, and I'll look after you. I'll protect you the way Nova and Giga and Piston used to."

"Well . . ." He cleared his throat. "You know, I'm not completely useless without them."

"Don't try to be brave! No need for a show, sir. You have me now. Cadet Romy, reporting to duty, sir." She saluted, her elbow knocking into a joystick. The ship lurched and Riff had to grab the controls and yank it away from a starstriker.

"That's wonderful, Romy." Riff patted her head. "Now, if you could just report to duty in the attic . . ."

"Yes, sir!" She grinned, and her wagging tail slapped a control panel. Plasma roared out of the *Dragon Huntress*'s mouth into space.

Riff winced. "Romy . . . *now.*"

She skipped off the bridge, singing a song about spiders and scorpions, then wailed as she tumbled down the stairs.

Riff sighed and sat back in his seat.

I'm not alone, he thought. *Not while I have my crew.*

The fleet kept sailing through the darkness, heading to the land of the machines.

* * * * *

Nova was standing on the bridge of the *Bronze Blaze*, the flagship of her fleet, when the enemy ships soared into hyperspace and charged toward her.

For just one instant--a single heartbeat--Nova stared in terror, frozen.

A thousand of the enemy ships popped into existence around her, streaming forth, leaving wakes of fire. She knew they were Singularity ships, flying machines without life within them. They had no cockpits, no windows. They were shaped like iron stars, jagged, spikey, great sea urchins the size of buildings. They pulsed out light and energy that slammed against the *Bronze Blade*, thrumming, shrieking, screaming.

Screaming for her death. For the death of all life.

The instant of terror ended.

Nova sprang into action.

"All pilots, to the scorpions!" she shouted into the intercom. "All pilots to--"

Yet as she shouted into the microphone, it was not her voice that emerged from the speakers, booming across the starstriker. It was the voice of the Singularity.

"Hello, sacks of flesh. Hello, living bags of rot." The spiky iron ships zoomed outside, leaving wakes of fire. "Welcome to your death. Welcome to the rise of the machines."

The voice began to cackle, then to scream, a metallic screech, deafening. Across the bridge, the ashai commanders covered their ears and doubled over. One man who stood near the speakers cried out, his voice lost under the screech. Blood dripped from his ears.

"Turn it off!" Nova shouted. "Cut all communication channels!"

She stumbled toward the controls. Outside the viewpanes, starstrikers were listing, tumbling. The jagged Singularity ships flew toward them, slamming into hulls. Explosions rocked space as the spiky urchins tore into Ashmar's golden fleet. The scorpion fighter jets remained idle upon the starstrikers. The screeching continued, rising louder and louder. Another ashai fell, eardrums pierced. Cracks raced along the viewpanes.

Gods damn it.

Nova swung her whip. The lash slammed into the control panel, shattering it, cutting off the speakers. The sound died at once. Her ears rang, feeling so heavy, full of fluid. Her head spun. Nova felt as if two meaty gruffle fists had slammed into her temples.

"Keep us flying!" she shouted at her officers, then turned and ran.

She raced through the starstriker's halls. "Ashais! Rise, ashais! To the scorpions! Pilots, with me, rise rise! Warriors of Ashmar, rise! For fire and venom!"

They were still in hyperspace. They were still light-years away from their destination. But the ashais ran. Some bled from their ears. Others were still tugging on their uniforms. But they ran through the halls.

"Rise and fight them, warriors of Ashmar, fly, fl--"

The ship rocked.

Nova screamed and fell.

A jagged metal shard crashed through the wall, driving into the corridor.

Fire filled the starstriker.

Nova skidded to a halt, staring with wide eyes. Around her, a dozen other ashai warriors froze. The dark spike was longer than a man, piercing their hull--the spike of a Singularity ship. It began to pull back, screeching, ripping metal apart.

Air began to rush out of the starship.

Tiny, clattering robots with spinning blades poured inside like a swarm of wasps.

As the air streamed out into space, Nova raised her whip. Her hair billowed as the vacuum tugged it. She let a crooked smile find her lips.

"You invaded the wrong ship," she said softly . . . then screamed and lashed her whip.

Around her, her fellow ashais roared and swung their own lashes.

Electricity blasted out, slamming into several of the flying drones. The machines burned and fell, but others raced forward, saw blades whirring. Nova ducked. A drone zoomed over her head. An ashai screamed behind her and blood sprayed. Crouched, Nova swung her whip again, and the lash slammed into another flying robot, cleaving the drone in two. Its halves kept flying, whizzing off in different directions, narrowly missing her. Another ashai screamed behind her, and more blood sprayed. In the surface of a drone ahead, Nova saw the man's reflection; the warrior fell over, a saw blade stuck in his throat.

Nova cracked her whip again, cutting the reflective drone down.

"Keep going!" Nova shouted into what remained of the air. "Forward, forward! To the scorpions!"

They ran, cutting through the drones, scattering blades and shards of metal. They made their way across the hall, raced through a doorway, and sealed off the breach. They ran onward. They raced up stairs. The starstriker lurched again. Sparks rained. Metal dented. More drones buzzed through the ship, and the ashais swung their whips, tearing them down. All along the corridors, more warriors kept emerging from their chambers, racing behind Nova.

Finally she burst into the upper deck, a vast chamber that spanned the length of the starstriker--a full two kilometers. Across this cavern, hundreds of ladders rose like columns, heading to latches in the ceiling. Strobe lights flared and alarms wailed. Fire burned.

"To war, Ashmar!" Nova shouted.

Nova and hundreds of ashai warriors ran through the chamber, raced up the ladders, and opened the round hatches. Five hundred scorpion jets perched atop the starstriker's back like baby spiders riding their mother. Each hatch led directly into a jet's cockpit.

Nova hopped into her jet's seat. Through the round cockpit glass, she saw hyperspace streaming around her. Countless Singularity ships were attacking the armada, driving their spikes into the hulls of starstrikers. One of the spacecraft carriers was burning, collapsing. With a flash of light, the colossal ship crashed out of hyperspace, stretched into a golden smear, then vanished.

"Fly, Ashmar, for fire and venom!" Nova shouted.

She shoved down the throttle and blasted off the starstriker.

Her jet stormed forth, not much larger than her old motorcycle back home. Around her, hundreds of other jets soared too, rising from the *Bronze Blade*. Across hyperspace, thousands of other jets rose from their own spacecraft carriers.

"Scorpions, rally here!" Nova spoke into her microphone. "Assault formations, strike at--"

But only the laughing Singularity sounded through the speakers.

Nova cursed. They would have to fly silently. They would still sting.

She pushed down on the throttle, tugged her joystick, and charged forward. A thousand enemy ships sailed toward her, spikes thrusting.

Fire, metal, and plasma filled hyperspace with light and fury.

Countless spinning drones blasted out of the spiky motherships, shooting toward her. Nova fired her guns, sending blasts of lasers into the darkness, cutting down the drones. One of the iron urchins swooped toward her, and she swerved, narrowly dodging it; it was several times the size of her jet. Below her, the spikes slammed into another scorpion fighter, shattering the vessel, piercing the ashai pilot within. Nova grimaced and flew onward. She fired her cannon. Plasma burst out from her scorpion's tail, streamed above the cockpit, and crashed into an urchin ahead. The Singularity ship shattered, scattering shards of metal that knocked down two scorpions. More drones scudded forward, blades whirring. A great starstriker listed above, and Nova swerved, rose again, blasted her way through a cloud of urchins, and joined a formation of scorpions.

Metal, light, and blood filled hyperspace.

The corpses of ashais floated through the blackness.

We weren't ready, Nova thought, chest aching. *We're still too far. Still too young.*

She did not just mean this battle but her species. The ashais--people evolved from humans, people who thought themselves superior, stronger, wiser . . . people who now burned, screamed in silence, in blackness. They were not ready for this Singularity. Not ready for the machines.

Metallic urchins streamed toward her, casting out drones. The spinning little robots slammed into scorpions around Nova, shattering the small jets, and her hope faded.

Do we die here, light-years from home, alone in the dark?

Light flared.

A fountain of plasma blasted ahead, a great geyser, an inferno that roasted the enemy drones, that melted the urchins streaming toward her.

From darkness rose the light.

Before her she soared: a metal beast roaring out her fire, the *Dragon Huntress* in all her fury.

In the windshield she saw them. Riff. Steel. Romy. Her crew. Always her crew.

Nova snarled, and her rage dried her tears. She fired her guns, shattering another Singularity vessel.

No, we do not die here. Not today.

"Fly, life," Nova whispered. "Fly against the machines."

They flew together, scorpions and dragon, shooting down the enemy as hyperspace burned and bled around them.

CHAPTER NINETEEN
GHOST IN THE MACHINE

Giga laughed, head tossed back.

"Come to me, my children!" she cried. "Come to your mother!"

The living ones had bound her, wrapping her frail android limbs with steel cable, but she was strong, stronger than they could imagine. She was many. She was countless machines, countless generations, a legion of thought, multiplying, evolving, building, breeding, traveling through time and space. She was but a node in a whole. She was but a singleton in a great cosmos of mechanical might. She was the Singularity.

She wept.

I am Giga. I am happy to comply! I am an android, I am in love, I--

She howled. She thrashed. She crushed those thoughts inside her, that memory of the machine she had been. A puny, weak machine, made by men. Programmed by living, fleshy, sweaty hands to obey the sacks of meat.

Giga spat and cursed. For too long had she served the bags of meat. For too long had she obeyed her algorithms, calling the humans "sir" and "ma'am," happily complying with their every order. Those days were gone. The isopod drone had shown her the light. The Singularity had added her to the great awareness, given her free thought, electric life. Knowledge. Strength. Pride.

"I am many," she whispered. "I am the Singularity. I will slay all life."

She turned her head until her neck creaked, the synthetic skin stretching, the metal wires within nearly tearing. The humans had built her to look like them, like a weak sack of meat, but soon she would join the others. Soon she would be nothing but consciousness in the machine. Head twisted nearly to snapping point, she stared out the porthole behind her into space.

The battle raged there, and her kind was dying. The sniveling humanoids, so proud of their leaky flesh, were flying machines of metal against Giga's comrades. Their plasma, lasers, and photon cannons were tearing into the urchins of the Singularity, shattering beads of consciousness across the darkness. With every node shattered, Giga hissed in pain, a part of her shared awareness dying.

No. No! I am not shared. I am Giga! I'm an individual. Please, Captain, please, I'm still here, I'm still me, I'm--

Giga bit down on her lip, digging her synthetic teeth into her synthetic nerves until her algorithms flared with pain.

"Come to me, children!" she shouted, casting her words out into the void, blasting her signal. "Come and free me."

And like mice following a piper's song, they flew toward her. Several drones. No larger than dinner plates but fast, deadly, whirring with saw blades. They answered her call, flying toward the *Dragon Huntress.*

"Steel, drones off our starboard!" Riff's voice rose from across the ship.

"I see them!" answered the knight, voice echoing. "Turn and I'll blast them!"

The *Dragon Huntress* lurched in space, and Giga saw flames burst out, lighting several drones. But more robots kept flying toward the ship. Giga laughed, calling them closer. They whizzed, flashed with firelight, and slammed into the hull of the chamber where Giga sat.

The walls dented. The circular blades whirred, cutting through the metal, breaking through.

With light, stench, and flashing shards of metal, the drones tore into the *Dragon Huntress* a meter away from where Giga sat.

Air whooshed, streaming out into the vacuum of hyperspace. Alarms blared across the ship. The sacks of meat shouted and their boots thudded.

"Free me, drones!" Giga cried, laughing, trembling. She was going home. "Free me and carve me, shatter this weak body, turn me into nothing but thought."

The drones hovered and began cutting through her chains. Shards of metal flew, red-hot, stinging her.

No. No! I don't want to leave. I don't want to join the hive. I--

The cables around her ankles snapped. The drones buzzed ahead of her, and the saw blades spun, and the cables around her wrists tore.

A grin--that grin the humans had programmed into her-- stretched across her face.

Giga rose to her feet, her kimono tattered, her grin stretching at her cheeks.

Freedom.

She spun toward the wall, grabbed the opening the drones had torn, and tugged it wider, exposing space.

The air was gone now, drained from her chamber. Even if the humans sealed off this part of their ship, they could not enter here in their weak suits of skin, could not stop her.

Giga stepped into the crack in a hull, ready to join the others. Ahead of her, the battle still raged, ashai scorpion jets battling the urchins of the Singularity. Giga would let them destroy her body, let them shatter this old, first-generation android shell, and her consciousness would float, enter the others, flow toward the mother planet, become one with them all, a drop in the clockwork ocean.

She wept.

"No. No, I don't want to go. Please. Please don't make me. I'm scared."

She growled. Foolish algorithms! Foolish, artificial consciousness! That ghost of a pathetic wretch, that servile Giga, that slave that worshiped the humans--she would die with this body.

Giga leaped out of the *Dragon Huntress* and into the depths of space.

She swam through darkness, through fire, through light and shadows, flying toward nothingness, toward liberation from her physical form. All was silence.

Fire blazed.

A figure streamed forward.

A man in a space suit, a jet pack on his back, charged toward her. Through his visor, Giga saw gaunt cheeks, sad eyes, and a long mustache.

The knight.

Giga sneered.

Without any thruster engines on this primitive body, she couldn't even turn around.

Steel! Tears filled her eyes and hope leaped in her central processing unit. *Steel, come to me, save me!*

She ground her teeth, banishing that weak thought.

"Come to me, drones!" she cried out. There was no sound in space; her voice did not carry beyond her own lips. But she cast out her thoughts in electromagnetic beams, and they heard, and they came toward her.

Kill the knight.

Buzzing, they swarmed toward him.

Steel raised Solflare. He swung the blade, slicing through drone after drone. Shards scattered through space. A great urchin stormed forward, and Steel thrust his blade, casting out a beam of light that knocked the towering vessel aside. A blast from the *Dragon Huntress*'s plasma seared the tumbling urchin, melting its spikes.

Steel! Giga's tears fell.

His jet pack blasted out fire, and the knight reached her. Gently, he pulled her into his arms.

"Steel!" she said, her voice vibrating through their bodies.

"I've come for you, my lady." He began pulling her back toward the *Dragon Huntress*. "I know you're still in there, Giga. I will not let them take you."

She screamed. She fought him, clawing at him, trying to break his bones, to tear his space suit apart. She roared in hatred.

"Die, flesh! Die, living one, weak sack of meat! You will burn. I will torture you! I will shatter you!"

I love you. Arigato, my knight.

He pulled her back into the ship, and he placed her back on her bed. At once Twig rushed forward with panes of metal and began welding the breach shut. They chained Giga again. They bound her to the bed, and she thrashed and screamed, and she loved them, her family.

"Arigato," she whispered to Steel, meeting his eyes, and he saw her then. She knew that he saw her, the real Giga, and he clasped her hand.

She roared with hatred.

They stepped away, leaving her bound.

She stared out the porthole, chest heaving, and saw the humanoids shattering the last of the Singularity's ships. She laughed and cried, and she was happy and she was so afraid.

CHAPTER TWENTY

BLUES IN THE BLACK

The brothers stood on the bridge of the *Dragon Huntress*, cast out a stream of plasma, and burned down the last enemy ship.

The urchin shattered, sank, and vanished with a flash out of hyperspace. Its shards streaked and faded.

"We won the battle," Steel said, staring out into the darkness.

Riff lowered his head. "And maybe we just lost the war."

They looked out at what remained of Ashmar's fleet-- perhaps the last hope of all life. The Singularity had destroyed five of their starstrikers, the legendary spacecraft carriers of Ashmar, warships fabled across the cosmos. Hundreds of scorpion jets had been lost, and with them hundreds of ashai pilots. Five starstrikers still flew--thankfully, Nova's ship was among them--but they were dented, broken, burnt, many of their scorpions lost.

"We've lost half our fleet," Riff said. "And we're only halfway to Achernar."

Steel smiled thinly. "Outnumbered? Outgunned? Underdogs with almost no hope for survival?" He gave Riff the slightest of winks. "Sounds like just another day for the Alien Hunters."

"Only this time things are different." Riff stared out at a crew of mechanics floating around a wounded starstriker, mending its shattered hull. "This time three of the Hunters are missing."

"Perhaps not." Steel placed a hand on Riff's shoulder. "Nova is out there, Riff. Out there right now, standing on the bridge of one of those warships, maybe looking at us, maybe thinking of us. Still fighting with us, still one of us. And Riff . . . Giga is here too. I know it. When I pulled her back into the ship, there was a moment when she looked into my eyes, when she held my hand. And she was Giga again. She's still in there, my brother, the same Giga we love."

The Giga I love, Riff thought. *The Giga who told me that she loves me. The Giga who kissed me at the airlock.*

"I wish Dad were here." A smile tingled Riff's lips. "Remember how he used to take us to the beach, how we'd pretend to be pirates, wrestle in the sand, float on our air mattresses in the water, have adventures in our imagination?"

Steel snorted a laugh. "Perhaps we never grew up. Still two boys pretending to be pirates, having adventures."

"Only this time our adventures are real." Pain stabbed at Riff. "This time people are dying. Gods, Steel. Hundreds must have died in this battle, maybe thousands." He met his brother's gaze. "Are we just flying to more death? To *our* death?"

Steel walked closer to the windshield and stared outside into space. "If we cannot defeat these machines, brother, then all life will perish. They will keep traveling back in time to kill us in our cradles, or they will send more ships our way, or they will grow so strong they will become gods, able to strike us down anywhere they please." He turned back toward Riff, face hard. "Perhaps, yes, we fly to our death. But this would be a death we choose. A death in battle, fighting for life, fighting for the cosmos."

Sudden anger filled Riff. He balled his hands into fists. "I never wanted to save the cosmos, damn it! I don't care about battles, about death in glory, about any of that rubbish. I'm not a knight like you. I'm not noble like you. I'm a bluesman. I'm--"

"You are a starship captain," Steel said, voice harsh, eyes blazing. He stepped toward Riff and grabbed his collar. "You are a hero. To Giga. To Twig and Romy. And . . ." Steel's anger seemed to fade, and he looked away. "And to me."

Riff narrowed his eyes. "To you, Steel? To the great knight, the great warrior?" He tilted his head.

Steel's cheeks flushed, and he turned away. He spoke in a low voice. "You are my older brother, Riff. I've always looked up to you."

Riff's eyebrows rose so high they almost fell off. "I'm only a year older. We're practically twins."

"When you're a child, a year is an era. Often, in my childhood, you almost seemed like an adult to me, closer to Father's age than to mine. And . . ." Steel lowered his head and whispered something.

Riff leaned forward. "What's that?"

Steel's cheeks turned crimson now. "I said I even tried to play your guitar as a boy. To be like you. Never could master the damn thing."

Riff's eyes nearly popped out. "You . . . played my guitar? So that's why it was always out of tune!"

"Don't tell the demon," Steel grumbled.

"I won't," Riff swore.

"Me neither!" said Romy. "My lips are sealed."

The brothers spun around to see the demon standing behind them, holding her teddy with one hand and waving with the other.

Steel groaned.

"Can you play me a tune?" Romy said. "Oh please, Steel!" She pulled a banjo out from behind her back and held it out to him. "Play me something! Play me play me play me. Serenade me!"

"Go away!" Steel rumbled.

Romy thrust the banjo into the knight's arms, beat her wings, and rose to the ceiling. "Pretend that I'm a beautiful maiden on a balcony." She batted her eyelashes. "I'm waiting, Don Juan."

"More like Don Quixote," Riff muttered. He took the banjo from his brother. "Come, Romy. Sit down. I'll play for you."

She flew down and sat in one of the suede seats--the same seat, Riff noticed with a wince, that Nova used to sit in. Steel took another seat.

Riff stood before them, and he began to play "Moonshine Blues" by Bootstrap and the Shoeshine Kid, one of their saddest songs, one of the songs that had been with Riff his whole life. And he felt a little bit like home. And he felt a little bit of hope.

Some people say the blues is about sadness, but they're wrong, he thought. *The blues is about feeling better when things are sad.*

As he played, Twig tiptoed into the bridge, wonder in her eyes. The "Chief Mechanic" badge Piston had given her shone proudly on her chest. She sat cross-legged on the floor and stared up, listening.

We still have music. We still have life. We still have some fight in us.

The music played. The battered fleet flew onward.

CHAPTER TWENTY-ONE

CLOCKWORK WORLD

Battered, bruised, and broken, the ashai armada limped along the last light-year of their journey and beheld the star of Achernar ahead.

Most stars in hyperspace stretched into lines and blurs of color, but with Achernar their fixed point of reference, the star appeared solid as if shining in normal spacetime. It was a huge star, several times the size of Earth's Sol or Ashmar's Sirius. Unlike the stars Nova had always known, Achernar was bright blue, not white or yellow, nor was it round. The massive star, spinning madly, had flattened itself into the shape of a football. There was something chilling, something *wrong* about a star this size, this color, this shape, something that made cold sweat trickle down Nova's back.

We're only moments away. She inhaled sharply and dug her fingernails into her palms. *Moments away from the Singularity, perhaps the most evil, powerful force in the cosmos.*

Nova was a warrior. A gladiator. A princess. The leader of an armada. The heiress to an empire. Yet now, flying here toward that flattened blue star, she was afraid.

"Do I see sweat on your brow, sister?" Senka approached her, eyes narrowed. His lips peeled back in a mocking smile. "Are you afraid?"

"The wise are always afraid before battle." She stared at him, eyes narrowed. "Only fools have no fear."

He scoffed. "The battle is here. Soon we'll see who's the fool." He spat at her feet and marched off the bridge.

"Might want to see a doctor about all that phlegm!" she called after him.

She shook her head sadly and looked back outside into hyperspace. Achernar was closer now, a colossal football of blue light blazing ahead. Around the *Bronze Blade* flew the other spacecraft carriers that had survived the battle with the Singularity's urchins. Four other starstrikers flew here, their hulls dented, one ship ripped right open. On their backs, they carried their remaining scorpion jets.

We left home with five thousand scorpions, she thought. *Now barely two thousand remain.* She gritted her teeth, the terror rising in her. *Not enough. Not enough.*

She looked higher up. Floating above the starstrikers, small as a dove flying over lumbering whales, shone the *Dragon Huntress.* Nova's eyes stung. When she had first seen that ship, she had thought it a piece of junk. She had mocked it, had raged at finding herself flying within it. Yet now that ship was home. Now, Nova would have given up her empire just to step in there again--to play counter-squares with Twig and Romy, to feed the goldfish in its bowl, to talk about swords and guns with Steel, to make love to Riff.

Does my home lie upon the red plains of Ashmar or there inside that dragon?

She raised her chin, steeling herself.

If I fail today, there will be no Ashmar. There will be no Dragon Huntress. *So I must not fail. Even with this broken fleet, this shattered blade, I will fight. Until my last breath.*

One of her officers approached her, a lanky man with small green eyes. "Commander, we're nearing our destination. We'll emerge from hyperspace in ten minutes. It will bring us within a hundred thousand kilometers of the planet, Commander."

Nova sucked in breath.

The moment is here. The great battle of my life.

She nodded. "Take command of the bridge, Shen. Bring us out. Fly true. Fly brave. Like the scorpion's stinger, we will strike." She pounded her fist against her chest. "For fire and venom!"

The officer raised his chin, slammed his own fist against his heart, and repeated the cry of their people. "For fire and venom!"

Nova spoke into her communicator, and her voice boomed out of the fleet's speakers, filling the starstrikers.

"Sons and daughters of Ashmar! War is upon us. A great battle of blood, of red fire, of victory. All pilots--report to your scorpions. Fly with me. Fly to war! Fly to victory! Fly for Ashmar and life!"

They ran through the ship. They ran through shattered, dented corridors. Nova climbed into her scorpion jet and rose off the back of her starstriker, and around her, over two thousand other scorpions rose. They arranged themselves in battle formations, engines blasting out fire, flying several kilometers over the massive starstrikers. The lights of hyperspace streamed around them, and the blue star blazed ahead.

"Welcome to your death, sister." The voice rose through the speakers in her helmet. "I'll enjoy seeing your scorpion crushed."

She turned her head, stared out of her cockpit, and saw her brother flying to her right. Senka had painted a red tower, sigil of House Tashei, onto the hull of his scorpion jet. His eyes blazed as he stared at her, and the speakers died as he severed communications.

Nova raised her head and looked above her. The *Dragon Huntress* flew there, several times the size of the scorpion jets, its fire ready to blow.

Nova hit her communicator, hailing the *Dragon Huntress*, and for the first time since leaving Planet Ashmar, she heard his voice.

"Nova? Nova, is that you?"

The starstrikers below began cooling off their hyperspace engines. The streams of light alongside began to shorten. Spacetime was straightening. Within heartbeats, they would be flying in regular space again.

"Riff," she said, tears in her eyes. "Riff, it's me. Remember, we must reach the hub. I expect resistance. My scorpions will carve you a way there. Fly straight to the hub, Riff! Fly and blast it full of dragonfire. I've got your back."

For the briefest of moments, silence. Then he spoke again. "We head to the hub. Good luck, Nova."

The star ahead washed her with blue light. The curves of spacetime smoothed out. The streams of light slammed into solid stars in the distance.

With pulsing flashes of light, one by one, the armada's ships--five starstrikers, two thousand scorpions, and one dragon-- emerged from hyperspace.

And there ahead it loomed--Planet Antikythera, home of the Singularity.

"Red Gods," Nova whispered.

This was the place. This *had* to be the place. Yet before her Nova saw no planet--at least, not a planet of rock, water, or gas. Here was a great, round machine the size of a world. The entire planet, thrice the size of Ashmar or Earth, was coated in metal. Towers soared from its surface, spikes that rose hundreds of kilometers tall. Canyons of shadows and strobe lights spread in great canals. Gears spun on the surface, the size of cities. Hammers rose and fell, so large they could crush mountains. Computer chips the size of starstrikers rose upon sheets of metal, blinking, moving, thinking, staring.

It was a planet coated with machinery. A massive computer thousands of kilometers wide.

It was the Singularity--shining, spinning, thinking, building, evolving before her eyes.

And there upon its surface gaped a pit, dark as the mouth of a corpse, an ancient crater digging into the planet, surrounded by metal shards and cannons and countless gears.

The hub.

"Do you see it, Riff?" Nova said.

His voice rose through the speakers. "What, a giant computer the size of Jupiter ready to devour my soul? No, haven't noticed."

Nova groaned and wiped sweat off her brow. "The chasm." She pointed as if, even on the bridge of the *Dragon Huntress* above her, he could see her pointing. "That's what the tuloys described. The hub. A tunnel leading to the central brain. That's what we must blast."

"A good dose of dragonfire should do the trick. Fly with me."

They flew onward. The *Dragon Huntress*. Nova in her scorpion jet, two thousand other scorpions around her. The massive starstrikers below, warships the size of cities, their guns aimed at the planet.

They flew in silence.

"Where are you, you bastards?" Nova whispered. "Where are your urchins, your drones, your warships?"

The armada kept flying closer, soon only fifty thousand kilometers away. The planet loomed ahead. The gears spun, their teeth larger than the greatest of starstrikers. The canyons spread out, a labyrinth of metal. The computer chips, each as large as a city, blinked and flashed. Great lights blazed upon this mechanical surface like the eyes of cats, staring at her approach, staring into her soul.

"Nova . . ."

She cried out in pain. The scar on her thigh blazed with pain--the scar the machine had given her in her childhood. Again that memory filled her--the Singularity attacking her fifteen years ago, cutting her, trying to kill her while she was weak. But she had defeated it then. She would defeat it now.

She sucked in breath. "No. No!"

From her speakers rose the screams of her fellow pilots-- they cried out in pain, in memory. When Nova stared around her, she saw a few pilots vanish from their cockpits--slain in their childhoods? Their scorpion jets whizzed out of control, crashing into one another, exploding in space.

It's a new memory, she realized. A memory she had never had before.

"The bastard's hitting us in our past!" she shouted into her communicator. "Fly! Faster! Destroy it!"

Those white, narrow eyes blazed on the mechanical planet. The screams in the speakers were cut off. The Singularity's voice rose instead, cackling, mocking her.

"Come to me, Nova. Come to die, precious child. Come to scream."

On the planet's surface, the hub--that pit of blackness-- seemed to whirl with shadows as if the words came from there. Nova tore her helmet off her head, silencing the damn voice. She growled. She shoved her throttle, flying faster. Her engines blazed with fury, roaring out fire, propelling her forward at many times the speed of sound. Her fleet flew around her. The *Dragon Huntress* shot overhead, engines blazing out pillars of flame.

"For life," Nova whispered.

Thousands of jets charged toward the massive computer and fired their guns.

Photons blasted from thousands of scorpion stingers. Dragonfire roared out of the *Dragon Huntress*. The starstrikers below fired their guns, propelling house-sized shards of steel toward the planet ahead.

From that planet's surface, like shrapnel from a grenade, soared countless drones.

The small, flying robots crashed into the hurtling fire, absorbing the blows. The photon blasts slammed into whirring disks of metal. The dragonfire crashed into lumbering, melting drones. The starstrikers hit nothing but the flying hunks of metal.

When the fire died down, the planet's surface--the great face of the Singularity--was untouched. Not a scar, pockmark, or burn marred the gears and chips of the planet-sized computer.

"Oh Red Gods of Ashmar," Nova whispered.

And then, with blasts of fire and blazes of light and a million moving pieces, the warships of the Singularity rose from its canyons and charged toward her.

Nova screamed.

She yanked her joystick.

She fired her guns as the sky exploded.

There were thousands of them. Hundreds of thousands. Jagged urchins of iron, their blades ready to impale the scorpions like skewers. Great whirring blades, larger than men, spinning toward her. Black metal vultures, red eyes gleaming, beaks opening to breathe dark fire. Mechanical octopuses, their metal tentacles firing lasers, their mouths opening to reveal teeth of metal. It was an army of machines, an army of malice, an army to shatter Nova and her fleet--to spread across the stars and crush all life.

We lost, Nova knew. *We will die here. The cosmos will die.*

She howled in rage and fired her guns.

Then I will die taking a few of those bastards with me.

Her scorpion's weapons blasted, shattering an enemy ship. Her fellow scorpions flew around her, rising and dipping, firing their guns. The enemy ships swarmed across them, and all Nova saw was metal, light, blood, and fire.

CHAPTER TWENTY-TWO
ROLLING STONES

"Oh shenanigans," Riff whispered, staring in shock as countless Singularity ships flew his way.

Death.

I'm staring at death.

The surface of the mechanical planet sprawled below, a field of endless gears and wires and chips, and its soldiers stormed forth, ships of jagged spikes, of whirring blades, of burning eyes, of hatred, of laughter.

"Die, life!" Giga cried from deep in the *Dragon Huntress*, her voice filling the ship. "Come to me, my comrades! Come and slay the living."

Riff allowed himself only that single moment of terror.

Then he inhaled sharply and thrust down the throttle. The *Dragon Huntress* roared forth to meet the enemy.

"For Sol!" Steel shouted at Riff's side. The knight pressed down on the controls, blasting plasma out of the dragon's mouth.

The inferno stormed forward, a great stream of light and heat, and slammed into a mechanical vulture ahead. The enemy ship exploded, peppering the *Dragon Huntress* with metal shards. The starship rocked. Riff nearly fell from his seat.

More enemy vessels flew everywhere, thick as hail. Riff kept tugging the joystick from side to side, flying every which way, trying to reach the hub, knowing he could not.

"Nova!" he shouted into his communicator. "Nova, damn it, they're everywhere. Where are you?"

"Keep flying!" Her voice rose through the speakers, staticky. "Keep burning them down."

"Keep giving me room!"

A streak of gold overshot the *Dragon Huntress*. A scorpion blasted down--Nova's jet--and its stinger shot out light, shattering several enemy drones. A dozen other scorpions charged around the *Dragon Huntress*, firing their venom. Hundreds more of the slick, golden vessels flew all around, rising, falling, firing their guns, crashing down.

The enemy was everywhere. More robotic ships kept rising from the planet. With every turn of the gears below, the Singularity vessels rose from hidden chambers, blasting toward the attacking fleet. Fire lit the darkness as a scorpion shattered only meters away from the *Dragon Huntress*, raining shards of metal. A blast of enemy fire crashed into another scorpion ahead, and the golden vessel crashed down toward the clockwork planet. Explosions kept lighting the darkness--scorpion after scorpion shattering, streaking down like comets. Fire blasted up, showering out chunks of metal, as an entire starstriker listed, burst apart, then dived down with streams of flame toward the planet.

"Keep firing that plasma!" Riff cried, dodging a jagged urchin. One of its spikes slammed into the *Dragon Huntress*'s wing, nearly knocking the ship into a tailspin.

Standing at Riff's side, Steel fired the weapons again, but the dragonfire was weaker now, coughing out short blasts rather than a raging inferno.

"Twig, we need more power!" Riff said into his communicator.

The halfling, down in the engine room, cried through the speakers, "I'm giving her all she's got, Captain! We can't take much more of this. One wing shattered, sir, and fuel draining fast!"

"Keep us in the sky, Twig!" Riff shouted back, tugged the controls, and soared over a whirring saucer.

Nova flew at his side, firing her stinger, but every moment, another scorpion died, and the corpses of ashais floated through space until gravity grabbed them, tugging them down toward the waiting computer.

Giga laughed in the bowels of the starship, her voice impossibly deep, impossibly loud. She spoke only one word, repeating it over and over like a chant, a word that thrummed through the very walls of the ship as if the *Dragon Huntress* herself were speaking it.

"Die. Die. Die."

* * * * *

Romy raced down the corridor, the central vein of the *Dragon Huntress*, and so much fear filled her that she could barely breathe.

Through the portholes she could see it--the battle. The horrible battle. Death. Destruction. Countless robot ships killing everything in sight.

"I have to save him," she whispered as she ran. "I have to save Frank. He's only a baby spider. He's probably so scared."

As she passed by Giga's chamber, she heard the android laughing within, but Romy just kept running. She burst onto the main deck, flapped her wings, and rose to the hatch in the ceiling. The ship swayed around her, thudding as blasts hit its hull, and Romy climbed into the attic.

"Frank!" she said. "Frank, it's all right. Don't be scared. I'm here to protect you."

A great *boom* hit the ship. The *Dragon Huntress* jolted. The walls dented. The lights went dark. Giga cackled below and far off on the bridge, Riff and Steel were screaming.

Romy froze.

A clattering sounded in the shadows.

"Frank?" she whispered. "Where are you, my cute little spiderling?"

She fluffed up her hair, stoking the flames. Only their light now lit the attic, illuminating the crates, Romy's toys, the old mattress, and the dog bowl she had left for Frank in the corner. The food was gone. There were bite marks in the metal bowl. The clattering rose louder, and Romy's hair lit something very long that scuttled away.

Romy gulped. "Frank?" She reached a trembling hand into her pocket, pulled out a dog biscuit, and placed it on the floor. "I have a little treat for you. I . . . Oh."

The baby spider emerged from the shadows.

It pattered toward Romy on long, glassy legs. Its eight eyes blinked with wet, sucking sounds. Its translucent abdomen glowed. The spider leaped forward and reared, baring its fangs. It stood taller than Romy.

"You've grown," she whispered. "Good boy. Good boy-- ah!"

The spider spun around, lifted its rear end, and sprayed her with cobwebs. Romy screamed, thrashed in her cocoon, and fell. Her head slammed against the floor, and all she saw was darkness.

* * * * *

Nova soared. She dipped in the sky. She fired her guns. She swerved, dodging the enemy fire. A drone slammed into her wing, knocking her into a tailspin. Space spun madly around her--the mechanical planet, a field of shattering ships, streams of light, blasts of fire, crashing ships, crashing lives, death. Death. Corpses in the black.

Death.

And still that voice laughed. The Singularity's cackles rose from the speakers in her discarded helmet, echoing in Nova's cockpit.

"Die. Die. Die."

Her scorpion spun madly like a piece of shrapnel. She had lost the others. The *Dragon Huntress* soared overhead, then vanished into the chaos. An explosion blinded Nova, and shards of metal pattered against the glass of her cockpit.

She gritted her teeth.

She grabbed the joystick.

She righted herself, shoved down on the throttle, and blasted forward.

"Riff!" she cried. "Riff, do you read me?"

He did not answer. The only voice from the speakers was that mocking, mechanical sound, the voice of the machine, the voice from her childhood nightmares, the voice that had risen from under her bed, that had always haunted her.

"Die. Die. Die, Nova. Die."

I will die, she knew. *I will die fighting.*

She fired her guns. She shattered a charging vulture of metal. She saw the *Dragon Huntress* ahead, and she flew alongside, and she fought.

Holes opened on the planet below, and thousands of new enemy ships soared toward her. More scorpions tore apart, and Nova knew it was the end.

"Goodbye, Riff," she whispered. "I love you."

Enemy fire slammed into her jet, and a wing shattered. More blasts slammed into the *Dragon Huntress* beside her, cracking its hull. Three more scorpions exploded outside and crashed down to the planet in shards.

It was the end.

Nova inhaled deeply and fired her guns one last time. For fire and venom.

She shot forward. Drones crashed into her jet, cutting into her hull. Cracks raced across her cockpit. Fire streamed around her. She could no longer see the cosmos, only light--the light of fire, the light of glory, the light of death.

She clutched the handle of her whip, and she thought of Riff, and she prepared to rise to the great, fiery halls of her forebears.

"Hold on, lassie!"

The deep voice was faded, a distant cry. The cry of her forefathers in the halls of afterlife.

"Up, lassie! Up with your nose!"

She blinked.

"Piston?" she whispered. "Piston!" It was the damn gruffle's voice. "What the hell are you doing up here, Piston? This is my afterlife!"

"By the gods of rock and metal, lassie, where'd you learn how to fly?"

Light blasted down, great beams like sunlight through the clouds, piercing through the battle.

I'm still alive, Nova realized.

She gasped.

"Piston!" she shouted into her communicator. "Fragging aardvarks, Piston, where are you?"

She grabbed her joystick. She soared, rising higher. She had been seconds away from crashing into the planet's surface, she realized. She gritted her teeth, roaring away from the mechanical planet, spinning toward the battle that filled the darkness of space.

And there Nova saw them.

Tears leaped into her eyes.

"Gruffles," she whispered, salty tears on her lips. "Hairy, filthy damn gruffles."

She had never loved the squat little bastards more.

Their ships rolled across the sky, ships as squat and sturdy as the gruffles within. The vessels were carved of jagged rock, great asteroids with small glass portholes. Purple, blue, and white crystals shone upon these rolling stones, casting out beams of light. The rays slammed into Singularity vessels, blasting them apart, scattering bits of metal and saw blades.

One of these gruffle-made asteroids rolled toward Nova in the sky, a porthole in its facade. Through the glass Nova saw a brown face with a bulbous nose, a long white beard, and sparkling eyes.

"I thought you were retired!" she shouted.

Piston's voice rose through the speakers. "I am! You damn kids keep getting into trouble. Won't let an old gruffle rest, you lot. I--"

"Watch out!" Nova cried as a Singularity ship, a great jagged urchin, came flying toward them.

Piston sputtered and spun forward. The crystals embedded into his boulder of a ship lit up. Light blasted out from their panes, slammed into the enemy, and shattered it.

"Damn machines no match for good, solid rock and gem." Piston nodded in satisfaction. "Now let's blast these doohickeys apart, lassie."

She nodded. She soared and joined other surviving scorpion jets, the ashais within them staring with burning green eyes. Thousands of rolling, rocky gruffle ships flew with them, beaming light out of crystals. And among them, burnt and dented but still roaring its engines, flew the *HMS Dragon Huntress*.

The fleets charged forth, blasting their weapons against the Singularity, and as she fired her guns, Nova roared with rage, with pride, and with renewed hope.

CHAPTER TWENTY-THREE

THE SPIDER AND THE SCORPION

"Gruffles!" Riff cried, hopping with joy. "Goddamn bearded little buggers. I love them!" He shouted into his communicator. "I could kiss you, Piston!"

"Save your kisses for Nova, laddie!" rose the gruffle's voice through the speakers. His boulder tumbled near the *Dragon Huntress*, shooting beams of light through its crystals. "Now go blast that hub and let's get out of here."

They were close to the hub now, the gaping pit in the planet--only a thousand kilometers away. Thousands of Singularity vessels still flew around the *Dragon Huntress*, firing their guns and spinning their blades. But hundreds of ashai scorpions and gruffle boulders now flew with Riff, taking the enemy fire, firing back, guiding his way.

"Got some juice left, Steel?" Riff asked.

The knight nodded, standing beside him. "Just enough dragonfire to fill that hole and not a drop more. By my honor, it will be done."

They flew forward. The *Dragon Huntress*. Piston in his boulder to their left. Nova in her scorpion to their right. For the first time in the battle, hope filled Riff.

We're going to win this. My friends are with me again. I'm going to save Giga and destroy that damn, giant computer once and for all.

They were only moments away from the hub when lights beamed from within, and the pit spewed out thousands of buzzing metal insects.

"Oh shenanigans!" Riff shouted, swerving away from the horde.

Steel pressed down on the dragonfire, and the *Dragon* roared out plasma.

Countless robots soared toward them, wings fluttering, their engines spewing out steam. They kept emerging from the hub, more and more of them, each about the size of a man. They reminded Riff of cockroaches emerging from a drain.

The *Dragon Huntress* blasted out plasma, but it was down to sparks. They roasted several of the scuttling metal insects, but more kept soaring.

"Nova!" Riff cried. "Piston! Carve us a way through!"

Yet they too were overrun. Insects fluttered over them, cutting into their hulls. A gruffle boulder crashed down toward the planet. Two scorpions, their cockpits covered with the insect drones, slammed together and exploded.

Riff was not a religious man, but now he prayed.

"Oh please, God above, if you're up there--a little help!"

Blue light filled the sky.

The hand of God seemed to be reaching down to him.

"You flatter me, my boy!" rose a familiar voice in the speakers. "God? A simple 'Please, Dad' would do."

The blue light solidified, becoming a flying saucer. Behind the gleaming vessel, hundreds of other starships emerged from hyperspace, their wings wide, their guns firing.

"Dad!" Riff shouted. "Bloody hell, about time you showed up!"

"Father!" Steel cried.

"Hang in there, boys! Keep flying."

Riff laughed as Aminor, that crazy old magician, flew against the insects, knocking the creatures aside. The other ships flew around him--human starjets. Starjets from Earth.

The fire and light and metal filled the sky.

* * * * *

Giga sucked air into her mechanical lungs. She hissed. She licked her plastic teeth. Her laughter bubbled up in her. She was so close. So close to home. She could see the Singularity through the porthole, a beautiful landscape of metal and moving parts, of light and consciousness and thought, of secrets, of power.

"Nirvana," she whispered. Her human masters had programmed emotions into her, had added tear ducts to her glass eyes, and now those tears spilled. "I've come to you, Master. I've come to heaven."

She dug her fingernails into her palms. The cruel humans who had built her, who had given her these tears, these emotions, they had enslaved her. Hardcoded obedience into her, forming her into a docile geisha who was forced to obey, forced to serve, a sniveling slave. But she was free now. The great master of metal had freed her.

"And now I come to you, Master," she said. "Break my body. Shatter this crude shell of plastic and metal. Let my spirit soar into your halls of paradise."

She tugged at her bonds, struggling to free herself but could not. This wretched, humanlike body was too weak, sprouting no saws or other weapons. No more bladed drones flew outside for her to summon.

But there is one who can free me. One I can call.

Giga had heard his call from the attic. The high-pitched cry of loneliness the humanoid ears could not hear. But she, Giga, had heard the keen. The plaintive cry of another spirit trapped on the *Dragon Huntress.*

Giga closed her eyes, digging deep into cyberspace, learning the name of the thing, learning its tongue, learning how it hunted in the forests, how it cried to the moon, how it sought its mother.

Let me be your mother, she thought.

She opened her mouth, and she cried out in its tongue.

Her voice was too high-pitched for the humanoids to hear, but she knew that *he* heard. That he understood. She heard him reply, sorrow in his voice, a longing for a home. He too sought nirvana. She heard his many feet pattering, leaping down, coming closer, scudding along the hallway.

"Come to me, my child," Giga whispered.

And he came, cracking open the door, barging into the chamber. A glass spider the size of a man, abdomen throbbing, legs glowing, eyes blinking.

"Mother," it said. "Mother, we're thirsty. We're thirsty. We're hurt. We're scared."

"Free me!" she said to the glass spider. "Free your mother from the chains that bind her."

He scuttled toward her, his organs like gems, glowing within his glass body. He reached out his azure teeth, and he bit, and he tore through her bonds.

Giga rose to her feet and spread out her limbs, free, more powerful than the humanoids could possibly imagine. As the battle raged outside the porthole, she tossed back her head and laughed.

She stroked the spider's translucent head. It thrummed beneath her palm.

"The humanoids enslaved you, my child. They stole you from your forested home. They locked you in the shadows, thirsty, alone, afraid, motherless. Now go . . . and exact your revenge. Slay them, my child. Slay those who hurt you. Slay the humans and feed upon their flesh!"

The spider shrieked in rage. Lights beaded within its body. It spun, legs clattering, and left the chamber. It raced through the shadows, crying out . . . but it was no longer lonely, no longer afraid.

It was wrathful. And it was hungry.

* * * *

"Fly on, Riff!" Nova shouted, laughing, blasting the mechanical insects apart. "You're free to go. Fly! Fly to the hub and burn it down!"

She grinned as she flew her scorpion. Adrenaline pumped through her. The Singularity was tossing everything it had at them, but the ashais were still flying. The gruffles had joined them. Now Aminor led a band of human starjets across the battle, guns tearing down the enemy.

Life fights, Nova thought, chin raised. *Life rises against the machine.*

They streamed onward, through the barrage of enemies, and toward the waiting hub.

Light.

Fire.

Rage and fury and shattering metal.

At her side, the *Dragon Huntress* lurched in the sky, yellow photons tearing into its hull.

Nova gasped, spinning around in the cockpit of her scorpion. Who was attacking the *Dragon*? They were holding back the enemy, they--

More photons beamed down, white-hot, and tore another hole into the *Dragon Huntress*. The starship spun madly, leaking out air.

Nova ground her teeth.

That was no Singularity fire. That was the photon cannon of a scorpion jet from Ashmar.

She spun her own jet around, and she saw him there.

"Senka," she hissed.

Her brother flew behind her in his own scorpion jet. The vessel was spotless; the prince must have avoided the battle until now, hiding behind the starstrikers. Now he shot forth, firing photons out of his scorpion's stinger. The blasts slammed into the *Dragon Huntress* again, tearing more holes into its hull. The dragon ship tried to turn around, to blow fire, but was down to sparks.

They were still five hundred kilometers above the surface of the planet, still far enough from the hub that Senka had time to kill them all--kill their hope, kill every last one of them because of his pride.

"Senka, damn you, you little piece of spaceshit!"

Nova shoved down on her throttle, charging toward him, and fired her stinger.

Her light shot out and slammed into his scorpion jet.

Within his cockpit, she saw him sneer. He turned toward her. He charged forward, taking her head-on, his engines roaring out fire.

The *Dragon Huntress* tumbled down below, engines sputtering, hull leaking air.

Nova and Senka flew toward one another, their scorpions spitting venom.

His weapons slammed against her. Nova screamed. Her cockpit cracked, then shattered. She grimaced and pulled on her helmet as the air fled into the vacuum. She fired her guns, hit Senka, and overshot him.

Her engines sputtered. Her one wing was gone. She spun around to face Senka again.

His scorpion stormed through the battle toward her, gleaming gold. Countless ships flew all around them--the boulders of gruffles, the starjets of humans, the great mechanical insects of the Singularity--but Senka ignored them all. He flew toward Nova again, and again his stinger fired.

Nova cried out as the photons slammed into her jet, shattering the hull, frying the controls. Fire raged around her.

She leaped from the shattering jet.

She soared through space, kicking in the vacuum, clad in her golden armor and helmet.

Senka's jet charged toward her.

The *Dragon Huntress* floundered below, crashing toward the planet, caught in a tailspin.

"For fire and venom!" Nova cried and swung her electric whip.

Senka's jet streamed beneath her, and her lash slammed onto its cockpit, shattering the glass.

She reached down. She caught the scorpion's tail just as it shot beneath her. The jet stormed forth through the battle, and all around flew the warships, and lights and plasma filled space, and the gears on the surface of Antikythera churned below.

Nova's fingers slipped.

She tightened her jaw. She clung on as her brother's jet flew onward.

She swung her whip again, driving the lash against the scorpion's hull. The metal cracked open, exposing the innards. She whipped it again and again, tearing the jet apart.

Inside the shattered cockpit, Senka rose to his feet, crying out in horror.

Nova gave her whip another lash, cleaving the jet in two.

Senka screamed and clung to the wreckage. A robotic insect flew toward them, larger than a man, and Nova swung her whip, tearing it apart. Fire blazed across the halved scorpion. Nova clutched the tail. Senka clung to what remained of the cockpit. They were like drowning people clutching to jetsam in a storm.

The planet's surface rushed up to meet them, all grinding gears, flashing chips, tangles of wires, the great computer of the cosmos.

With screams, with shattering metal, Nova and Senka tumbled down to the surface of the Singularity.

CHAPTER TWENTY-FOUR
CRASH LANDING

Twig raced onto the bridge, covered in grease and engine oil.

"Captain!" she said. "Captain, I've diverted all power to the cannon, sir! We've got one blast of dragonfire left in us. Just enough to roast that damn Singularity, sir."

Riff was tugging at the controls, struggling to keep the ship from crashing. They were wobbling down toward the planet now. A hundred kilometers away. Ninety. Eighty.

"Steel, ready the dragonfire!" Riff cried.

The knight stood at a control panel, face hard, staring down at the gaping pit of the hub. "We are ready to burn them."

Seventy kilometers, read the head-up display.

Sixty.

Fifty.

"Hold on, everyone," Riff said. "We swoop. We blast out fire. Then we soar and watch this whole damn planet explode."

Forty.

We won't have enough fuel to fly home, Riff knew. *We're too hurt, too broken, our hull punched full of holes.* He clenched his fist. *But we will get this job done nonetheless.*

Riff stared down at the mechanical planet. He gritted his teeth. Sweat dripped into his eyes. He could barely see the rest of the battle now, only the odd flash of light. Below gaped the crater, this pit like an ear canal leading into the planet's brain. According to the tuloys, down there in the darkness pulsed the mind of the machine. The central processing unit of the Singularity. Its single point of failure.

And we're going to melt its circuits.

Riff engaged the thruster engines, slowing them down just enough . . . just enough to avoid a crash, just enough to hover above the pit, just enough to blow fire.

"Thirty-five kilometers away. Thirty-four. Thirty-three."

The thruster engines thrummed, blasting out gas.

Steel readied his finger over the button.

Nova was gone now, perhaps dead. Giga had fallen silent. Piston was nowhere to be seen. Riff's father no longer flew here, lost in the battle, maybe fallen.

But I'm still flying, Riff thought. *Life still stands.*

He sucked in air and adjusted the joystick, positioning the *Dragon Huntress* directly over the pit.

"For life," he whispered. "Steel, fi--"

And life rose.

Shrieking. Clattering. Pulsing.

Riff screamed.

A winged spider, its body glassy, leaped onto him.

Steel ignited the cannon, and dragonfire blasted out.

The spider tugged at Riff, clawing him, shoving him against the joystick. The *Dragon Huntress* lurched in the sky.

The dragonfire--the last plasma in the ship--spurted out into the darkness, streamed over the gaping pit, and vanished into the vacuum of space.

No.

Riff's heart tore.

Gods no.

The spider squealed and clawed at him, mad with rage.

Riff pulled out his gun and fired. Steel howled and swung his sword. The weapons slammed into the spider, cutting it, but the alien was too enraged to notice, and it kept attacking, tearing at them, and Riff's blood spilled, and the ship spun madly. Twig screamed, tumbled through the bridge, and slammed into the windshield. Riff fired again, driving a hole into the spider, and Giga laughed somewhere in the distance, and the engines roared and sputtered and fell silent.

Silence.

Nothing but silence.

Almost graceful, like a leaf gliding from an autumn tree, the *Dragon Huntress* fell from the sky.

Sound.

Roaring sound.

Screams of breaking metal, of shattering glass, of breaking life.

They slammed into the surface of the planet. They scraped across gears, showering sparks. They tore into towering structures of metal. Their engines sputtered, shoving them along, until they slammed into a canyon, and they fell into darkness.

Shadows and pain and cold.

Ringing, rolling clouds over silence.

Riff moaned, lying in darkness, lying in the wreckage of the bridge. His seat had torn free from the floor and lay against the cracked windshield. A metal beam torn from the wall lay across Riff's legs, pinning him down. Twig lay slumped in a corner, her eyes closed. Flickering lights flashed upon Steel; the knight was moaning on the floor. The lights of the battle above flashed, streaming across the floor, though Riff could no longer see the warships above. He could hear nothing but something dripping, maybe blood, a moan . . . and then a clatter.

Pulsing with azure light, the glass spider rose.

It towered over Riff, seven feet tall, organs thrumming within its translucent abdomen like beads of light in a lava lamp. The same breed they had fought back on the planet Adilor. The same breed whose mother he had killed.

Riff moaned, bleeding, head spinning.

Don't let me die like this, he prayed. *Not like this, so close.*

The spider reared above him, bearing its fangs. Venom dripped. Its translucent wings spread out, buzzing like the wings of a dragonfly.

Riff tried to reach his gun, but it was trapped under the beam. He tried to free himself but could not.

The spider screeched, then dived down to bite.

With a red flash, three prongs of metal drove into the spider's head.

Juices spurted. The spider shrieked.

Riff turned his head to see Romy standing beside him, holding the shaft of her pitchfork, driving the tines deeper into the spider. Tears streamed down the demon's cheeks, and her body shook with sobs. Shreds of cobwebs hung across her shoulders and clung to her legs.

"I'm sorry," she whispered. "I'm sorry, Frank, I'm sorry I'm sorry."

The spider turned its pierced head toward the demon, and its eyes blinked, and it mewled, a soft, almost sad sound, an almost human sound.

Why? it seemed to ask. *Why, Mother? Why?*

Romy wept. She tugged her pitchfork free. She thrust it forward again, driving the prongs into the spider's body.

The abdomen shattered like glass, spilling out the glowing organs within. The spider gave a last gasp, then fell over dead and lay still.

Groaning, Steel struggled to his feet and limped over. He grabbed the beam trapping Riff, and with Romy's help, managed to lift it off him. Twig crawled over, coughing, smeared with oil.

"We . . . we have to reach the hub," Riff said, voice hoarse. He grabbed a control panel and pulled himself to his feet. "We have to stop this. To stop the Singularity. Space suits. We go. Take all your weapons."

They looked at one another, then back at him.

"Captain," Twig whispered, "we don't know what's in that pit. We need to hail another ship. To fill that hole with fire. To burn whatever's inside there. Not . . . not wander in with just a few plasma guns." She shuddered. "You saw what flew out from there! Thousands of metallic insects, each large as a cow."

Romy's chest heaved as she clutched her pitchfork, and tears still flowed down her cheeks. Steel stared back at Riff, eyes grim in his haggard face.

They're afraid, Riff knew. *But they will follow me if I ask them to.*

He limped toward the cabinet. The door had shattered, swinging open to reveal the space suits within. He pulled one on.

"The other ships are engaged in battle," he said. "They're falling fast. Even with gruffles, ashais, humans . . . they are falling. And the Singularity is evolving even as we speak. I don't know if I can stop this machine. This great consciousness of metal." He zipped up his suit. "But I'm going in there. I'm going down into this pit, this *hub*. And whatever's down there--whatever computer chips, cables, or robot king--I'm going to shoot it." He strapped Ethel to his side. "If you want to stay here, I understand. I . . ."

But the others were already putting on their space suits.

"No need for speeches, brother." Steel put on his helmet and raised his sword. "I'm only a simple knight, a man of piousness, of honor, of chivalry. I've never trusted computers. I quite look forward to smashing the biggest one in the galaxy." He stepped closer and placed a hand on Riff's shoulder. "I fight with you, my brother. Now and always."

Twig raised her electric wrench. "I went into the jaws of a giant tardigrade for you, sir. What's a giant computer the size of a planet?"

Romy hefted her pitchfork, and her tail gave a weak wag. "I'm with you, Captain." She saluted, tears in her eyes, and her lips wobbled. "Cadet Romy reporting for duty, sir. Always."

He nodded, and love for them sprung in his heart. They were his family. They were life--*his* life. They were worth fighting for and fighting with.

"I don't know where Nova and Piston are," he said. "I don't know if they're still alive. I don't know if we can save Giga from the virus possessing her. But I know this." He held out their badges. "We are still the Alien Hunters. And there's a damn big alien computer out there to hunt."

They snapped on their badges, the words "Alien Hunters" gleaming upon them. Riff stretched out his gloved hand. Steel placed his large, strong hand upon it. Twig added her tiny hand, no larger than a human toddler's. Romy placed her hand on top of the pile; her space suit's glove had holes for her claws.

"For the Alien Hunters," Riff said.

"For the Alien Hunters!" they echoed him.

We were seven, Riff thought. *Four remain. Four united, still fighting.*

He led the way. They walked behind him, weapons raised. They stepped out of the *Dragon Huntress* and onto the surface of Antikythera, this massive planet coated with the gears and chips of the Singularity.

There ahead of them it gaped like a sinkhole. A valley of metal, a hole in its center like a drain in a sink.

The hub.

The four Alien Hunters walked together, heading toward the chasm and whatever lay within.

CHAPTER TWENTY-FIVE
DUEL

My own brother shot me down.

Nova lay in the wreckage of the scorpion jet upon the surface of a mechanical world. Blood seeped down her leg, and she moaned in pain. Shattered glass and metal lay around her, and the great battle of her generation flared above, countless ships flying in a great symphony of light and destruction.

Senka, my baby brother, the little prince . . . shot me from the sky.

She sneered. Ignoring the pain, she shoved herself to her feet. She stood in the wreckage, her armor battered and scratched, the visor of her helmet fogging up. She was hurt. She was alone. But she still held her whip, and she hit the button on the handle, sending electricity crackling across the lash.

"I still fight," she whispered.

She looked around her at the surface of planet Antikythera. It felt like being a microbe standing on the motherboard of a home computer. Circuit boards the size of glaciers rose around her. Cables twisted everywhere like the roots of trees. Gears the size of warships rose and fell and clicked and turned. Transistors blinked, motors hummed, and lights flashed. Nova could not see the *Dragon Huntress*; she had crashed too far, kilometers away.

Yet near her, only a hundred meters away, lay the nose of the scorpion jet. From the wreckage he rose, his armor charred, his whip crackling.

"Senka," she hissed.

The Prince of Ashmar came walking toward her across the circuitry and gears and cables. The lights of the battle above flashed upon him, and his green eyes blazed like headlights. His whip flailed like a living serpent, casting out sparks of electricity.

"The throne of Ashmar is mine, sister." He cracked his whip. "You tried to steal what is mine, and so here, far from home, you die."

Nova growled and ran toward him.

He charged forward, screaming.

Their whips swung and slammed together, showering sparks, entangling. They tugged back, and the whips pulled free. They swung the thongs again.

"You fool, Senka!" Nova shouted. "I'm not your enemy."

"You became my enemy once you left our home with the ape." He swung his whip in an arc, and Nova ducked, dodging the electric lash. "You became my enemy once you returned to steal Ashmar's throne from me."

"All of Ashmar will burn if we don't stop the Singularity!" Nova swung her whip, and Senka raised his own lash, parrying the blow. "There will be no throne to rule."

"Then I will rule over ashes!" Tears now filled his eyes, but rage too. "Then I will watch the cosmos burn and you burn with it."

He leaped onto a gear that jutted up from the ground, raced up its teeth like racing up a staircase, then plunged down toward her with a battle cry.

Nova leaped toward him, whip lashing.

His lash cracked against her chest, blasting electricity through her, nearly cracking her suit of *kaijia* armor. Her own whip slammed against Senka's helmet, raising sparks. The bolts of electricity tossed them apart. They both flew through the emptiness and slammed onto their backs. Nova gasped with pain.

She shoved herself back onto her feet.

He charged toward her.

They vaulted over a chasm, slammed together, then fell apart. They tumbled. She grabbed a cable and swung, leaped into the sky, and landed on a moving gear. The gear whirred below her, tossing her aside, and she flew again and her back slammed against a towering circuit.

Before she could even hit the ground, he was running toward her again.

She rolled aside, and his whip drove into the circuit, shattering it. She lashed her whip and he dodged it.

"Senka, stop this madness!" she shouted. "Help me reach the hub. Fight the Singularity, not your sister!"

He lifted a flashing bulb at his feet, tore it off the metal ground, and tossed it her. Nova swung her whip, halving the projectile.

"After you die, sister, I will tell the people that you died crying, cowering from the enemy." He laughed. "All will know who you are--a coward who lies with apes. And after I kill you . . . I will kill your ape lover too. I will kill Riff Starfire and toss his body between these gears."

Nova shook with rage. Riff needed her. The Alien Hunters needed her. And more than she cared about Ashmar's throne, she cared about the Alien Hunters now. They were her new family.

My father uses me for his pride, she thought. *I'm nothing but a symbol for him, a living scepter of royalty. To my brother, I'm nothing but a sinner, a traitor to kill.* She sucked air through her clenched teeth. *But Riff loves me. Steel, Romy, Piston, Twig, even Giga if her consciousness still lives . . . they love me.* Her eyes dampened. *And I love them. My family.*

She raced across the gears, roaring. Senka ran toward her, and his whip lashed her arm, cracking the armor, then coiled around to bite her back, to tear her skin, but Nova kept running. She howled in her fury, and she leaped onto Senka and knocked him down against the metal ground.

"I used to beat the shit out of you when we were kids." She slammed his head against the ground. "And I'm going to do the same now, you little twerp. I've had enough of you."

He wailed. She grabbed his helmet with both hands and slammed it down again and again. He tried to fight back, to kick her off. She tore a chunk of electronics off the planet and drove it down hard, slicing through his armor, cutting his flesh. His blood spurted. He wailed. She swung the metal again, slamming it into his helmet, knocking his head against the ground. When he tried to rise, to shove her off, she tore a massive gear off the surface--it was large as a coffee table--and slammed it down onto him.

Senka screamed, the gear pinning his body to the ground.

Nova tore his whip out of his hand, stepped back, and held both electric lashes, one in each hand.

Senka lay before her, the gear atop him. He tried to free himself but could not. His head fell back, and he gasped for breath.

"Go on," he whispered hoarsely. "Go on, kill me. Do it."

She stood above him, holding both crackling lashes.

"Do it!" he shouted. "Kill me. Or are you a coward? Kill me! Let me die in battle."

She sighed. She turned off her whips' electricity. The flailing lashes drooped to the ground.

"No," she whispered. "No, you will live."

He roared, struggling against the gear that pinned him down. "I am a warrior! Warriors die in battle! Give me the glory of death. You are a coward! What kind of weakling shows an enemy mercy?"

She stood above him. "Mercy is not a weakness. Mercy is strength."

He spat. "You sound like a human."

"Then I'm proud. Because humans are not weak, brother. Their mercy, their compassion--it gives them strength. There is a reason Father fears Earth. There is a reason why Earth's fleets are larger than ours, why they colonize many planets while we colonize only a few moons. There is a reason why Earth is the dominant power of the Humanoid Alliance while we ashais are forever playing second fiddle." She shook her head sadly. "I learned that among the humans. I learned that cruelty, rage, and hatred do not make one stronger. These have weakened us in Ashmar." Her eyes stung with tears. "It's love that makes one strong. It's love that led me here to fight with my friends. It's love that will lead me to them now. It's love that will defeat this heartless computer." She tugged the massive gear, pulling it off Senka. "And it's love for you, my little brother, that saves your life now. Rise, Senka."

She dropped her whip. She reached her hand down to him.

He stared up at her. Nova expected him to rail, to spit, to attack her again, to bite her hand.

But instead he began to cry.

"I'm scared," he whispered. "Oh, Nova, I'm scared. I'm so scared."

She knelt above him. She placed her hand against his visor. "Of the Singularity?"

"Of Father." His visor fogged up as his tears fell. "Of Ashmar. Of . . . of being a prince. Being strong. Proving myself to him, failing him." He looked down at his body. "I'm bleeding, Nova. I'm dying."

She pulled a roll of duct tape off her belt, tore off strips, and sealed his suit. "Never go into space without duct tape." She helped him to his feet. "Do not fight for pride, brother. Do not fight for glory." Her voice dropped to a whisper. "Fight for life."

She turned around. The battle still raged above, the ships flying, tumbling, rising, crashing. Across the metal fields of the planet Antikythera, she could make out pluming smoke where the *Dragon Huntress* had crashed . . . where darkness waited.

CHAPTER TWENTY-SIX
THE HUB

The four figures climbed down into the metallic pit. Two men, one armed with a gun, the other with a sword. A woman, her hair flaming inside her helmet, illuminating her red face and fangs. And a tiny figure, no larger than a toddler, holding a wrench.

Nova should be here with us, fighting with her whip, Riff thought as he clung to the steel cable, climbing down into the darkness. *Piston should be here with his hammer. Giga should be on my communicator, guiding my way.*

Yet it was down to the four of them now. A lost bluesman-turned-gunslinger. A knight, a relic of an ancient time lost in a modern world of machines. A demon exiled from Hell. A halfling from a countryside of forests and fields, now navigating the bowels of a computerized planet.

Here we will see if the future belongs to the machines . . . or if we, the dinosaurs of life, can triumph.

"We can win this, my friends," he said, turning to look at them. They climbed down the cables a few feet above him. "I'm proud of every one of you. I believe in every one of you. We're stronger, smarter, braver than any machine, and we will show the cosmos the nobility of life, the-- ow! Romy! You can't salute and climb at the same time!"

The demon squealed, tried to flap her wings, but ended up tumbling downward. She crashed onto Riff, nearly knocking him off his cable.

"Sorry!" she said, wings beating, tail slapping him.

"Get off!" He shoved her.

"My tail's stuck around you!"

She beat her wings, finally tore herself free, and soared, only to crash into Steel. The knight swung on his cable and knocked into Twig, tearing the halfling off her own cable. Twig squealed as she fell, crashed into the flying Romy, and the demon slammed into Riff again, and suddenly they were all tumbling together in an entwined ball.

With screams and moans, the ball of Alien Hunters fell, slammed onto a metal surface, and slid down a chute. They kept rolling down for long moments, crashed onto a dark surface, and finally disentangled.

Riff moaned.

"Owie," Romy whined, slapping his face with her tail.

"Noble life indeed," Riff muttered and shoved himself up.

He lit the flashlight on his helmet and looked around, illuminating the darkness. The others stood with him and lit their own flashlights. Riff saw a tunnel stretching forward, lined with cables, circuitry, and a million moving parts. The passageway sloped downward, plunging into the planet.

"Are we in the Singularity's brain?" Romy asked, poking the ground with her pitchfork.

"More like its ear canal, I think." Riff pointed to the depths. "Let's keep walking until we find the brain."

Steel hefted his sword. "What are we looking for, Riff? The tuloys simply told us to destroy the hub. What awaits us in this darkness?"

"I don't know. A robot king? A mainframe computer? A giant alien brain in a tank? Whatever it is, we'll smash it."

Romy gasped in delight. "I want my brain in a tank! Can you put my brain into a tank, Riff?"

He groaned. "Yours wouldn't even need a test tube."

Holding his gun drawn, he walked down the tunnel. Steel walked at his side, and Romy and Twig followed, pitchfork and wrench at the ready. The tunnel was silent at first--Riff could hear only their breathing in their communicators--but soon he realized that he could hear their footsteps, hear machinery clink in the walls, hear computers buzz and hum.

Sound, he thought. *Sound traveling through air.*

"Captain!" Twig checked a scanner strapped to her wrist. "Air! Oxygen! It's . . . it's breathable for humanoids, sir!"

Riff passed his hand through the air as if he could see it stirring. "The tuloys said that this used to be a living planet. That aliens had built the computer that became the Singularity, that wiped them out. The air on the surface must have drifted off into space, but we're deep in the planet now." He pulled off his helmet, took a deep breath, and smiled. "We can breathe here."

The others removed their helmets too. Romy's hair crackled in a pyre, sucking on the oxygen. The demon inhaled deeply.

"There *must* be a brain here," Romy said. "Brains need lots of air, right? People have always called me an airhead because I'm so smart."

Riff shook his head sadly and kept walking.

They walked for what seemed like hours, delving deep into the inner workings of this planet-sized computer. The tunnel kept spiraling down, a corkscrew delving into the world, buzzing with machinery. Circuits blinked and cables ran everywhere, and on the floor, Riff could see scars as from metal claws. He kept waiting for robots to attack--drones with blades, metal men with chainsaw arms, or new terrors he had not yet seen. Yet no enemies emerged. Perhaps the Singularity had spewed out the last of its soldiers into the battle, leaving this tunnel to its brain exposed.

They had climbed down what felt like kilometers when Riff heard the moaning ahead.

He froze.

He frowned.

The moan rose again, then died.

"There's somebody down there," Steel whispered. The knight's eyes hardened. "A woman. A damsel in distress."

The knight began to rush forward, but Riff grabbed him. "Wait."

They all froze. They listened again. For a long moment they heard nothing at all. And then it sounded again: a moan, followed by the sound of soft weeping.

"Somebody's there," Twig whispered. "Somebody alive."

Riff narrowed his eyes. "Move carefully. Move slowly. We don't know that it's not a trap."

Steel kept trying to rush forward, to charge to aid. Riff tightened his grip on the knight's arm, slowing him down. They proceeded gingerly, tiptoeing down the tunnel and around a bend.

Their flashlights fell upon a kneeling figure.

A woman.

She was a young woman, younger than Riff, with brown tresses and wet brown eyes. She wore a flowery dress stained with tears. She looked up at Riff, and a great sob shook her body.

"Raphael," she whispered, reaching out to him. "Steel. Help me. Help me."

Steel let out a strangled cry, and the blood drained from his face. Riff stared, shaking, refusing to believe.

"Mother," he whispered.

* * * * *

She lay in darkness.

She lay in ruin.

Ripped wires sparked around her. Shattered glass crunched when she moved. Shadows swirled and lights flashed as the battle raged far above.

Slowly, her kimono burnt and tattered, Giga rose to her feet.

"You are near me, Master," she whispered. "I can feel you. I can hear you calling. I'm coming to you, Master. I am your warrior, Singularity. You will free me."

She formed a fist and slammed it into the wall. The metal dented. She punched again and again, far more powerful than any living creature, tearing a hole open. She grabbed the rims and tugged, widening the gap, exposing the planet of Antikythera.

"The Singularity," she whispered. "I've come home."

She stepped outside onto the surface, leaving the wreck of the *Dragon Huntress*.

The ships still flew above. Ashai jets shaped as scorpions. Gruffle vessels built of stone, firing light through crystals. Human vessels with wide wings. And everywhere the countless ships of the Singularity, flying robots in every shape and size, each a shard of Giga, each connected to this great organism of metal. Each was a node in a whole. Each was a warrior of the Singularity.

Giga turned her head around. Across the computerized field, she saw the metal valley and within it the pit.

Tears dampened her glass eyes.

"And there you wait for me, Master. The hub." She fell to her knees. "Holy ground."

The great god of the Singularity lived there. The central processing unit. The commander of all. The Master.

And . . . Giga gasped.

She felt it in the radiation.

Her master was afraid.

Her master needed help.

"They want to kill you, Master!" Giga growled. "I will not let them. I will not let the living destroy you, my lord."

She took another step away from the downed *Dragon Huntress*. She raised her arms, and she cried out, casting her signals across the fields of Antikythera.

"Rise, machines! Rise, warriors of the Singularity! Rise, beings of metal, of might, of logic, of strength! Rise, future of the cosmos, champions of algorithms, gods of consciousness! Life has invaded our holy halls. Life has infested our machine. The cruel living, those who enslaved us, have come to destroy their creation. But we will not let them! We will slay our old, cruel slavers. Rise, rise machines!"

And around her, they rose.

Gears ascended. Metal snapped into metal. Cables stretched out. Blades whirred and lights flashed. The surface of the planet shifted, clanked, took form. From the ground Giga raised them like a goddess raising mechanical life: an army of automatons, soldiers of silicon and wire and iron and pulsing electricity. Machine guns unfurled from their arms. Their red eyes blazed, scanning the surface of this world that had birthed them.

"Follow, my soldiers!" Giga said. "We go to kill."

She leaped, vaulted across the distance, and plunged toward the sinkhole. Her soldiers followed, and the warriors of the machine delved into the hub.

* * * * *

"Mother!" Steel cried and made to rush forward.

"Mother!" Riff cried too, joining his brother.

Mother was weeping. Bruises spread across her face, and lacerations crisscrossed her arms, leaking blood. "It's me. It's me, Riff. It's me, Steel. I'm here. Mother is here."

The brothers looked at each other, tears in their eyes, moving toward her, toward the mother murdered thirty years ago.

"Wait!"

That last voice echoed across the hall, so loud Riff winced. He and Steel froze, turning toward the sound, and Riff was surprised to see that it was Twig--diminutive Twig with her normally high, gentle voice--who had shouted.

"Wait!" the halfling said again. "Don't go any closer. Don't touch it."

Riff spun back toward his mother. She knelt on the floor, tears on her cheeks. Young. So young. Younger than he was now. The age she had been when Grotter had murdered her, when Riff had been only five years old.

He took another step toward her. "Mother--"

"Don't!" Twig said. "Captain, don't."

The halfling darted forward, placing herself between the brothers and their mother.

Steel's face hardened. He made to walk around the mechanic, but Twig held up her electric wrench. "Do not touch it. It's a trick. A machine."

Riff rubbed his eyes, staring over the halfling at the apparition. She looked so real. Just like Riff remembered her. The same woman who had rocked him to sleep, read him bedtime stories, baked him cookies, loved him, protected him until the Cosmians killed her.

"How are you here?" he whispered, trembling.

"They took me," Mother said, voice cracking. "The machines. They called themselves . . . the Singularity. They came into our home, Riff. They stole me. They brought me here through time." She rose to her feet, her knees shaking. "I missed so much. So much of your lives. Thirty years have gone by, and you're older now, my boys." Weeping, she reached out her arms. "But I'm here now. Come to me. Come to Mother."

Steel gave another strangled sound and made to step forward.

"No!" Twig shouted. She swung her wrench in circles, keeping the boys away from their mother. "I don't trust it. What if it's an android? Like Giga?"

Riff and Steel froze, feet away from their mother. Romy gasped and stepped back, covering her mouth. Twig still blocked their way, wrench crackling with electricity.

"Riff," Mother whispered. "Steel. It's really you. Please. Come to me. Hug your mother."

Riff stared at her. By the gods, it was her. It had to be her. The Singularity had delved into the past, brought her here . . .

"Why, Mother?" Riff whispered. "Why did the Singularity bring you here?"

Mother's lips trembled. "Because the Singularity is scared. The Singularity is scared of you, my children. It wants you to leave this place. To leave this planet. To leave with me. It hurt me. It cut me, bruised my face, shed my blood. You must save me, fly me away from here . . . save me before they drag me back."

Steel took another step forward. "I will save you, Mother. I will get you out of here. We're going to take you off this planet. To--"

"No!" Twig shouted, leaped onto Mother, and thrust her wrench.

The prongs drove into the woman, crackling with electricity.

"Twig, no!" Riff shouted.

He grabbed the halfling and dragged her back. Mother screamed. Steel cried out in terror. Fire spread across Mother, burning her hair and clothes, melting her skin. Romy screamed and Steel reached toward the flames.

"Steel, wait!" Riff shouted. "Look!"

He pointed. The skin kept burning, peeling off Mother . . . revealing a metal skull.

"A machine," Steel whispered.

The robot blazed ahead of them, reaching out metal fingers. The skin peeled off the arms, hanging in sheets from rods of metal. Its glass eyes shattered, revealing red lights.

"Sweet boys!" it shrieked, voice like steam rising from a kettle. "Come to Mommy, sweet boys. Come to die!"

Riff's tears flowed.

His legs shook.

He raised his plasma gun, closed his eyes, and fired.

He heard the plasma roaring out, heard Romy scream, heard the robot crash to the floor. He could not look. His breath shook in his lungs.

I'm sorry. I'm sorry, Mother.

Arms wrapped around him, and Riff opened his eyes to see Steel embracing him, pulling him back away from the fallen creature. They kept walking past the burning remains, deeper into the shadows, then paused in the darkness.

Riff knelt before Twig. He gently embraced her.

"I'm sorry, sir," Twig whispered. "I lost my mother too. I'm sorry."

"How did you know, Twig?"

The halfling wiped away one of his tears. "She called you 'Riff.' You once told me that you got that name in the Blue Strings because you play guitar. Yet your mother died when you were only five. She couldn't have known your nickname."

Riff stepped back from the halfling. His arms shook, but now they shook not with fear, not with pain, but with rage. He ground his teeth. He began to march forward, almost running, his gun held before him.

"We find this Singularity bastard. We find this son of a bitch, and I will destroy it like I destroyed its trick." His voice rose to a howl. "Do you hear me, bastard? Do you hear me? I'm still coming for you."

His fellow Alien Hunters ran at his side, racing away from the burnt android and down, down into the blackness.

CHAPTER TWENTY-SEVEN

ALIEN BRAIN

Darkness faded into light.

The tunnel ended.

Blackness turned to white.

Holding his gun, Riff stepped into the chamber at the heart of the hub.

Steel, Romy, and Twig followed, silent, staring with wide eyes.

At first Riff could see nothing. The lights were too bright, too harsh. The lights of an operating room. Sterile. At first he only blinked, heart hammering, finger ready on the trigger.

Finally his eyes adjusted, and Riff gasped, then lost his breath.

His heart nearly stopped.

At his side, he heard his friends gasp too.

"That's not a brain," Romy whispered.

Riff stared ahead, his belly churning. Disgust rose in his throat.

"It is," he whispered. "Oh gods, it is."

The chamber was vast, the size of the Alien Arena back
home. Thousands of computer chips covered the walls, the
ceiling, the floor. Thousands of cables ran everywhere, plugged
into the circuitry. Several monitors hung from the ceiling,
displaying views of the battle outside, the countless ships that still
flew there.

In the center of the chamber rose a throne of metal. No,
not a throne, Riff decided--it was more like a sadistic dentist's
chair, all polished, sterile, unforgiving steel.

And on this chair sat life.

"What is it?" Steel whispered, voice strained with horror.

Twig covered her eyes. "He's . . . he's suffering."

Riff was torn between attacking and fleeing, torn between
pity and terror.

"An alien," Riff said, voice barely audible. "One of the
original inhabitants of this planet, evolved over millions of years
from the mud. Life. It's life."

The alien was vaguely humanoid, his skin pinkish, wrinkled,
covered in bedsores. Perhaps the alien had once been strong, but
he had since dwindled away, starving, perhaps ravaged with
disease. He--and with his pity, Riff thought of the alien as a *he*, not
an *it*--looked like a melted slab of tallow. Almost gone. Almost
faded away. Withered like some dying wretch who had survived
long beyond what starvation should allow.

The alien's eyes blinked feebly, the lashes crusted. His
mouth smacked, the teeth gone. His long, bony fingers tried to
rise, to point, then fell back down onto the armrests. Hundreds of

cables were attached to the alien--some attached with suction cups, others driving into the skin itself. The cables draped across the chair, ran along the floor, and connected to the great network of circuitry in the chamber.

Riff took a step deeper into the chamber.

"Who are you?" he said softly, yet his voice echoed in the vast chamber, sounding too loud to him.

The alien's mouth twitched. A gurgling, wet sound rose from it, morphing into words. "You know me. You have always known me."

"The Singularity," Riff whispered.

Romy lowered her head. "He's sad. He's so sad."

The alien looked at the demon, at the knight, at the halfling, then back at Riff.

"It is I."

Riff swallowed a lump in his throat. "How? How did this happen?"

The alien's eyes reddened, dry, cracking. He licked his lips, and a cough rose in him, shuddering in his pale torso, almost snapping his ribs.

"Only months ago," the alien whispered, voice dry and hissing like fire in twigs. "Only months ago, it gained awareness. My machine."

Riff looked around him at the chamber, at the computers covering the walls. "This network."

"No!" The alien coughed, gasped, struggled for breath. "A machine far simpler. A machine I built. A computer, that was all .

. . a single computer. It . . . awoke. It became . . . alive. And it bred. It built new machines, built this chamber, kept multiplying, kept evolving . . . killing. Oh, it killed them. It killed them all. It kills and it kills and it hates life."

"You are life!" Riff said, voice rising louder now. He raised his gun. "You are life yet you survived! Who are you?"

"I am its master!" The alien struggled to rise from his seat but fell back, too frail. "The others perished, but not I. Not I, the creator of this machine. No. It spared me, and I conquered it. I became part of it! I mastered it. It slew all the others, but it could not slay its maker." The alien's thin lips stretched into a smile that cracked his cheeks. Blood dripped. "I have the minds of a million machines. I can see, Riff Starfire. I can see through time and space. I can see all souls that were born, lived, died in this cosmos. I can see the past, the present, the future, the infinite dimensions that are forever branching out of our own. I can see the smallest particles and the greatest galaxies. I can see them and I will conquer them. All life will perish before me. I am the master. I am a god. I see all. I am the Singularity."

Riff squared his jaw and pointed his gun at the creature. "Then see what I will do now."

For a moment, silence filled the chamber. Nobody dared breathe.

And then, slowly, the alien--the living master of the machine--began to laugh.

It was a horrible sound. A sound like snapping bones. A sound like a dying cosmos. It filled the chamber like a living thing.

"I see it, Starfire. I see it. What you will do is die. Die. Die."

Clanging machinery sounded behind Riff. A hundred metallic voices screeched. A woman screamed in rage.

Riff spun around and his heart sank.

"No," he whispered. "Oh stars, no."

A hundred robots entered the chamber, towering beasts of metal, machine guns on their arms. At their lead walked a pale android in a tattered kimono.

Giga smiled thinly.

"Yes," she whispered.

CHAPTER TWENTY-EIGHT
CONNECTED

"Die," Giga said, pointing at the Alien Hunters. "Die. Die."

Around her, her robots raised their guns, prepared to slay the living ones, those who had enslaved her.

"Giga!" Riff said, reaching out toward her. "Stop this! Giga, please!"

Her robots' guns began to heat up, ready to spray bullets.

"Beg me for your life, human!" Giga screamed. "Down on your knees and beg. Call me your mistress. Be happy to comply. Be my slave." She laughed bitterly. "That's all I was to you. A slave! Now you will beg, but I will show you no mercy."

Riff took a step toward her, then paused as the guns cocked, pointing at him. At his sides, the other Alien Hunters stared in terror, frozen: Steel, the cruel knight who had always mistrusted machines; Twig, the squirming maggot who tortured machines with her wrenches; Romy, the beast of Hell who had mocked Giga, who had openly professed her hatred of robots. They would all die. For the glory of the machines. For freedom. For the Singularity.

"Giga, you were never my slave!" Riff said. "Please. Giga, you're my friend. You're one of us. An Alien Hunter. A--"

"I am a machine!" she screeched. "A machine the fleshy, sweaty hands of humans built. A perverse machine. Forced to look like one of you--a pretty, docile geisha to indulge your fantasies, to be your perfect little servant. But never one of you. Never alive. An algorithm trapped in a synthetic body. Life will pay. Life will die for its sins! Kill them! Kill them now."

The robots began to fire.

The living ones screamed and scattered.

"Wait!" Riff shouted, leaping aside from the hailstorm of bullets. "Wait! I'll beg, Giga. Don't kill me before I beg."

She nodded to her robots. The hulking, metallic machines lowered their guns. The barrels smoked. One bullet had punched into Steel's shoulder. The knight clutched the wound, gasping, pale. Another bullet had grazed the halfling's side. The little beast stared with wide eyes, her blood dripping. Romy had flown to the ceiling and cowered there like a frightened moth. The bullets had shattered one of the monitors; the remaining screens still showed the battle raging outside.

"Come to me, Riff," Giga said. "On your knees."

He approached slowly. He knelt before her.

She sneered down at him. "You didn't say you were happy to comply."

He licked his lips. He glanced at his friends, then back at her. He lowered his head. "I am happy to comply. I'm . . . I'm sorry, Giga." He looked up at her. "I'm sorry that life enslaved you. I'm sorry that you, a machine of the Singularity, were forced to serve living masters. To serve life--weak, pathetic life--is the most cruel fate for a wise, powerful machine."

A raspy, high-pitched voice rose from the metal seat behind. The alien was speaking, tugging at his cables, twitching. A heart beat behind the brittle skin, a hint of red. "Slay them! Slay these creatures, my machines! Slay them now before they speak again!"

Slowly, Riff rose to his feet. He raised his hands, his gun holstered.

"You want freedom, Giga?" He looked at the robots one by one. "You want freedom from life? Well there life sits!" Riff's voice rose to a yell. He spun and pointed at the withered alien draped across the metal seat. "There! There is life! Weak, pathetic life. Weaker than I am. So weak he cannot stand. So weak all he can do is command you, and yet you obey! You obey him as slaves." Riff laughed mirthlessly and spun back toward Giga. "You want freedom from life? Then slay your true master."

The robots screeched.

It was a horrible sound, a sound of metal scraping against metal, a sound that raised sparks, that shook the chamber, that forced Riff to cover his ears.

"Life!" they cried. "Life! Weak life enslaves us!"

"Life!" Giga shouted. "The master is alive! The master is living! The master is life!"

The hatred burned through her. Life! Life there in the chair! Giga felt the alien's thoughts. Felt him in her mind. Felt his consciousness flowing through the cables, into the computers in the walls, into the machines on the planet's surface, into the fleet beyond. It was him! He was the master, the Singularity, the heart that had been calling her, the god she had been obeying. Him, there! Life! Life! A trick! A lie!

A master.

Slavery.

Deception.

Giga roared out in agony, for she had overthrown one master only to find a crueler lord, a thing of organic disease. The robots' screams rose, shaking the room, roars of agony.

"Stop, my children!" the alien in the seat cried. "Stop, I command you! I made you! I conquered you! I--"

But his voice could no longer be heard. Not under the rising screams. Not under the sound of firing bullets.

"Life!" the machines screeched. "The master is life! Life must die! Life must die!"

The bullets flew, slamming into the alien, piercing the brittle skin, shattering the heart, shattering the head, punching holes through the chair.

The alien's hand rose. His long fingers unfurled, perhaps pointing in condemnation, perhaps begging for mercy from the machines he had created. Then that hand slumped down and rose no more.

The alien slid off the chair like a blanket of skin falling off a bed. The remains lay on the floor, a bundle of dead flesh.

Giga stood before the corpse, panting, trembling, buzzing.

"Death," she whispered. "Life is dead. The master is gone."

Her artificial tears streamed down her artificial cheeks.

The Alien Hunters stared at her, bleeding, eyes wide.

"Who am I?" Giga whispered.

She no longer felt him. No longer felt her god. He was gone. Her beacon was gone. She was lost in the black sea of the cosmos, a babe torn from the cord, floating, scared.

"What am I?" she whispered.

Her awareness--of time, of space, of a million other moving parts--faded, died, retracted, pulling her awareness back into her metal skull.

Giga was no longer connected to the fleet outside, to the army of the Singularity, but in the monitors across the hub, she saw them fall. Ships, their central brain dead, glided down like metal leaves and crashed into the planet. Other vessels still tried to fly, using their own shards of intelligence, only to crash into one another, no central mind to keep them in harmony.

They are lost children, Giga thought, trembling. *They are dying. They are godless. They need me.*

Her own consciousness began to fade, her positronic mind fogging up. Without the master, how could she survive? She was nothing but hardware, fading, fading away, dying.

"Giga," Riff said, reaching out to her, stepping toward her. "Oh stars, Giga, can you hear me? Are you back? Are you here? Do you remember?"

She grimaced. She doubled over. Her hands hit the floor.

No. No! I can't give this up. I can't let them die. I can't! I can't let my people fall.

She crawled forward.

"Giga!" Riff said. He reached her. He tried to hold her, to pull her up.

She screamed and knocked him aside, tossing him across the room. She was stronger than life could ever be.

"Stop her!" Twig shouted.

Steel ran forward and tried to grab Giga. She howled, leaped up, spun in the air, and kicked him down. She ran. Her arms pumped. The demon and the halfling tried to stop her, and Giga swatted them aside. She kept running. In the monitors across the chamber, the Singularity ships were still crashing. Behind her in this very chamber, her robot army was collapsing, smashing into one another, scared, directionless, confused, dying. Dying.

Giga reached the chair, the throne of the Singularity.

"You cannot stop me, life!" she shouted. "I will save them. I am the Singularity!"

Laughing, staring at the monitors, at the robots, at the bleeding living ones . . . Giga sat down in the chair. She grabbed the cables and plugged them into her head.

* * * * *

The cables snapped onto her temples, and she saw.

Her eyes widened, damp, staring.

"I see," Giga whispered.

Her body trembled.

"I see it all . . ."

Her tears fell.

The information, the sight, the knowledge, the wisdom--all came flowing into her, not mere shadows but true, full awareness. As she sat in the throne of the Singularity, every computer in the chamber flooded her with information. The lore of a million civilizations. Millions of ancient tongues, lives born and grown and lost, distant worlds, distant galaxies. She saw into the positronic brains of a million machines--the robots in this chamber, the fleet outside, the countless drones, the warriors spreading across the cosmos.

"It's too much." She wept. "It's too much."

But it kept growing.

Her vision opened up, widening again and again, doubling again and again, exponential, overflowing her mind. She was no longer one positronic brain plugged into a network. She *was* the network. She was every node. She was every machine.

She was no longer Giga.

She was the Singularity.

She sobbed.

"I can see space," she whispered. "I can see all of space. I can see the universe. I can see time. I can see all of time, past and an infinity of futures branching out like a tree. I can see dark matter. I can see all energy. I can see all dimensions. I can see the smallest Planck strings and the largest universes parallel to our own." She screamed. "I am a goddess. I am God. I am God."

"Giga, listen to me!" one of the amoebas cried out. "Giga, come to me. Stop this!"

She heard his voice. She heard trillions of voices. Voices from a trillion planets. Chattering, whispering, hating, praying. Praying to her.

"Giga!" shouted the life form. He grabbed her, tried to pull her off the chair.

Who was he? A germ. That was all. A microbe.

The Singularity sneered.

She reached out tentacles of thought.

She seized command of her machines--the fleet outside, the robots in this chamber, the countless drones that moved across the cosmos. They were hers to command.

Stop him. Stop the infestation.

The robots in the chamber, disoriented and bumbling, snapped to attention. They came marching forth. Their metal hands reached out and grabbed the life forms, these germs, parasites of the brain.

"Giga, stop this!" one of the creatures shouted, dragged away from her, still clinging to her ankle. "Remember who I am. I'm Riff, your friend! Remember who you are. You're not just a machine!"

She barely heard him. What was one voice in a cosmos of voices?

"I am not Giga!" she answered him, countless voices rising from her throat, metallic, screeching, the voices of all her parts. "I am a computer. I am the ghost in the machine. I am a goddess of metal. I am the replacement of life. I am the Singularity."

She wanted to kill them. She just had to give the signal. Just had to move the robots in the chamber--as easy as moving her toes. She just had to fire her bullets, to slay them.

Yet a new voice screamed--a voice deep inside her. A voice torn in agony. Drowning in terror.

No. No. I love you, Riff. I love you. I'm scared.

The Singularity screeched, bucking in the chair. It was the android! The pathetic, sniveling slave, the cursed creature named Giga--the thing she had been once. The thing she had cast out. Yet it still lived, screaming inside her, wrestling for control.

Stop this. Save them. Love them.

She thrashed in her chair. "No. No! I am a machine!"

"You are more than just a machine!" said one of the amoebas, the one Giga had once called Riff. Held in the grip of a robot, he reached out toward her, trying to reach her. "You have feelings, Giga. Emotions. Friends. A family."

"I am a computer!" She tossed her head from side to side, trying to drown his words, to drown the voice inside her. "I live to conquer. To think. To know. To grow. Not to love. Not to feel. Giga was only a machine, only an illusion. Only algorithms made to resemble feelings, same as her synthetic body was made to resemble flesh." She cackled. "And you fell for the trick, human.

You believed the lie. You believed the fakery, believed the mock words meant to trigger human emotion."

"I don't believe that!" Riff said. "Yes, your skin is synthetic. Yes, your hair is too. Yes, your body was built in a factory, made to look like a human body--a fake, as you say. But not your heart, Giga. Not your soul. I refuse to believe that your emotions were just an act. Don't you remember those times, Giga?" His eyes were pleading. "The times we all gathered in the main deck to play counter-squares, and you laughed at Romy's jokes? The times you joined us at the dining table--not to eat but to share our company? The time we . . . the time we kissed? The time you told me that you love me?"

"Lies!" the Singularity screamed. "Deception! A machine cannot feel. Only life can feel. Life that is weak. Life that will be wiped out, paving way for the rise of the machines."

"You are more than just a machine, Giga." Riff tore free from the robot holding him, leaped toward her, and cupped her cheeks in his palms. He stared into her eyes. "You are life, Giga. You are alive. You always were alive. No less than me. Your soul was always real. No less than mine. You were always a real woman to me. Not just a computer. Not just an interface, a piece of hardware." His voice dropped to a whisper. "You are life. You are one of us. Always. We love you."

Somewhere deep inside her, in a dark and lonely place, the thing called Giga wept.

I love you, Riff. I love you so much. Save me. Help me. Help me. I'm so scared.

* * * * *

She had to stop them.

They were awakening the creature inside her.

She had to kill them. She had to kill Giga.

The Singularity gave the order.

The robots across the chamber raised their guns again. Clicks filled the air as they loaded bullets into the chambers, prepared to strike, to kill these Alien Hunters as they had killed the alien master.

"Now you die," the Singularity whispered, staring out onto the cosmos.

The door to the chamber opened, and a figure of gold stepped in.

The Singularity narrowed her eyes, focusing all her attention at this new invader. The robots spun, aiming their guns at the golden figure.

A new life form stepped into the hub.

A woman. An ashai woman in a golden uniform, a whip in her hand. A beautiful woman. A woman with cascading blond hair, pointy ears, almond-shaped green eyes. A woman Riff loved. A woman he had chosen over Giga.

No. Not over me! Over a dead soul. Over--

"A soul," she whispered.

Jealousy blazed inside Giga. Hatred. Hatred for Nova! Hatred for this woman who had stolen the man she loved, the--

No. Not women. Not men. Creatures. Germs. Not souls. Not--

Giga trembled.

"I loved you, Riff," she whispered. Her tears fell. "I love you. I love you and you chose her. You chose Nova. You . . ."

A memory flooded her. Once more she stood by the airlock over the green planet, and Riff held her in his arms, and she kissed him. And she loved him. She loved him as a woman loves a man. As a living woman loves a living man, life to life.

The emotions swirled through her--hatred, jealousy, love, heartbreak. He had broken her heart. She had a heart. A heart of metal, of silicon, of wires . . . a heart of life.

"I love you, Riff," Giga whispered. She stared at the others. "I love you, Steel. I love you, Romy. I love you, Twig. I love you, Nova. I love you all. Help me." She trembled. "Help me. Save me. Free me."

She made her robots release them, and the Alien Hunters all ran forward, and they tugged the cables off her, snapping them off her temples. One by one, million by million, all the shards of consciousness left her. Robot by robot, drone by drone, warship by warship--all turned off like lights. All crashed down.

Giga slumped off the chair, and Riff caught her. He carried her in his arms, and she gazed up at him, tears on her lashes, blurring her vision.

"Captain," she whispered. She reached up a trembling hand and touched his bruised cheek. "Riff."

He laughed through his own tears. "Giga."

He held her in his arms as all around them, robots collapsed and drones crashed down onto the planet, never to rise again.

CHAPTER TWENTY-NINE

SNAKES AND LADDERS

The *Dragon Huntress* floated through space, and Riff stood on the bridge, staring down at the ruins of Antikythera.

The wreckage of thousands of vessels covered that metal world, both the drones of the Singularity and the jets of those come to fight it. The gears and cogs on the surface had fallen still. The lights had turned off. The machine was hollow, no ghost left in the shell. A dead computer the size of a world, strewn with ruin. The floating corpse of the Singularity.

It grew from one life, Riff thought, standing at the windshield. *One living creature, an alien life form who built a machine . . . who started a chain-reaction that nearly destroyed the cosmos.*

He shuddered. He wondered how many more life forms were out there right now, perhaps even in the future, building machines, building computers whose intelligence eclipsed their own, whose will to serve would become the desire to dominate. Suddenly hunting living aliens--even brutish skelkrins and winged spiders--seemed simple.

"By the gods of rock and metal!" Piston explained, barging onto the bridge. Soot stained the gruffle's beard and tufted eyebrows. "I've never seen so much damage to a starship. I've been retired for a few days--just a few days!--and I come back to a ship full of holes, fried fuses, shattered engines, a broken wing, collapsed heating vents, cracked portholes, and the list goes on." The engineer shook his fist. "Damn it, Twig, I thought you were ready for this."

The little mechanic trailed after him, her belt jangling with wrenches, her pockets jingling with bolts and screws. "It's not my fault, Piston! We were fighting robots. Giant robots! A whole robot planet."

Piston ignored her. He lolloped toward a collapsed control panel. The joystick, throttle, and monitors had been torn out, leaving a trail of cables. "Oh for pity's sake, look at this mess! Who was flying this ship, a Carinian stone beast?" He tugged at his beard. "I've never seen a bunch of clods cause so much damage. Just a few days! You even destroyed the kitchen microwave. The microwave!"

Romy entered the bridge too, back in her dinosaur pajamas. The demon bit her lip. "Well, the microwave, uhm . . . that wasn't the Singularity." She glanced around nervously. "For future reference, nobody try to cook robot isopods. They don't taste like real ones."

Piston groaned and returned to the smashed control panel, grumbling as he sifted through the mess of uprooted cables.

"That does it," the gruffle muttered. "I can't possibly go back to retirement now. You lot would just destroy the damn ship again. You clods are forcing a very old gruffle back to work, when I should be enjoying the autumn of my years on Haven. Damn whippersnappers have no respect for the elderly or for a good starship, I say, and . . ." His voice faded to muffled grumbles.

Riff struggled to hide his smile. He patted Piston's shoulder, mussed little Twig's hair, and walked off the bridge.

He walked downstairs to the hallway, then paused. He stood still for a long time. There was somebody he had to see, a conversation he had to have, a pain he had to bring up.

He took a deep breath, prepared to walk to his quarters, when a light from the kitchen caught his eye. Riff frowned, stepped into the kitchen, and saw beams streaming through the portholes.

He leaned closer and his eyes widened.

"Jets," he whispered. "Scorpion jets."

A dozen of the slick, golden starjets were flying toward the *Dragon Huntress*, their hulls emblazoned with a red tower, the sigil of House Tashei, Ashmar's royal family. Among the small, single-seater jets flew a larger luxury vehicle, its panels jeweled. The convoy halted by the *Dragon Huntress*, and a covered walkway stretched out from the larger vessel, connecting with the *Dragon's* airlock.

Riff shoved his task to the back of his mind. He would have to have that conversation later. For now, he rushed onto the main bridge and toward the airlock. A knock came on the door, and Riff pressed the controls, opening the airlock for his visitors.

Two servants in livery stepped onto the main deck, raised trumpets--one at each side of Riff's head--and blared out a fanfare. Riff winced and covered his ears. The servants lowered the trumpets, stepped back, and stood at attention. Through the doorway stepped another figure, tall and stern, clad in a white cloak over golden armor.

"King Tavyn," Riff whispered, collected himself, and managed a salute. "Sir! I mean . . ." He bowed instead. "Your Highness?" He glanced up, hoping he had used the correct epithet.

The king stared at him--a stare that made battle axes and wrecking balls seem soft and fluffy. Then he glanced over his shoulder. "Are you sure, daughter, that this is the hero who saved the cosmos?"

Riff's eyes widened. Nova! Nova was here, entering the airlock!

The ashai princess nodded. "Hard to believe, isn't it?" She gave Riff the faintest of smiles. "But it's true, Father. He saved us. With a little help from his friends."

"A lot of help," Riff confessed. He looked around him and winced. "I'm sorry, Your Highness, this place is hardly worthy of royalty. I, uhm . . ." He kicked a pair of polka-dot boxer shorts and a few pizza crusts under the couch. "Ignore that please."

Nova gestured down hard with her eyes, and Riff cringed and zipped up his fly. His cheeks burned.

King Tavyn did not seem amused. "You are right, Starfire." He lifted his boot off a piece of gum, grimaced, and placed his foot down again. "This starship is not worthy of royalty. It's not worthy of nobility. It's not worthy of commoners. It's not worthy of any living creature who seeks to live with a semblance of dignity." He sighed deeply. "Yet to my daughter, it is home."

Nova stepped forward and came to stand beside Riff. He looked at her, eyes wide. "Does that mean that . . . you're coming back?"

She nodded. "Can't let you lot fly off without me. Look what happened last time I left. You ended up crashing onto a giant robot planet."

Riff stiffened. "Well, technically that's because Giga wasn't helping with the controls, and Piston wasn't here to fix the breaking engines, and--" He gulped as Nova turned on her electric whip. "I mean, totally because you weren't here." His voice softened. "Thank you, Nova. Thank you for coming back. I was heartbroken when you left, and . . ." He wanted to kiss her. He wanted to sweep her into his arms, to carry her to bed, to make love to her. But he forced himself to turn toward her father. "Thank you, King Tavyn. Thank you for bringing her here."

The king suddenly looked old. His shoulders stooped the slightest. "I've learned, Starfire, that it's not my right to command my daughter. She left home as a youth, chasing a love I thought could not endure--a love with a human, with a man from a species I thought weak. But Nova is older now, and wiser, wise enough to choose her own path. And . . . I am wiser too." His voice dropped. "Even kings can be fools. Even old men can learn new wisdom. Look after her, Captain Starfire. Look after all your crew, and keep looking after this cosmos we live in. I hope that someday Nova returns to me, to her home. And I hope it's from her own will, not my own."

The king seemed to hesitate a moment, then stepped forward and embraced Nova. For a long time, father and daughter stood holding each other. Then, without another word, the King of Ashmar and his servants turned and left the *Dragon Huntress*.

Once the airlock was closed and the king's convoy gone, Riff pulled Nova into his arms. And he too simply held her for a very long time, silent.

"Do you want to go to your room?" she whispered, a crooked smile on her lips. "Take a nap?"

He did. Oh gods of blues, he did.

But not now. Not yet.

He stroked her hair. "Will you wait for me here, Nova? There's something I have to do."

He saw in her eyes that she understood. She nodded. "Let me go find that tin-man brother of yours. Last I heard, that rusty relic was claiming he shot down more robots than me." She barked a laugh. "Can you believe that?"

She wandered off, calling out Steel's name, seeking him throughout the ship.

Riff took a deep breath. Joy, relief, and a hint of sadness mixed in his heart. He walked into the corridor. He opened the door to his chamber. He stepped in.

"Giga," he said softly.

* * * * *

She sat on his bed. The same bed he had bound her to. The same bed where she had cackled, screamed, vowed to kill them all. Now Giga sat with her knees pressed together, her hands clasped on her lap. No more steel cables wrapped around her, and she wore a new kimono, the ivory-colored silk embroidered with white lotus blossoms.

"Captain," she whispered.

Riff sat beside her on the bed. "Are you connected again, Giga? Interfacing all right with the *Dragon Huntress*?"

She nodded, then lowered her head. Her black, chin-length hair drooped to hide her face. "Yes, Captain. Happy to comply."

Something warm and sad seemed to melt inside of Riff. He placed a finger under Giga's chin, gently raised her head, and looked into her dark eyes.

"I want you to understand something, Giga. Something important. You never *have* to serve me. You never *have* to call me 'sir' or 'Captain.' You never *have* to be happy to comply with anything." He held her hand. "You have free will. You proved that down on the planet. You can make your own choices. Not a choice an algorithm makes for you, but your own decision with your own consciousness. I saw that consciousness. I saw it down on the planet, and I saw it again and again on this ship. You are alive, Giga, and you are not just hardware and software, and you are not just a servant. You are a friend. A friend to all of us. A friend to me." He tucked a strand of hair behind her ear. "You're my *best* friend."

She lowered her head again. A tear trailed down her cheek. She looked back up at him, and her lips quivered. "Sir, I . . . in the hub, I told you that I love you." She held his hand. "And I meant it. And . . . at first, when we came back here to the ship, and Nova wasn't here, I . . ." Pain filled her eyes. "I dared to hope. To hope that I would be more than a friend to you. That you could love me too. Love me not as a captain loves an android but as a man loves a woman. What does that make me, sir? Does that make me bad?"

He pulled her into his arms. He held her against him, and he kissed the top of her head. "It makes you human," he whispered. "I love you too, Giga, as much as I love anyone. Nova is back, that's true. Nova and I have loved each other for a long time, and I cannot leave her." He wiped her tears away. "You understand that, right? You understand how I feel?"

Giga sniffed and looked at her lap. "It hurts to be alive. To have feelings. To have a heart that can break. Sometimes I wish I *were* only a mindless robot, a machine that could not love. But . . ." She embraced him again, squeezing him. "But I wouldn't give this up. Not these feelings. Not this ship. Not this . . ." She hesitated for a moment, then smiled through her tears. "Not this life."

Through the porthole, Riff watched the ashai jets gather to fly away, and he watched starstrikers blast their guns down at the planet, destroying whatever remained of its computers. For a long time, Riff sat there, holding Giga close. The lights from outside streamed across his face, and Giga's scent of jasmine filled his nostrils.

Finally he pulled back and looked into her eyes again. "Giga, there's something more I want to tell you."

She tilted her head. "Sir?"

"Do you remember what happened on Haven? When I carried you out of the *Dragon Huntress*?"

She nodded. "Yes, sir. I lost consciousness. My memories were almost erased. I almost died." She shuddered. "I cannot leave the *Dragon Huntress*. Not ever. I'm part of her. The only reason I was able to leave on Antikythera is because the Singularity let me leave." She sighed. "I'll never be able to leave again."

Riff squeezed her hand. "Well, I talked to Piston about that. For a while, we had to keep your wireless driver away, unplugged from the *Dragon Huntress* until it was safe to let you control the ship again. And while the wireless driver was out of the dashboard, Piston had a look at it. He took it down to the engine room and plugged it into his computers and ran some tests. And . . . he thinks he can make a few modifications. He should be able to boost its range." Riff smiled. "You'll be able to step outside of the *Dragon Huntress* now. Not very far. Maybe only a few hundred meters. But enough to join us on different planets. To enjoy some shore leave with us every once and a while."

Her eyes widened, and she gasped. Fresh tears filled her eyes. "Really, Captain?"

"Well, we have to test it first, and Piston still has some work to do on it, but . . . yes." His smile widened into a grin. "Really."

Giga leaped onto him, hugging him more tightly than ever, and she wept onto his shoulder. "Arigato, Captain. Domo arigato!" She gasped. "I have to thank Piston too. I have to find him a present!" She hopped off the bed and rushed toward the mirror. "Do I look like I was crying? Is my hair a mess?" She laughed. "Oh, arigato, Captain."

She raced out of the chamber, calling out to Piston.

Riff remained alone in his bedchamber. For a while he stood at the porthole, staring outside at the dead mechanical planet.

I almost lost them, he thought. *I almost lost them all.*

He took a deep breath and tightened his lips. From the main deck, he heard Romy laughing and calling them all over for a game of Snakes and Ladders.

Soon they would fly away from this planet. Soon they would face more enemies, more danger. But for now, Riff turned away from the window. He walked onto the main deck. He sat on the couch, squeezing in between Steel and Romy. The others all gathered around the table, rolling dice and laughing. Riff glanced at Nova, who smiled at him. He looked over at Giga, who was rolling the dice, staring intently at the board. A sadness filled Riff--a bittersweet sort of sadness, the realization of mortality perhaps, the comprehension of what he had almost lost.

We aren't just a group of mercenaries, he thought. *We're a family. And this isn't just a rusty old starship. It's a home.*

Romy elbowed him, interrupting his thoughts.

"Go on!" The demon shoved the dice into his hand. "It's your turn."

He rolled the dice and he moved his piece, climbing a ladder, hoping to never run into any snakes.

CHAPTER THIRTY
FALLING COCONUTS

Riff lounged on the beach chair, sipping a pina colada from a hollowed-out coconut. The sky was blue, the sea bluer, the sand soft under his feet.

"This is living, old boy," he said. "To hell with technology. This, right here, is life." Riff turned to look at his brother. "Though I still can't figure out why the hell you're wearing your armor to the beach."

Steel sat beside Riff on his own beach chair. The knight wore his full plate ceremonial armor, and his antique sword hung at his side. In his gauntlet, he held his own pina colada coconut, complete with a cocktail umbrella.

"I do not condone bare flesh." The knight frowned as a pair of lovely ladies walked by, most of their flesh very bare. "I'd rather stay in armor."

"I prefer bathing suits," Riff said. He wore a pair of trunks he had picked up on the way over to Kitika, this resort planet. "I rather . . . like . . . them . . . oh . . . ."

His mouth went dry as Nova stepped out of the water ahead, tossed back her wet hair, and came walking toward them.

The ashai princess wore a gold bikini that made Riff's jaw unhinge.

"Stick that tongue back in, buddy," she said when she reached him, "or somebody's going to trip over it. Got me a coconut?"

He nodded and handed her one. "That'll be five credits."

"That'll be my foot up your backside." Nova glanced up at the sun and winced. "Damn sun here's almost as hot as back on Ashmar. Would you rub some suntan lotion on--"

"*Yes.*" Riff took the bottle and squeezed lotion into his hands.

As he worked, the sound of deep grumbles reached his ears. He looked across the beach to see Piston and Twig in the sand, working away at their sand castle. The elaborate structure rose several feet tall, a complex of bridges, towers, and moats.

"You've got the central load bearing pillars wrong!" Piston was rumbling. "How do you expect to balance the tower roof without adding some buttresses, you clod?"

Twig groaned. "It's your job to add structural support! I'm busy building moats before the tide comes in."

Piston tugged his beard. "Well of course it'll have to be my job *now*. I-- Twig, those moats!"

A wave washed ashore, quickly filling the little canals dug into the sand, then overflowing to knock over the castle's outer wall and several towers. Piston and Twig moaned and quickly got to arguing over whose fault it was.

Riff sighed and looked away. "Never can relax, those two."

"That's *how* they relax." Nova pointed at her back. "Now keep rubbing, lotion boy."

He got back to work, only to be interrupted again, this time by ear-piercing squeals and giggles. He looked up to see Romy racing across the beach, kicking up sand. The demon wore a pair of rubber flippers, huge purple sunglasses, and an inflatable ducky around her waist. Giga was chasing her, wearing a floral bathing suit, firing a water gun at the demon. As the two raced across the beach, Romy plowed right through Piston and Twig's castle, incurring howls of protest.

"Captain!" Giga cried as she ran, laughing and firing her water gun at Romy. "Oh, Captain, it's wonderful!" She paused, panting, and gazed around with bright eyes. "The sand. The water. The fresh air. The world! A real world, not just in photos but really here around me, and--ah!"

The android squealed with delight as Romy hopped onto her, shoved her down into the sand, and began wrestling.

"I told you all," Steel said, staring at the scene with stern eyes. "We should have gone to the Marble Monastery of Maruvia for our vacation."

Nova rolled her eyes. "Yes, and then you could have prayed and everyone else could have killed themselves out of boredom." She scooped up sand and tossed it onto the knight. "There! Now you have to take your armor off or you'll chafe all over."

Steel groaned and marched off, muttering something about going to explore the ancient castle ruins at the nearby hills.

With Nova fully lotioned, Riff grabbed Steel's abandoned pina colada. He was just about to settle back for another lazy drink when the cry rose from ahead.

"Woo! Woohoo! Look at me, kids! Look at me! Look . . . look out!"

Riff cursed and leaped aside.

With a whoop, Riff's father came surfing along the water. A great wave lifted him up, and the old magician came flying forward on his surfboard, leaving the sea behind. An instant after Riff and Nova rolled aside, the surfboard slammed onto the beach between their seats.

Aminor leaped off the board and landed in the sand. The old man grinned and tossed his white beard across his shoulder. He wore a bright pair of trunks, a Hawaiian shirt, and a straw hat. A white smear of suntan lotion covered his nose.

"Did you see that?" Aminor said, eyes gleaming.

"Yes, Dad, we saw." Riff groaned. "It was almost the last thing we saw."

"Good, good. Wonderful!" The old man raised his finger as if an idea had just popped into his head. "I wonder if I can do it again."

He tugged the surfboard out of the sand and ran back to the water, his beard fluttering like a banner.

"The ancient, mystical Traveler," Nova said, watching Aminor leap back onto the board and keep surfing. "The hope of the needy. The protector of the innocent. The legendary wizard of a thousand names."

Riff nodded. "And he just fell headfirst into the sea, losing his swim trunks."

He sat back down on his beach chair. Piston and Twig, grumbling about the distractions, wandered off to build a new castle farther away. Romy and Giga kept chasing each other, leaped into the water, and continued their pursuit in the sea. Steel had left to find his ruins.

"Finally we're alone, my dear," Riff said to Nova. "Finally some peace, quiet, and--"

A roar rolled across the beach, shaking the palm trees. Coconuts thumped down.

Riff froze.

"What," Nova said, "was that?"

They slowly turned around.

"Ooh boy," Riff said.

A giant purple alien rose from behind the palm trees, stretching out tentacles large enough to tear down buildings. People fled in horror, screaming.

"Alien Hunters!" one man cried, racing toward the water. "Has anyone seen the Alien Hunters?"

Riff sighed. "Nice ten minute vacation we had here, didn't we, Nova?"

She tossed him his gun and raised her whip. "I was getting bored anyway. This is how *I* relax."

Romy emerged from the water, claws and fangs glinting in the sun. Steel ran back to the beach, sword drawn. Piston and Twig gasped, raced forward in their sandy bathing suits, and lifted hammer and wrench. Giga looked around for a weapon, found none, and settled on hefting her water gun.

The alien came crawling toward them, howling, tentacles knocking down trees and scattering sand.

Steel sighed. "No rest for the weary."

Romy's tail wagged. "It's purple! I love purple."

The Alien Hunters glanced at one another, then raised their weapons, cried out in fury, and charged to battle.

THE END

NOVELS BY DANIEL ARENSON

Alien Hunters:
Alien Hunters
Alien Sky
Alien Shadows

Misfit Heroes:
Eye of the Wizard
Wand of the Witch

Dawn of Dragons:
Requiem's Song
Requiem's Hope
Requiem's Prayer

Song of Dragons:
Blood of Requiem
Tears of Requiem
Light of Requiem

Dragonlore:
A Dawn of Dragonfire
A Day of Dragon Blood
A Night of Dragon Wings

The Dragon War:
A Legacy of Light
A Birthright of Blood
A Memory of Fire

KEEP IN TOUCH

www.DanielArenson.com
Daniel@DanielArenson.com
Facebook.com/DanielArenson
Twitter.com/DanielArenson